Froggy Style

Also by J. A. Kazimer

Curses!
A F***ed-Up Fairy Tale

Published by Kensington Publishing Corp.

Froggy Style

A F***ed-Up Fairy Tale

J.A. KAZIMER

KENSINGTON BOOKS
www.kensingtonbooks.com

KENSINGTON BOOKS are published by

Kensington Publishing Corp.
119 West 40th Street
New York, NY 10018

Copyright © 2013 by J. A. Kazimer

All Kensington titles, imprints, and distributed lines are available at special quantity discounts for bulk purchases for sales promotion, premiums, fund-raising, educational or institutional use.

Special book excerpts or customized printings can also be created to fit specific needs. For details, write or phone the office of the Kensington Special Sales Manager: Kensington Publishing Corp., 119 West 40th Street, New York, NY 10018. Attn. Special Sales Department. Phone: 1-800-221-2647.

Kensington and the K logo Reg. U.S. Pat. & TM Off.

ISBN-13: 978-0-7582-6913-3
ISBN-10: 0-7582-6913-7

First Kensington Trade Paperback Printing: March 2013
10 9 8 7 6 5 4 3 2 1

Printed in the United States of America

To Lisa Birman and the odd Land of Oz,
for many things, but mostly for introducing me
to fairy floss, bliss bombs, and a kangaroo named Skippy

Froggy Style

Prologue

Once upon a time (about twenty-two years, seven days, twelve hours, twenty-one minutes, and forty-seven seconds ago) in a land not so far away sat a forlorn frog, his lime-colored skin pale under his frogger's tan.

"Ribbit," he croaked halfheartedly, and then sighed, bored by his unending amphibianness, if not his shiny reflection in the khaki-colored water. His days passed in a jaded blur of flies, hopping, and the occasional real-life game of Frogger.

The most excitement he'd experienced in his eight years of frogitude was a questionable wart. He groaned again, closing his bug eyes against the harsh afternoon glare. Hours passed. The sun sank lower in the sky, shading it a princess-pink color.

The frog's nose twitched. Something approached, something that smelled a lot like sugar and spice with just a hint of wet dog. Not unpleasant to his froggy sense.

From the enchanted underbrush tumbled a girl child. She clutched a tattered blanket coated with dirt and chocolate. The frog, surprised by his stubby visitor, did what frogs do. He croaked once and dove into the pond, sinking below the surface to avoid a confrontation with the seemingly sticky child. Frogs, and their toadish counterparts, were known for two things: double-sided sticky tongues and the ability to avoid any conflict. With the exception of the horny toad.

Those guys jumped anything.

The child bumbled her way toward the pond, closer to the hiding frog. Her blond hair burst from her head like a deranged troll, sticking up at odd and geometrically impossible angles.

The nearer she came to the edge of the water, the more nervous the frog became. What if she fell in? he pondered in his pea-sized brain. Or worse, what if she didn't and the frog was once again left all alone to live his fly-eating existence?

The question proved moot. The girl child stopped at the rim of the pond, her purple lollipop eyes searching the watery depths. For what, the frog couldn't say, but she piqued his interest.

Could she be the One?

Apparently finding what she desired, the child let out a small squeal, dropped her blankie, and jammed her hand into the murky water.

The frog's head wobbled with disgust. If she was indeed the One, he was in trouble.

The girl shrieked and yanked her arm from the water. A miniature golden ball emerged in her mud-coated hand. She beamed at the ball and then stuffed it into her mouth.

Ew. The frog shivered with repulsion, and he was a frog who ate flies for three meals a day.

As soon as the golden ball passed the girl's lips she began to choke, grabbing at her throat with chubby hands. Tears streamed down her cheeks as her lips turned the brightest shade of blue the frog had ever seen outside the reflection of his own gaze in the pond.

Panic set into the frog's tiny brain. Was the blanket-carrying, golden-ball-eating, sticky girl about to drop dead in front of his very eyes? What if she was the One and she died? What would happen to him then?

Blinded with terror, the frog did the only thing his frog brain could think of. He jumped on the little girl, landing with enough force that she and her frog-stowaway tumbled to the swampy ground in a heap of child and amphibian parts.

The golden ball popped free from the girl's mouth. It rolled down the embankment and into the murky water once again. The child watched it with a frown, which she then turned on her frog savior. Her fat fingers pointed at the pond. "Ball," she muttered with a yawn.

The frog responded with a ribbit.

The child frowned harder, her brow wrinkling under the curls of her hair. The frog paused to watch the child. There was something about her. Something that he wasn't sure boded well for either of them.

A second later, without warning, the girl scooped up her guardian froggy angel and stuffed his slimy body into her drool-coated mouth.

Thunder rumbled overhead. A flash of lightning lit the sky. With a shriek, the child abruptly spat the frog out. He tumbled downward, spinning faster and faster in the air until he hit the pond water with a loud splash. The sticky girl's violet eyes widened two times their already bug-eyed size. Blackness quickly descended, turning day to night in the blink of a milky toad's eye.

As quickly as it came the storm vanished, leaving the little girl standing at the edge of the pond, a confused look upon her chubby face. She glanced down at the eight-year-old boy in front of her. A very naked, slightly greenish eight-year-old boy, who was standing in three feet of stagnant pond water where the frog had dropped only moments before.

The boy gazed down at his naked arms, legs, and boyish parts with surprise. *Free, free at last from the dreaded curse,* he thought with a grin.

A grin that quickly faded under the little girl's gaze. She

slowly looked him up and down and shook her head, nearly poking out her own eye with the point of her hair in the process.

The boy's face flamed red and he quickly covered himself with a lily pad. "The water's cold," he said like a million men before him.

The little girl smiled.

The frog prince scowled.

And they lived happily ever after.

Or so the tale goes. . . .

Chapter 1

"Bullshit," I said to the gin-soaked fairy godmother standing next to me in the Royal Tux-We-R Shoppe. She shrugged her massive shoulders swaddled in pink chiffon. "Come on, Elly," I added. "No one lives happily ever after."

Elly smacked me in the back of the head with her wand and scowled. "Hush your mouth. I happen to know for a fact that fairytales do come true."

I rubbed the back of my neck. "Not this one. I don't love her and I never will." The wand rose again, but I danced away, nearly colliding with an overly well-endowed mannequin.

"Johnny, why do you want to marry her, then?" She paused to look down her long, pointed nose. "In a week."

"Ten days!" Ten days. Ten frogging days. "And you damn well know why. And don't call me Johnny. My name's Jean-Michel. Jean-Michel." How many times did I have to tell her that? I hesitated, considering my fairy godmother, a woman who'd spent the last twenty-two years of my life annoying me as much as fairyly possible. "Never mind. Are you sure she's the One?"

"What do you think of this? For your wedding tux?" Elly picked up a baby blue boutonnière from a rack of rainbow-colored boutonnières. "It matches your eyes."

Baby blue? Was she kidding me? If anything, my eyes were a manly indigo, maybe even sapphire, in the right light, with enough mead. "Don't change the subject," I said. "Are you sure Sleeping Beauty is the princess from the pond?" I shuddered, remembering my meeting with the sticky, drool-coated child. She'd broken my curse, sure, but what eight-year-old boy wanted his first kiss to be with a drooling, pint-sized princess? And it wasn't even a real kiss.

The girl had tried to eat me!

I had the scars from her tiny teeth on my forehead to prove it. Elly's voice drew me back to the present. "Of course I'm sure, Johnny." At my evil look she amended her words, "Jean-Michel."

"Okay then."

"I mean, really, how many twenty-six-year-old blond princesses with a frog fetish could there be in the City?"

"What?!" I snatched the matching baby blue bow tie from her large, almost manly hands. "Are you saying that you don't know if this is *my* princess? Are you crazy?"

Elly patted my arm, leaving red welts on my olive skin. "Relax. I'm ninety-five percent sure." She hesitated, her head tilting to one side. I wasn't sure if she'd stroked out or was thinking. Either way, I didn't want to interrupt. "Eighty-seven percent, if we factor in her . . . affliction."

Affliction, my ass. I had a term for the affliction where a healthy princess suddenly fell asleep at the drop of a tiara: laziness.

Ah, poor tired princess needed a nap.

What a hard burden to bear.

Her "affliction" didn't bother me much, though. After all, I'd spent the last thirty years of my life doing absolutely nothing worthwhile or even a tad bit noble.

Just the way I liked it.

"We'll know for sure if she's the One after we meet her

this afternoon," Elly said with a smirk. "Now try this on."
She handed me a black tuxedo made by none other than
Geppetto. The fabric felt stiff, almost wooden, under my
fingers, but I nodded and did as Elly ordered. Mainly out
of fear.

My godmother packed one hell of a curse.

"I'll be waiting right here." She motioned to a tuffet
next to the dressing room. Oh goody, I wanted to reply,
but again, my survival skills kicked in.

I was in bad enough shape without adding another
curse. The one I already had was plenty. It went something
like: Poof, you're a frog. Shazam, a princess, albeit a slight
one, gave you a kiss. Then, whammo, if you don't marry
said princess on the day you turn thirty (which I would do
in ten days), you'll be turned right back into a frog.

Forever.

Or so Elly warned me at least ten times a day.

Hence my hasty marriage to the sleepy princess I'd
never truly met, unless one counted that time she'd stuffed
me in her mouth.

I heaved a sigh and adjusted the sleeve of the fashion-
able tuxedo jacket. The blackness of the tux suited my
olive skin tone and jet-black hair that tickled my collar.
Hair I kept longer than was in vogue. But what the hell. I
was going to be hairless and a lot greener in a few days. I
brushed back a wayward lock and smirked at the man in
the mirror. "Mirror, mirror on the wall," I began. "Who is
the finest damn prince of them all?" I didn't expect an answer, and was pleasantly surprised to hear:

"You are, sir."

I turned around, narrowly avoiding my servant, Karl,
standing a hairsbreadth away. I stepped back and stifled a
grin. Karl was all decked out like a jester in my royal colors of emerald and white. He wore a jewel-encrusted hat
and bells on his slippers. The poor guy looked ridiculous,

but by the pride on his face he was clueless as to how much. I grinned. Eagerness, loyalty, and stupidity were all traits to admire, especially in a servant.

For the last ten years, since my father hired him fresh out of the Butler Did It Academy, he'd kept all my secrets, large and small, lime and slimy. "I have your tunic and leggings, sir," Karl said, holding up a pair of avocado-colored leggings and an off-white tunic with a large "P" across the chest. As if the tights weren't bad enough.

"I'm not wearing that."

"But, sir, it's for your meeting with"—he lowered his voice—"the One. You have to look your best."

"I'm still not wearing it." I gave a slight laugh. "I don't care who I'm meeting. No man looks good in tights." Even a male specimen as perfect as myself. After all, poets wrote sonnets in my name while women swooned at the mention of my manliness. What could one lazy princess possibly take exception to?

"But, sir—"

"Forget it." I motioned to a rack of dinner jackets hanging like a little pig on a rotisserie. "We'll compromise. Go pick out a jacket and I'll wear it to meet the princess." I grabbed his arm as he turned to go. "Nothing green," I reminded him for the thousandth time. The very mention of the color sent chills down my spine. The taste of partially digested flies bubbled in the back of my throat, but I managed to swallow it down.

Karl nodded and practically danced across the room. I groaned. Marrying Beauty was becoming quite tedious. First, I had to beg her father, the king, for her hand, followed by the submission of proof of princelyship, in the form of three picture IDs and a long-form birth certificate. Hell, it was almost easier to hop across the New Never City border than spend five minutes with the tired chick.

I hoped all my trouble was worth it. If Beauty proved not to be the One, I was out of options. Still, the thought of marrying her or anyone, for that matter, grated on me. I should choose who to love. Who to marry. Who to frog for the rest of my days. Not some damn curse cast before I was even born.

"Suck it up." Elly swatted me with the pointy edge of her wand. "You'll get married. Settle down. Have some babies. And forget all this 'I don't want to marry her' nonsense. You'll see. She is the One, Johnny."

"Excuse me," said a woman standing next to Elly. She was young, maybe twenty, with auburn hair and a sweet cherub face.

I returned her smile, adding a wink for good measure. "Yes, luv?" I asked. "What can I do you for?"

She giggled prettily. Elly rolled her eyes. I waved off the annoying fairy godmother and took the young lady's hand. The warmth of her skin eased a bit of the tension lingering in my shoulders.

"Is it true?" she asked. "Are you really him?"

I nodded, bowing low. "Indeed. I am Jean-Michel La Grenouille."

Her eyes narrowed. "Who?"

"The Frog Prince, mademoiselle," I said in a perfectly affected French accent. "The Frog Pr—"

Before the last syllable left my mouth, the girl grabbed my neck and planted a kiss on my lips. Her mouth tasted of sugar and spice, but not a hint of wet dog or drool presented itself. A pity since my body reacted instantly, wanting more.

But she wasn't the One.

So after five hot minutes of saliva and groping, I gently pushed her away, damning the hack reporter from the *New Never News* who first reported on my "quest" for love's eternal kiss, an article nearly as poorly written as the recent exposé on a Cin City assassin with a fetish for flora I'd read this morning over my smiley face pancakes.

Ever since the story of my plight hit the airwaves,

women practically attacked me in the street, longing to be the one who could save me from my greenish fate. Not that I minded the public displays of affection. A part of me liked to think that their attraction was due to my winning personality and stunning good looks, but the curse's promise of riches beyond compare might have had something to do with their interest.

"Sorry," I said to the girl as I wiped a string of slobber from my lips. She promptly burst into tears and ran from the shop, the imprint of my hand on the back of her skirt. I stared after her.

Feelings I rarely allowed to surface did just that. My life wasn't my own. It never had been, nor would it ever be. Not until I was finally free once and for all from this curse.

Chapter 2

A half hour later, dressed in my princely finest, which included a dark blue suit jacket, freshly pressed trousers, and beyond-shiny loafers, I stood outside the bedroom doorway of the woman I would soon marry and felt true terror.

What if she wasn't the One?

I fingered the tie around my neck. This was it. I was about to meet my future bride, a woman who'd either ultimately save or destroy me. With the way my luck was running, my money was on the latter.

"Prince Jean-Michel La Grenouille." Karl announced my arrival in a shout.

"Who?" asked the crusty-faced butler.

"The Frog Prince," he began, and then quickly rushed on, "not that he's a frog. Or ever was a frog. He's just French. Not a frog!"

I closed my eyelids. Sometimes Karl went overboard in his quest to keep my past a secret. I couldn't blame him, though. My own father refused to accept my early tadpole-hood, and instead claimed to anyone who'd listen that his son spent the first eight formative years of his life at charming school in France.

"I repeat, he's not a frog." Karl bowed low and motioned me into the room. "Never was."

I strode through the ornate doors of Sleeping Beauty's bedroom and grimaced. Not at the wasted opulence of the gold-plated ceiling or even the pink shag carpeting thick enough to drown a blind mouse, but at the woman sleeping on the silk sheets of a four-poster bed, the woman wearing enough flannel to make a lesbian jealous. Kinky flaxen curls sprang from her head in all directions, giving her the demented look of a troll after a visit to Fairy-Clips.

This was the One?

Shit.

Elly must've read my hesitation because she grabbed my arm and tugged me deeper into the room. "Well hello," Elly called to the princess, who didn't seem to hear her. Instead, the princess let out a loud snore. "My lady." Elly tried again, adding a finger wave. "Yoo-hooo."

When we reached the edge of the bed the princess shot up and screeched like the Wicked Witch of the East after the fall of the housing market. I jumped back, nearly toppling over Elly, who now lay sprawled on the floor, her wings twisted underneath her.

"Wrong. Wrong. Wrong," Beauty shouted from her bed. "He did it all wrong."

I glanced around, unsure. Was Beauty sleepy and a wee bit crazy? The look on her face was a pretty good indication, but I decided to give her the benefit of the doubt. It was the princely thing to do.

Helping Elly to her feet, I raised my hand for quiet. Of course, Beauty continued to scream, her pale face growing a splotchy red. The screeching sounded familiar, like that of the four-year-old girl from the pond. That made me less than pleased. I didn't want to marry this crazy woman.

"What the hell is wrong with you?" I yelped after a particularly loud burst of squealing. Elly shushed me, and when that didn't work, she smacked me in the head with the sharp edge of her wand. I glared at her, but said no more.

"He did it wrong," Beauty complained again.

"Hush," chirped a voice from across the room.

Squinting into the harsh glare of sunlight drifting through the windows, I tried to place the voice. There, in the corner by the bookcase, a cockroach wearing a top hat and a monocle stood, arrogantly twirling an umbrella.

"My God. Jimmy?" Elly said in a whisper. "Is that you?"

"You know that...thing?" I asked, nodding to the roach. Elly got around, sure, but a cockroach? Then again, who was I to judge? I was about to marry a cranky lesbian with bad hair. Did they make white flannel wedding gowns?

Elly leered at the roach and then turned to frown at me. "That's not a thing, but a who. Jimmy Cockroach. Marriage broker to the stars. If he doesn't find you suitable to marry Beauty..." Ever the drama fairy, Elly hesitated for a second before continuing, "We're screwed."

"A roach decides my fate?" I gave a bitter laugh. "You've gotta be messing with me."

Jimmy glared at me as if he'd overheard our heated exchange. Elly bowed low. "My apologies, Jimmy. Jean-Michel's a bit nervous, as you can imagine. Meeting Princess Beauty has...well, been a dream of his for a long time."

Now Elly got my name right?

"He did it wrong," Beauty repeated. "Wrong. Wrong. Wrong. I won't marry him." She emphasized the "I won't" for good measure.

"What's she babbling about?" I asked the roach.

"There are rules, your lordship," he sneered. "Undeniable rules." His voice grew higher as he warmed to the topic. "In Beauty's tale, consistency is key. And you failed to follow the script. There will be no marriage. Not to you."

With that decree the little bastard jumped from the bookcase and disappeared into a hole in the wall. Beauty stopped whining and settled back against her pillow, a small satisfied smile hovering on her lips. "Have a nice life, loser," she sneered as she drifted off to sleep. A few seconds later a soft snore escaped her mouth.

"What the hell was that?" I spun to confront Elly.

"Shame on you, Johnny." Elly fanned her flushed face. The strong scent of gin wafted in the air between us. "Why, you broke the poor girl's heart. Now she'll never marry you and you'll turn back into a toad. Is that what you want? To give the ladies warts? She's the One, and you've ruined everything."

"A frog, not a toad," I reminded her. "What the hell happened anyway? What could I have possibly done so wrong? I didn't say a word to the chit, and yet, she called me a loser? Me? The frogging Frog Prince!"

Elly shook her head, sending her glittery silver hair bouncing in all directions. "It's not about what you said."

My brain began to ache. "Then what's her problem?"

Rolling her bloodshot eyes, Elly smashed her wand against the palm of her hand and glared. "Women want to be wooed. To be appreciated. To be wanted."

"Is that so?" I took a step toward Elly. "Sage relationship advice from a woman who's been married eight times. Thanks, but I'll pass."

Elly raised her eyebrow as well as her wand.

"Fine." I released a harsh breath. "I'll woo the chit."

"Too late." The roach reappeared, this time wearing a greatcoat with a ring around a rosy collar. "In Beauty's fable, her prince arrives and is stunned by her beauty, so much so that he drops to his knees." He tapped his cane against the floor. "You didn't. Hence you are not her prince. Now, if you'll excuse us, we have another applicant coming at three."

"This is ridiculous." I glared at the roach. "No one said anything about a cockroach, let alone some master script I'm supposed to follow." I lowered my voice to a dangerous level. "The king gave me his blessing to marry Princess Beauty last night. We will wed in ten days."

"Good luck with that." The roach snorted.

"Hey—"

"Good day, sir." The little bastard spun on his Kenneth Cole heel and headed back toward the hole in the wall.

"Wait!" Elly yelled loud enough to wake the dead. Beauty let out another volley of snores. "Johnny will get it right. Give him another chance."

Jimmy checked the small watch on his antenna. "Fine. He has two minutes. *Go!*"

Who did this roach think he was dealing with? "I'm not dropping to my knees. Not for you or any man." I winced. That had sounded much better in my head. "You and your lazy princess can bite me." I nodded to Elly. "We're outta here."

I started to walk away, but inside I was seething. Beauty was the girl child from the pond. I was almost positive of it. She had the same golden hair and the same grape-colored eyes, and she smelled a little like wet dog. How many princesses could there be like that?

I couldn't just walk away. Not after I finally located my wayward princess. But I'd never bend, literally, to her will. I was the Frog Prince, damn it.

Thwack!

Elly's wand smashed into the back of my knee, and I dropped to the floor, grabbing at my throbbing limb. Manly tears burned my eyes, but I blinked them away. "What the hell did you do that for?" I yelled at the fairy godmother innocently picking lint from her dress.

"Do what, dear?" She batted her eyelashes.

I glared at her, a litany of curse words charged up my throat. But before I could utter a single one of them, a loud, choked gasp filled the room.

My eyes flew to Beauty, who'd awoken in time to see me fall to my knees. Her lollipop eyes grew as big as stars and just as bright. "You . . . ," she whispered, her voice tart as if she'd swallowed a lemon.

"I . . . ah . . ."

"But . . . he's . . . he's," she sputtered, her lips curling with disgust, "French." After making that borderline racist statement, my bride's eyes rolled back in her head and she fell instantly asleep, a string of drool slipping from her curled lips.

Jimmy Cockroach nodded his head, his thin lips twisting into something that resembled a smile. "To the happy couple!"

Chapter 3

"Congratulations, sir," Karl said to me in the rearview mirror, his hands tight on the wheel of the bright orange stretch-limo pumpkin. We'd just left Beauty's palace, all i's dotted with little hearts and t's crossed. It was now official. I would marry Beauty in ten days.

God help me.

"Let's skip the heigh-hos for now." I glowered, watching Cin City flash by in a swirl of lights and sounds. Normally I loved the excitement of the fairy strip. You could win or lose everything in a blink of a frog's eye. But not tonight. Tonight my heart just wasn't in it. Of course, I still leered at the tanned women standing at every corner.

It was the princely thing to do after all.

The pretty girls waved back, squealing with delight. "Oh my God! It's him. The Frog Prince," they screamed with high-pitched giggles. I rolled up my window and shifted deeper into the leather seat. My sigh reverberated around the limo.

"Are you not pleased with your upcoming nuptials?" Karl asked.

I grunted. "Overjoyed."

"But she's the One. The One who can save you from your curse." Karl hesitated. "Is she not?"

"I guess." I sighed again, loud enough that Karl nearly

swerved into a flock of Cinderellas. Ever since she was killed, you couldn't walk ten feet in Cin City without running into a Cinderella impersonator. And not the young, sexy, pre-run-over-by-a-bus version either.

"Sir," Karl said after he straightened the wheel. "Sleeping Beauty is the One. I can feel it. Things will work out. You'll see."

I had my doubts. But it was too late to worry about them now. After all, in less than ten days, I'd be married to a xenophobic, pajama-wearing whiner who smelled like sugar, spice, and wet dog. What more could a prince want?

Damn, I needed a drink.

Two hours and six shots of whiskey later, disguised in a *New Never City Knicks, Knacks, Paddy Whacks* cap and opaque glasses to ward off the most eager of Frog Prince groupies, I plopped down on a bar stool in the center of the casino bar, plunking a dollar into the video porker machine. Three little pigs squealed in delight, spinning on their reels. Pig. Pig. Wolf. Another dollar wasted. Luck had deserted me.

Almost one year ago to the day. I remembered it well. My twenty-ninth birthday. Elly had stood, swaying slightly in front of me, her pudgy lips mouthing words that my brain could not understand, no matter how many times she said them, words like "marriage" and "happily ever after," and the final, most damning words of them all.

Sleeping Frogging Beauty.

I downed another shot and shook off the memory. Around me, slot machines clanged and shouts of joy and/or despair filled the room. Fairies, witches, and the occasional troll strolled by, eyes glazed with greed, fanny packs stuffed with pilfered food from the buffet and hooker trading cards.

"Waitress," I said to a chestnut-haired, down-on-her-luck princess in a short shirt. She quickly bounded over to take my order, her eyes sizing me up like Georgie Porgie at recess.

"Hi, handsome," she said in a husky voice. "I'm Jaz."

"Jean-Michel."

"You look really familiar." She tilted her head, showing off the slender column of her neck. "Are you a prince?"

Hidden behind the black lenses of my sunglasses, I gazed into her hard, greedy eyes and smirked. "Nope."

"A pity." She spun on her heel and pranced away, my drink order forgotten. I called after her. "Whiskey. Make it a triple."

She extended her middle finger in acknowledgment and vanished into a crowd of high rollers.

I wanted to get so drunk that I forgot how to one, two buckle my shoe, let alone remember the next ten days. Thanks to the half a bottle of whiskey I'd consumed already, I was well on my way. My eyes grew fuzzy, my body warm and liquid. The thought of Beauty still made me a bit queasy, but drunk, the prospect of wedding her held more appeal. Not by much, mind you, but a little more than returning to eating flies three meals a day.

"Bastard!" A fist smashed into the side of my face, knocking me from my musing, the sunglasses from my face, and my butt to the floor. Pain radiated into my brain, slowly, absorbed by the tide of alcohol surging through my bloodstream. I blinked away the hurt. Then I turned to glare at my attacker.

"RJ?" I whispered to my former best friend.

He stood over me, his fists clenched, his face red. A lock of black hair fell rakishly over one of his hate-filled eyes. Not a new look for my one-time villainous friend. "Get up," he ordered through clenched teeth.

I wiped a trail of blood from my split cheek and grinned. "Are you going to punch me again?"

"Of course."

"No thank you, then." I crawled to a sitting position, adjusting my cap lower on my face. "I think I'll stay right here."

His boot lashed out, catching me under the chin. My head snapped back, sending my baseball hat flying. Tiny princesses circled my vision. I scrunched my eyes shut and quickly opened them. The princesses vanished.

"Get up, you wuss," RJ repeated with less violence. "People are staring."

My eyes narrowed. Since when did the infamous villain Rumple Stiltskin (only taller) care what other people thought? After all, he'd made a name for himself beating up hapless princes like myself. "Your new bride has made you soft," I said, slowly rising to my feet.

"Don't even think about my wife." His glower grew darker, and for the first time, real rage entered his expression.

I swallowed hard. "Guess you still hold a grudge?"

"You think?"

"I did you a favor, you know."

"You slept with my wife," he yelled.

I poked him in the chest. "I did not!"

"Yeah, you did." He grabbed my finger and twisted. "In my bed."

"Oh." I grinned, pulling away from his death grip. "You mean your former wife, Natasha. Not your current one."

In truth, I had slept with Natasha, in RJ's very own bed. To be fair, Natasha was smoking hot. She was also evil, which added a certain appeal. For a few days I even thought she might be the One until she absconded with half my coffer and my cobbler.

Good pie was so hard to find.

"You were my best friend and you betrayed me," RJ said. "That's not something I can simply forget."

"I did you a favor by taking Natasha," I paused to grin,

"off your hands." RJ hoisted his fist, and I quickly added, "If it wasn't for me, you'd never have met Asia," referring to his new bride, RJ's perfect match in every villainous way.

RJ glared. "Don't even think about Asia. If you so much as smile at her, I will break your stringy frog legs."

Hurt whipped through me. RJ knew better than anyone how his threat affected me. Not the fear for my physical well-being. No. I'd had my ass kicked plenty of times by better, bigger villains. But to mention my slightly bowed and green former legs, how dare he? We used to be like brothers, damn it.

Half brothers at least.

Close cousins at best.

Before considering the consequences of my drunken actions, I lunged at him, knocking him back against the video porker machine. He stumbled under my weight, but righted himself quick enough, too quick actually since I was in mid-lunge, flying through the air toward the floor with amazing velocity.

RJ grabbed me just before my nose smashed into the ground. He hefted me up and threw me onto my bar stool, but not before, he tossed two jabs into my kidney. Much-deserved jabs.

After all, I had done his wife. Froggy style.

"I'm sorry about Natasha," I said once the pain from his kidney punch subsided. "I really was doing you a favor."

"I know."

"She was evil."

"Yeah." His lips curved into a wicked smile. "It really was her best quality."

"To Natasha." I hoisted my half-empty whiskey glass.

RJ snatched my drink from my hand. "May she roast in hell."

The grin quickly left his face when a woman in red leather grabbed my drink from him and downed it in one gulp. "I'll drink to that," she said with a princess-like belch.

RJ shot me a glare that said "Don't even think about her." "Hello, pumpkin," he whispered to his new bride. "I missed you."

Pumpkin? Oh, how the mighty villain had fallen. I vowed two things. One, I would never, under any circumstance, call any woman "pumpkin" or any other cutesy pet name. It just wasn't dignified. I was a prince, after all. And second and more importantly, I would never let RJ live this down.

"You have a piece of gum stuck to your forehead." RJ's bride, Asia, motioned to my noggin. "And is that a boot print on your chin?"

"Size twelve, baby." RJ pointed to his combat boot. Asia's eyes grew hot, and she looked as if she'd rip his clothes off right in the middle of the casino.

I cleared my throat to gain the happy couple's attention. When that failed to work I tugged on Asia's dress. "Why yes, yes, it is a boot print." I glowered at RJ and then turned to Asia to plead my case. "Your husband kicked me when I was down."

"An accident," RJ declared with a wink.

"Then he sucker punched me in the kidney."

"A love tap, really."

I lifted an eyebrow.

His face flushed red. "You know what I meant."

"I ask you." I waited a beat, my grin widening. "Is that any way to treat a member of the family?"

"Family?!" RJ asked, his voice rising two octaves.

"About that," Asia began.

Chapter 4

The look of horror on RJ's face was worth every sucker punch, every bruise, and every foul word he'd perpetrated on my person. I grinned at my former friend, enjoying the swirl of emotions racing across his face as my cousin, Asia, explained our family history. Rage, disgust, and finally resignation flashed through his eyes.

The last one was my favorite by far.

"I thought he was French." RJ nodded at me, grasping at straws, like the little pig right before the wolf blew his world apart.

"Wee, wee," I said with a laugh.

"Your parents are bad enough." He blew out a long, tortured sigh. "Now I'm related to this idiot too?"

I snickered again. Poor RJ. Good old King Maldetto was truly insane, and his wife, well, she made the mad hatter appear stable.

Asia winced, taking a second to smack me in the head with the palm of her hand. "Stop laughing. It's not funny," she said to me and then patted her husband's arm. "I'm sorry, RJ. I should've mentioned it sooner, but . . ."

"You didn't want me to know," he said with a groan.

She nodded.

"What am I going to do with you?" He leered, his eyes shining with lust and a wee promise of revenge. Asia shivered prettily, which made me want to gag. What was wrong with these people? RJ tugged Asia close, wrapping his arm around her waist. He leaned down to kiss her.

"Enough!" I shoved between them. "Any more of this kissy-kissy crap and I won't be responsible for my actions."

"Fine. It's almost midnight anyway." She gave RJ a quick kiss on the lips. "I'm going up to bed. To change. See you upstairs."

I puckered my own lips.

"Night, Jean-Michel." She patted me on the head like a kitten missing a mitten. "Try not to goad my husband into murdering you." With that parting shot, Asia disappeared into the crowd of gamblers, leaving RJ and me alone at the bar.

I studied my former friend's lovesick face, a slow grin filling my own. "Second."

"Second what?"

"Cousins, my friend." I waggled my sculpted, dark eyebrows. "Asia and I are only second cousins. By marriage. No blood ties to speak of."

Bam!

RJ's fist connected with my head. For a second time that night, I dropped to the floor, a smile on my bloody lips.

The rest of the evening, or what I can remember of it, went a lot like the first part. I'd wind up on the floor, usually wiping away a copious amount of blood; yet with each punch, our strained friendship healed a bit.

Or so I thought.

"Ow!" I yelped as RJ smashed his fist into my face yet again. Not that I felt it. I'd passed the point of feeling anything an hour ago. Rubbing my jaw, I asked, "Are we even yet?"

RJ chuckled.

Not a good sign.

"Waitress," I called to a bare-chested fairy carrying a tray of pink umbrella drinks. "Another round."

She gave me the finger.

Our drinks arrived a half hour later. I glanced at RJ, ready to duck or cover depending on his mood. He took a sip from his mug of beer and set it down on the table, so I ventured a question. "What brings you to Cin City?"

His snort was loud enough for the stripper on stage, dressed in a Little Miss Muffet costume, to pause mid-grind, her face, along with other parts of her anatomy, pinched. "Some stupid wedding," RJ said. "One of Asia's cousins is getting married in a couple of days."

"Ten days."

RJ tilted his head, his eyes boring into mine. "What?"

I exhaled loudly. "The wedding is in ten days." I squinted at my watch. The numbers floated around, finally settling on 2:34 a.m. "Oops. Nine days."

RJ let out a bark of laughter. "You!" He pointed at me with two equally fuzzy fingers. "You're getting married. What poor princess sank so low as to marry the likes of you?"

"You don't know her," I said quickly. Much too quickly.

"Spill or I'll punch you." He grinned. "Again."

I tried to roll my eyes, but they had taken on a will of their own. "Fine. Her name's Beauty."

His smile widened. "As in Sleeping Beauty? The chick who fell asleep at Baby Bear's Coming Out Ball? The one they had to wake up with a hose? That Beauty?"

My face flushed with embarrassment and alcohol. Beauty wasn't that bad, or so I told myself for the twentieth time today. So she had a bit of an attitude and slept a lot. Big deal. I wasn't Prince Fucking Charming either. Besides, I needed her to break my curse. I drunkenly slurred the whole sordid tale to RJ, from the day Elly foretold of the curse to my not-so-happy meeting with my future wife and my impending nuptials. Like an annoying cricket, my conscience, the unpickled part, screamed "shut up," but I was too far gone to heed the desperate warning.

But rather than laugh in my face as I expected, a warm glint entered RJ's eyes, which in hindsight was a bad sign. "Happily ever after, you say?"

I nodded, resigned to living out the rest of my days with my bitch of a bride. "Till death do us part."

"How about another drink?" RJ flagged down our waitress and ordered another round.

Chapter 5

The next afternoon, I awoke in the bathtub of my hotel suite, a bathtub brimming with ice, having no recollection of how I'd gotten there. Chills racked my naked body. My teeth chattered. My stomach rolled. And my head felt like Mary's Little Lamb after being sheared.

I was too old for this party-like-a-prince lifestyle. I shifted in the tub. Water and ice sloshed over the side and onto the marble floor. A pain exploded in my lower back. A pain so intense I screamed like a witch during a sponge bath. With shaking hands, I staggered from the tub and flopped on the floor. Vomit crawled up my throat.

Closing my eyes, I prayed for death. The pain in my back increased. I moaned. Groaned. And cried just a little.

All in a manly sort of way.

What the hell had happened last night? My mind flashed to the old fairy legend about a man who woke up in a very similar situation in a very similar city with one less kidney. *This is bad,* I thought. The last thing I remembered from the night before was RJ's face floating over me, an evil smile on his lips. Was it possible? Had RJ taken his revenge in the form of my kidney?

When the waves of nausea passed, I opened my eyes and glanced around the water-soaked bathroom. A Post-it note hung on the elongated mirror. I squinted at the block letters.

It read: *Now we're even.*

Two hours later, after a brief nap, a pot of coffee, and a bowl of pease porridge, lukewarm, mixed with a hearty dose of ketchup, I felt much more like myself. Of course, I looked more like something the farmer had left in the dell. Bags circled my eyes, matching the dark rings left by RJ's fists. My skin drooped, appearing greener than I liked. All of which diminished my stunning good looks. But only a little.

Luckily, I still had two kidneys.

Unfortunately, I also had a brand-new tattoo on my lower back, and not a cool "hey, I'm a badass" tattoo either. In fact, one might say it resembled the outline of a pocket full of purple posies.

I considered the tattoo in the reflection of the gold-trimmed bathroom mirror. Was this what RJ meant by "we're even"? I'd slept with his former wife, so he'd marred me for life? Seemed fitting, but I doubted RJ was finished torturing me just yet. Letting me off this easy wasn't in my former friend's villainous nature.

Something tickled at the back of my brain.

Something very bad.

A vague memory my brain couldn't quite capture.

I squeezed my eyes shut trying to conjure up anything about last night. Grape lollipops came to mind. They floated in and out of my consciousness like the dancing snack food at a movie theater. Then another vision surfaced—a rose with sharp barbed wire crisscrossing around the flower.

My stomach clenched. Picking up the house phone, I dialed the operator. A woman answered, her tone bored. "Aladdin's Palace. How can I help you?"

"This is Prince La Grenouille."

"Who?"

"Just connect me to Stiltskin's room."

Through the phone line the click of manicured nails on a keyboard sounded. French manicure, I'd bet, long and pointy, sharpened like talons as they flew across the worn letters. There was a brief pause and my bored maiden was back on the line. "I'm sorry, sir. But we have no one registered under that name."

Shit. "Try Maldetto," I said, using Asia's maiden name.

"I'm sorry. No listing," said the woman. But she didn't sound the least bit sorry. "Can I try another name for you? Prince Charming, perhaps? Or how about Snow White? I hear her sugar dwarfs are in town for a mining convention."

I scratched my chin, thinking, and again a sense of doom pooled in my intestines. Something bad had happened last night. Something my subconscious didn't want me to remember. I hoped it didn't involve a foursome with Eeny, Meeny, Miny, and their uglier sister Moe. "Did anyone leave a message for me?"

The receptionist sighed, as if my request was almost too much to bear. "No messages, sir."

"Oh." Damn.

"But someone did leave . . . something for you," she said. "Shall I have a bellhop bring it up?"

"Something?"

"I believe it was a red rose, sir."

"Was?"

She paused. "Now it more resembles rose-scented mulch. A potpourri, if you will. A very nice scent," she added with glee.

"A mulched rose?" I repeated, unsure I'd heard her correctly.

"Yes, sir. And a note." When I didn't reply, she said, "I suppose you'd like me to read it."

"That would be nice."

"Fine," she said with a drawn-out sigh. "There's just one word . . . scrawled in blood."

I swallowed the rush of bile crawling up my throat. "Blood?"

"Oh, sorry." She paused. "Not blood. Red ink."

I rolled my eyes. "What's the word?"

"Beauty."

I hung up, my mind racing. What the hell had happened last night? And what did it have to do with Beauty? The mulched rose was clearly some sort of threat, but for who? Was Beauty in danger, or was the message more personal? Maybe the less I knew about last night, the better. Yet try as I might, I couldn't quite convince myself to ignore the warning. Something was very wrong.

A few minutes later, a light knock sounded at the ornate French doors of my hotel room. I wrapped a robe around my body and went to open it. Karl stood on the other side, his jester hat replaced with an umbrella hat. The pink of his scalp shined through like a diamond and nearly blinded me with its intensity.

Shielding my eyes, I nodded to my manservant. "You do know we're in a desert, right? That it hasn't rained in Cin City for three years."

"Of course, sir."

"So what's with the hat?"

"Just in case."

"I see," I lied, too tired and hungover to apply logic to the ridiculous answer. "I'm glad you're here. I need your help."

Karl nearly jumped for joy. "Of course. Your wish is my command. But, sir, what happened to your face?"

I fingered my bruised cheek. "I ran into RJ last night."

"A lot of times, apparently."

"A few cuts are the least of my worries."

"Oh?"

"I blacked out," I admitted sheepishly. "Don't remember a damn thing after three A.M."

"Have you checked your pockets?"

I patted my robe. "No pockets."

"I meant the pockets of the trousers you wore last evening." He tapped his umbrella hat. "Dark blue slacks, with a crease in the left thigh region. Two front pockets. Two back pockets."

A bit creeped out by Karl's intimate knowledge of my wardrobe, I ran to the bedroom in search of my wayward pants. They lay on the floor tied into a bow. How they'd gotten there or that way was a mystery best left unsolved. I quickly dove into the front pockets, finding fifty cents and a matchbook from a strip club called Old Mother Hubbard's All Bare Cupboard. The back pockets bore little more—a scrap of paper, my credit card, and a red rose petal.

I laid my trinkets on the coffee table in front of Karl. We stared at each, my mind searching for any faded memory. My eyes kept returning to the rose petal. What did it mean? Was it from the same rose left at the hotel desk? I glanced at Karl, unsure what he was thinking or even if he was thinking. He could've fallen asleep, if his expression was an indication. His mouth hung open and his eyes were closed. A string of drool slid south of his chin.

Come on, I thought, *remember.* What did these things mean? A credit card, a matchbook, fifty cents, a rose petal, and let's not forget, a pocket full of posies tramp-stamped across my back. Whatever had happened last night, it was bound to be one hell of a tale. If only I would survive to tell it because, deep inside, I knew my memories were a matter of life or death.

An image of a rose flashed inside my brain again. This time the barbed-wire rose thorns dripped with purple blood spelling Beauty's name.

Chapter 6

I dressed quickly, tossing on a pair of dark khakis and a lightweight button-down shirt while Karl poured hair gel onto my black locks. When all was said and coiffured, I looked like my normal princely self, which was to say I looked damn good. Neither Jack nor his beanstalk had anything on the Frog Prince.

Before I changed out of my robe, Karl had called my credit card company for a list of charges from last night's debauchery. There were seventy-one separate charges from four different places totaling over a hundred thousand dollars. A portion of the money went toward drinks and cash advances, likely to pay for numerous lap dances. I supposed that explained the finger-shaped bruises on my thighs.

I really hoped that explained the finger-shaped bruises on my thighs.

Now it was a matter of returning to the scene of whatever crime I might've committed last night. Karl suggested we start with the first charge and work our way down the list. As far as suggestions went, it wasn't bad. And I didn't have a better clue to last evening's events, barring the mulched rose at the concierge desk, which I decided to keep to myself for the time being, so I nodded to my servant. He beamed in response.

"What's our first stop?" I asked Karl, a feeling of dread weighing my natural enthusiasm down, not to mention a liver the size of Humpty Dumpty before his supposed suicide.

"Knowing you, sir, it's to the free clinic for a shot of penicillin," Karl called as he charged out of the room.

I scowled, snatching up the rose petal from the table before pulling on my baseball cap and sunglasses. "What'd you say?"

"Nothing, sir."

"Mademoiselle, do you remember me?" I asked a stripper at Old Mother Hubbard's All Bare Cupboard, our third and hopefully final stop on my quest for answers. I was tired, still hungover, and cranky to boot, but I couldn't stop searching for clues now. Last night had changed my life.

And not in a good way.

The tattoo above my butt proved as much.

Damn RJ. When I got my hands on him . . .

The stripper halted briefly in her gyration to stare down at me. I lifted off my baseball cap and sunglasses. Her eyes narrowed. I beamed my most charming smile. She shrugged her thin shoulder, making her pink tassels spin in a circle. "Not really."

"I think I was here last night. With another guy. Not nearly as good-looking." I flashed a twenty-dollar bill her way.

"After a while you all kinda look alike."

"Excuse me?"

"Princes, I mean." She scissor-kicked her leg, nearly slaughtering a wolf with her spiked stiletto heel. The wolf ducked, his granny glasses falling to the stage.

I straightened to my full six-foot height. "Madam, I assure you. I am one of a kind." What was wrong with her? I was more than just a prince. I was the Frog Prince.

Women fell at my feet. Other princes wished they could be me, just for a day or two. Damn it, I was special!

"Excuse me, sir." Karl patted my shoulder. "If you would allow me to handle this?"

I nodded, sweeping my hand toward the half-naked chick grinding onstage. "Be my guest. But be leery, my good man." I boosted my voice over the throbbing beat of the canned music being pumped into the club. "She's obviously demented."

"Obviously." Karl stepped around me and faced the poor deluded stripper. "My lady," he began. "It is with the utmost urgency that my employer requests your help."

Pulling a hundred-dollar bill from his pocket, Karl held it out to the stripper, his eyes never wavering from her face. "If you could pause in your," he cleared his throat, "daily grind and assist us, I would be eternally grateful."

The stripper glanced down at the money and then up to Karl's earnest face. She stopped mid-gyration. "You got it, hon."

The lady stepped off stage. A gaggle of businessmen on their lunch break groaned in dismay. She shot them a lascivious wink and then motioned Karl and me toward the back room, a place where, for the right price, a prince might encounter a wealth of STDs. Not that I'd ever personally partaken in the seedier sections of a strip club—or so I told Karl.

I was a soon-to-be-married prince, after all, I assured my faithful servant as we arrived at the steel door. The stripper gestured to the plaque on the door. It read "Paid for by a generous donation from the La Grenouille Foundation."

Karl frowned.

What could I say? I was a humanitarian at heart, altruistic in every endeavor. We entered the shady room, our feet sticking to the cement floor. I shook my head at Karl and mouthed "Don't ask." Thankfully he didn't.

The stripper led us to a small alcove in front of a stage complete with the requisite gleaming silver pole. The room smelled of desperation, perspiration, and a hint of black sheep wool. Two bags full, if I wasn't mistaken.

The stripper pointed to a throne-like chair with a high back and golden trimmings. A pale and sweaty Karl eyed the tassels and then me, as if begging for a stay of execution.

"Buck up, chap." I gave him my brightest smile. "It's all in a day's work."

He swallowed hard and wiggled in his chair.

When Karl finally settled, the stripper draped her long leg over his upper thigh and plopped down on his lap. Karl's face went a few shades whiter and a bead of sweat dribbled down his bald head.

"That's a good lad." I patted the air above his shoulder. "Now think of baseball or that sport with the gloves."

"Boxing, sir?"

"They use gloves in that? Seems sort of barbaric." I scratched my chin. "Very well then, think of any damn thing you like, but find out if she remembers me from last night." I crossed my arms over my chest and glared at my faithful servant.

A hardcore rap song by Snowy W and the Midgets, "Who You Callin' a High Ho?" burst from the speakers loud enough to drown out the wail of distress from my manservant as the stripper began to grind against his manly parts.

A few minutes into her lap dance, Karl sprang from his chair. The surprised stripper slipped from his lap and fell to the floor. With a gasp, Karl reached down to help her up while he apologized again and again. "My lady, please forgive me. I . . . ah . . ."

"It's all right." She ran her hand down Karl's arm, leaving a trail of sweaty glitter in its wake.

"Don't get me wrong, you are ama—" he said.

"Yeah, yeah. She's a peach." I waved my hand to gain their attention. "Now, do you remember me from last night or not?"

She squinted, tilting her head to the side. "You look sort of familiar."

The poor girl obviously suffered from brain damage. It figured, with the amount of twirling around a pole she did in one evening. There was no other explanation for her faulty memory. I started to say as much.

"My lady." Karl cut me off and reached for the stripper's hand.

"Candi," she said. "My name's Candi."

"Candi," Karl, the dope, said with a genuine smile. "Please tell us what you can remember about last night. It might trigger my employer's memory."

The stripper tapped her finger against her bottom lip. "Well, some guys were arguing in the corner by the second stage. Your employer," she motioned my way, "might've been one of them."

Karl smiled at the stripper and then pulled me aside. "We found a clue, sir. I knew we would."

Damn servant started jumping around like a Great Dane on the trail of a mystery. I grabbed his arm. "Calm down. All's we know is that I was here last night, with RJ. Which we already knew from the credit card charges."

Karl eyed the stripper. "Do you . . . want me to . . . ?"

"Naw. I'll handle her." I strode to the dancer, flashing my most charming smile, the one that drove ordinary princesses to their knees.

She flinched instead and backed up a step. "I was wrong," she began. "I didn't see or hear nothing."

I held up my hand. "Hold on, mademoiselle."

"I swear it." Her eyes widened and her lips began to tremble, quite a feat for the sheer amount of collagen injected into them. "Please don't hurt me," she whispered.

"Hurt you? Why would I do that, luv?" My brow wrinkled as I took a step toward the frightened lady. "I am in need of your help, not wishing you injury."

Her eyes peered into mine. "But last night, you . . ."

"Candi." Karl took her hand in his. "My employer is very sorry for whatever cruel word or deed he perpetrated on your person last evening."

"Hey—"

"Rest assured, he is not normally abusive to anyone," Karl turned to glare at me, and then returned his gaze to Candi, his tone soft, "let alone a woman as beautiful as you."

Candi blushed, surprising for a woman over eighteen, and truly amazing coming from a woman with glitter on her naughty parts. "You think I'm pretty?" she asked, a hitch in her voice.

Karl shook his head.

Her face fell.

" 'Pretty' is too diminutive a word to describe your beauty." Karl dropped to his knees in front of the stripper. "You are a lady beyond compare. Poets weep when they look upon your face."

"How sweet," she said, helping my flowery-speech-spouting servant to his feet. A circle of wetness coated the knee of his jester suit.

"Burn those," I said, pointing to his tights, and then turned to the stripper. "Listen, madam, I swear you are completely safe from me," I nodded to Karl, "and anyone else in my acquaintance. No matter what. You have Jean-Michel La Grenouille's word."

"Who?"

"Just tell me what happened last night!" I stomped my foot. Candi flinched, earning me a glare from my faithful moron of a servant.

My tone had the intended result, though. "I overheard you and your friend talking," Candi blurted.

"Yeah, I kind of figured that out." The tiniest flicker of

a memory flashed through my mind, and then it was gone. "What were we saying?"

She swallowed, her throat bobbing up and down. Her eyes glanced around the room, as if she'd rather be anywhere but here, with me. What the hell had I done to scare her this badly?

"Please, mademoiselle." My eyes burned into hers. "I really do need your assistance. I can't help but feel that my life is at stake."

She bit her bottom lip and shook her head.

"What do you mean?" Karl's eyes narrowed.

"Not his life."

I scowled. "Excuse me?"

Candi lowered her voice. "It's not your life that's at stake. It's your fiancée's." She paused to lick her plump lips. "You hired someone to kill her."

Chapter 7

In the backseat of my stretch-limo pumpkin, I shut my eyes and considered the stripper's accusation. Was it possible? Had I truly hired someone to off my future wife? And if so, how? I knew absolutely nothing about how to hire a killer. An escort with a pancake fetish, sure, but a killer? Where did one even begin to look? Kill-Mart? Murderers-R-Us? A National Woodsmen's Meeting?

As hard as I racked my brain for an answer or even a glimmer of a memory, the only thing that came to mind was a rose entwined in wire, which made no sense unless I'd hired a sadistic garden gnome to off my fiancée.

"Sir," Karl said. "What're we going to do?"

Good question. I tapped my finger against my bottom lip, hoping for inspiration. Damn RJ and his revenge. This was his fault. I was fine with marrying Beauty.

Well, not fine exactly.

But I hadn't subconsciously hired anyone to bash her head in until RJ showed up. Yet. And to think I'd sent him a gravy boat for a wedding present. Asia deserved better.

Asia! That's it. I scrolled through my p-Phone in search of her cell number, finally locating it under the folder "Chicks I'd Do if We Weren't Related." A fairly long list. I pressed Send and waited while the phone connected.

"Not a good time, Jean-Michel." Asia's warm voice crackled through the phone line.

"Put your husband on the line."

"He's a little preoccupied at the moment." She yelled to someone on the other side of the phone. "Duck and cover, baby."

"Damn it, Asia," I yelled. "Put RJ on now!"

A loud crash followed my demand, and for a moment, I thought Asia had hung up. A few seconds later RJ picked up, breathing heavy. "What?!"

RJ had ruined my life, and all he could say was "What?" Rage replaced my attempted murder–induced stupor. I wanted to reach through the phone and choke the life out of my former villainous friend. "I hired someone to kill Beauty!"

RJ snorted. "You did?"

My lips curved into a frown. "Yes, I did. Because of you!"

"Oh yeah?" RJ said, distracted.

"Yes! Damn it!" I stomped my foot.

"Is that why you're calling? Because I'm a little," he yelped, "busy at the moment. Asia, honey, hand me those nail clippers."

Asia's muffled response drifted through the line, and it was neither sweet nor particularly loving. RJ laughed and then sobered as another voice boomed, "Fee-fi-fo-fum."

"Shit." RJ fumbled with the phone. "Jean-Michel, I don't have time to listen to you whine right now. So spill whatever it is you want or I'm hanging up."

"I have to stop Beauty's murder."

"So stop it."

"You don't understand." I clutched the phone, panic lacing my every word. "I don't remember anything about last night."

"So?"

"So I don't remember who I hired or even where to find him," I explained through clenched teeth.

"Ah. I see." RJ guffawed and then groaned. "Asia, quit that, sweetheart. You're only making him madder." RJ hesitated as Asia's voice mumbled in retort. "What do you mean he's the wrong giant?" RJ asked. "He's green, right?"

I growled into the phone. Stupid RJ. We were talking about me now. But no, it's always RJ, RJ, RJ. Even as a kid RJ could never focus on my problems.

"Yeah, I can see he's not jolly," RJ was saying to his bride. "But who'd be jolly when being chased by a villain with toenail clippers?"

"RJ!" I screamed into the phone. "Pay attention! This is a matter of life and death."

"Oh, sorry, Jean-Michel. Forgot you were there." RJ gave a trifling chuckle. "So you think you hired an assassin to kill your fiancée, but you don't remember any of it. Is that what you're saying?"

"I remember . . . a rose and grape lollipops." My voice went cold. "That and my new tattoo. Remind me to thank you for it. A lot."

"Well, there's your answer."

"What?"

"Sorry, mate. You'll have to figure it out all on your own." RJ laughed and then quickly sobered. "I gotta go. A husband's work is never done," he said and hung up the phone.

Damn villain. I'd show him. I'd find Beauty's assassin and stop her impending murder. I didn't need his help. I didn't need anyone's help.

"Karl, I need your help!"

"Sir?"

I replayed my conversation with RJ to Karl. When I finished, Karl bit his bottom lip and scratched his chin. His eyes grew distant; the pupils shrank as his mind wandered. *We could be here a while,* I thought, cracking open a window. A rush of hot air slipped into the air-conditioned limo. It smelled of stripper sweat and desperation. I took another whiff and grimaced. The stench wasn't coming from the outside air.

"Well, sir," Karl said with a sigh. "If we apply logic—"

"Are you mad? When has logic ever worked before? What I need is a miracle!" I pounded on the leather seat. Just then my miracle fell from my pocket in the form of my credit card. We still had two charges left to check.

I squinted at my credit card receipt and frowned as a voice-over sounded in my head.

Hangover from hell—$257
Multiple lap dances—$3,542
Tramp-stamped tattoo—$200
Bridal assassin—Priceless

The last two charges were to a business called the Rose. A flicker of recognition buzzed in my head. Could it be that easy? Then again, what self-respecting assassin named his business something as girly as the Rose? Hell, the Three Guys in a Tub nightclub sounded less gay.

Unfortunately, name aside, I didn't have a clue where to find the Rose, and the receipt didn't help; it bore no address, only a smiley face after the neatly printed name.

"Now what?" I asked Karl.

"Try Wish Upon Star." Karl pointed to the bright blue button on the dashboard of the limo with a large white star emblazoned across it.

I grinned and scrambled into the front seat, slamming my finger against the button. Instantly, a perky female voice responded, "Wish Upon Star, how can we help you tonight?"

"This might sound like an odd request," I began.

"At *Wish Upon Star* no request is too anomalous, sir."

"Right." I cleared my throat. "Here's the thing—"

"Why, just last week," the chick on the other end of the button broke in, "I had to find a prostitute for one of our big, bad, and furrier clients."

Big deal. This was Cin City, after all. Hookers were a dime a baker's dozen. They came in all shapes and sizes, from Thumbelina to Jack Sprat's overweight wife.

Ms. Perky added with a laugh, "The client wanted her to eat a basket of pastries while he watched. And I'm like, 'hello, what self-respecting hooker eats carbs?'" She paused, as if gathering steam for another long-winded tale of debauchery and diet tips.

"Anyway," I interrupted. "I need to find a business named," my cheeks heated, "the Rose."

"One moment, sir." Ms. Perky blew out a breath. "Here we go. The Rose is located on Eighth and Fairily Way. It says here they specialize in tattoos, taxes, and taxidermy."

Well, I guess that explained my tramp stamp. But the more important question was, did the Rose also specialize in murder?

Chapter 8

"Bugger," I yelped as a droplet of melting chocolate ice cream dribbled down my hand and onto my thousand-dollar silk shirt. I rubbed at the stain with the edge of my jacket. "Damn, this was one of my favorite shirts."

Standing in the doorway of the Rose, Karl glowered at the growing brown stain across my chest and then at me. "I told you we shouldn't have bought ice cream. That we should've come straight here to stop your fiancée's murder. But you just had to have an icy treat."

"I was hungry," I said with a shrug. A prince had to eat, right? And I felt bad about the whole Beauty thing. Really. I'd messed up by hiring a killer, but in the scheme of things, was murdering my intended that big a deal?

"Yes!" Karl yelled. "Murder, by definition, is a big deal, sir."

Oops. Hadn't meant to ponder my withered morality aloud. My lack of principles always made Karl a wee bit nervous. Go figure.

But Karl wasn't finished with his moral outrage. "A woman's life is at stake. A woman you vowed to love, honor, and cherish."

I stifled an eye roll, but just barely. Karl was blowing this whole thing out of proportion. It wasn't like I purposely hired an assassin. Sure, I didn't want to marry Beauty, or any woman, for that matter, but would I go as far as hiring an assassin? It had to be a mistake, like when one of the dwarfs "accidentally" caught Snow White coming out of the shower. These things happened. Sort of like a late-night booty call, but rather than a blow job, I got an assassin. I'd fix my mistake and everything would work out. It always did. It always would. I was the Frog Prince. Bulletproof, baby.

"Think of what could happen if, for some reason, you cannot stop Sleeping Beauty's assassination." Karl's voice fell as he gestured to the shiny doorway of the Rose.

I glanced at Karl. "I never thought of it that way."

He nodded. "It does give one pause."

"Shit," I said, the full weight of what I'd done rushing over me. "If I can't stop Beauty's murder, I very well might turn back into a frog."

Karl stared at me as if I'd grown an extra head or perhaps frog legs. His mouth opened and closed, but no sound escaped. Finally he took a shuddering breath. "That wasn't quite what I meant, sir."

"Well, it's a moot point anyway. Five minutes from now, Beauty will be safe and we'll be on our way back to the hotel." I grinned. "No one the wiser."

"You can say that again, sir."

I glared at my sarcastic servant and set my dripping ice cream cone in a trash can next to the doorway. In the reflection of the window, I adjusted the sleeve of my jacket and ran a hand through my black curls. The image of a rose wrapped in barbed wire graced the window, obscuring a part of my face.

This was the place.

"Let's get this over with," I said with a yawn.

Karl gave a diminutive shake of his head and opened the front door of the Rose. The sweet scent of fresh blood swept over us as we entered the dim interior of the shop. A sign on the wall stated "The Rose: We Cater to Your Every Happy Ending." I grinned at the irony.

A dwarf with curly red hair and paint-by-numbers eyebrows glanced up from a stuffed Brer Rabbit in her hand. Cotton fibers leaked from its every orifice. "Can I help you?" she asked with a bored air embedded in the genetic code of a short hipster.

"Um . . . yes," Karl began. "My employer, Jean-Michel La Grenouille—"

"Who?" the dwarf asked.

A woman wearing a white tank top and black leather pants, her arms colored with enough ink to cover Mother Goose and her whole gander twice, walked out from the back room. Her opaque, nearly black eyes met mine and she smirked. "What can we do for his lordship?"

I took a step back, surprised by the beauty in front of me. This woman was beyond gorgeous. Blue-black ringlets of silken hair fell around her shoulders and down her back. Silver hoop earrings, six in all, lined her earlobes. I imagined her long legs wrapped around me, and my mouth went dry.

She tilted her head to the side. "What's the matter? Did an Isty Bitsy Spider crawl up your waterspout?"

Her words penetrated my fantasy. My eyes narrowed on the leather-clad chick. "Mademoiselle, I assure you, my waterspout is in perfect working condition."

The beauty snickered. "Mademoiselle? How formal." Her hand hovered over her heart. "Call me Lollie. Lollie Bliss. I own this tattoo shop."

"Uh-huh."

"What's that supposed to mean?"

"Your name." I chortled. "It's obviously a fake."

Her lips curled into a frown. "Oh, and Jean-Michel La Grenouille isn't?"

Touché. I considered the pale beauty with a small diamond chip sparkling on the right side of her nose. She looked vaguely familiar, but from where? Was she here last night? Was that why the curve of her lips and her mysterious dark-eyed gaze sent a shiver down my spine? Or was there something more? A connection of sorts. Like two equally attractive sexually active ships passing in a one-night stand?

The red-haired midget jumped from her chair and came around the reception desk. She looked at the brunette and then shot a glare my way. "What is it you want?" she growled.

"Well, my lady," I sneered. "I believe I was here last evening . . . on a business matter of . . ."

"Grave importance?" the taller woman suggested with a grin.

"One might say that." I nodded. "As I was saying—"

Lollie held up a hand. "Sorry, I've never seen your pretty-boy face before. You?" She nodded to the midget, who answered with a grunt.

"Perhaps another person in your employ?"

"Nope."

"But I have a receipt from last night, for a two-hundred-dollar charge, and then there's another, much larger cash advance." Enough of a cash advance to hire a killer and have a little bit left over for a nice steak afterward. "The credit card company said both charges originated here." I yanked the paper from my pocket and shoved it toward her. "Care to explain?"

"Explain what? A receipt? Yeah," her lips thinned, "you charged something somewhere. By the smell of you, I'm guessing a brothel. But it wasn't here."

"But—"

"Listen," her eyes skimmed over me with indifference, as if my superior manly form was of little consequence, "I've never seen you before and we closed up shop early last night. Are we done here?"

My eyes narrowed. Something wasn't right, something besides her obviously poor eyesight. This had to be the place. Had to. The sign on the door. The vague familiarity of the bitchy brunette. She was lying for some unexplainable reason. Perhaps meeting me last evening had ruined her for all men. Ah, the peril of being me.

"Then explain this." I twirled around and yanked my pants down.

"Sir," Karl said, "I don't think—"

I held up my hand for quiet, waiting for the woman to speak, to acknowledge our association, or at the very least apologize for the large girly flowers tattooed across the small of my back. When she failed to respond, I ventured, "Well?"

"The tattoo's nice," she said, and then motioned to the door. "Now, if you'll excuse me . . ."

"Mademoiselle, you don't understand—" I spun back around to glare at her. "This is a matter of life and death. If you refuse to aid me, I'll be forced to take action. . . ." I let my threat trail off.

"Oh, I understand plenty, Kermit." Her eyes shrank to slits. "Now get out of my shop before I take some actions of my own." Sadly, her threat carried much more weight, in the form of a Fairyville Slugger wooden bat that she picked up from underneath the reception desk.

Using the bat like a cattle prod, she pushed me toward the door. The wood dug into my spine, bruising my already multicolored back. "This isn't the last you've heard from Jean-Michel La . . . ," I said as my feet hit the sidewalk. "Oh, forget it."

Karl followed, his knees scraping the cement as the woman shoved him out of the door after me. She waved the bat in good-bye and then slammed the door in my face.

"Sir, I guess we were mistaken about your final stop last evening," he said.

"Not quite."

Karl's eyes narrowed. "Huh? The woman . . . Ms. Bliss . . . she said she didn't remember you. Vehemently, I might add."

"That's what she said, all right."

"Then why do you look so pleased?" His brow knit in confusion. "We're no closer to stopping Princess Beauty's murder."

"Not true." I helped my manservant from the sidewalk and watched with disgust as he dusted off his tights.

"I don't understand, sir," Karl said. "What did I miss?"

"She called me Kermit."

Chapter 9

Twenty minutes later, I'd finished explaining to my manservant the significance of Ms. Lollie Bliss's apparent slip of the tongue, and leaned back against the leather couch in the center of my suite with satisfaction. I was right. I could feel it in my formerly aquatic bones.

"But how can you know for sure?" Karl asked. "Maybe you misheard?"

"She called me Kermit. I'd swear to it. That means she knows who I am." I lowered my voice. "Who I truly am."

Karl scratched his chin. "So what? That doesn't prove anything. She could've read that article about you in the paper, or seen you on *Fairyland Tonight*." Damn *FT*. Those hack paparazzi followed me everywhere. It was getting so bad a prince couldn't drive recklessly and run down innocent peasants anymore without some video showing up on FairyTube.

As much sense as Karl's explanation made, I suspected there was more to Lollie's reaction. Why else would she kick us out of her shop? She knew more than she was letting on, most likely about the upcoming murder of my neither sweet nor innocent future wife.

I'd bet my castle on it.

Maybe just the west wing. It was far too drafty for my taste anyway.

A moot point, anyhow. Unless I found the assassin in the next eight days and four hours Beauty would be much less beautiful, and so would I. Green wasn't a great color on anyone, let alone a prince with my smooth complexion.

"E-mail Georgie," I said to Karl. "Get me everything he can on Ms. Lollie Bliss." Georgie Porgie, a gelatinous fellow who often smelled of pudding and pie, worked in my employ gathering intel when the need arose. And what I needed now was information, and a lot of it. Mostly regarding a tattooed woman named Lollie Bliss.

Karl nodded, yanking his BlackFerry from his pocket and quickly sending off a missive to my less-than-attractive employee. When he finished with his task, Karl turned to me. "I have a thought." He scratched his chin, his eyes scanning my opulent hotel room. "Since we can't find your assassin, why don't you tell Princess Beauty the truth?"

I chuckled. "Good one."

"Sir, I'm not joking." He stood and started to pace, his chubby thighs wobbling like little piggies in the clingy fabric of his tights. "There is a murderer after your sweet and innocent bride."

Partly true, I supposed, at least the part about the killer. But Beauty sweet? Innocent? I had my doubts. After all, Beauty was a twenty-six-year-old spinster. Who knew what sort of debauchery she was into? I started to say as much, but Karl shushed me. "How can she protect herself from the threat if she does not know about it?" he asked with a weary air.

What a drama queen. I wouldn't let anything happen to Beauty. I'd protect her with my life.

If I had to.

"You have to tell her the truth."

"But—"

"Tonight." Karl stopped pacing to glare at me. "At dinner."

Shit. I'd nearly forgotten all about my impending

disaster/dinner date with Beauty and her family at one of the fancier restaurants in Cin City. A "get to know you" dinner. I suspected there might be more to it than that, like Beauty's relatives scamming me for a free meal.

"What time's dinner?" I asked with a sigh and glanced at my watch.

"Eight o'clock, sir."

That left me with an hour to kill. I contemplated the liquor cabinet. Dinner with the future in-laws was bad enough, but a sober dinner with the future in-laws seemed like a death sentence. Add the complication of telling Beauty I "accidentally" hired someone to kill her, and bingo, it was the stuff of fairytales. And not the Happily Ever After kind either.

The Grimm ones.

I rose from the bed and strode across the room to the well-stocked bar. The plush carpet tickled my bare feet. "I can't tell Beauty the truth."

"Why not?"

"Because she won't marry me," I said very slowly, as if Karl was the village idiot. "What woman would marry a prince who doesn't love her, and worse, hired a killer to murder her?"

"But—"

"No." I poured a healthy dose of brown liquor into a highball glass. "The less Sleeping Beauty knows about this . . . about me, the better." For me, at least until she said "I do." I wasn't ready to risk the rest of my life on the truth. Tossing my servant a figurative bone, I added, "Would you mind picking out appropriate dinner attire while I grab a shower?"

Karl sprang into action, running to my closet to inventory the mass of suits, jackets, and starchy shirts in an array of colors, except for any variation of green. "Of course, sir. Right away."

"Thanks," I said, slamming my drink and then heading to the bathroom for a quick and much-needed shower. I still smelled faintly of strip club and sadistic tattooed chick. The things I did in order to save Beauty's life. I hoped her pajama-wearing self appreciated it.

Chapter 10

A half hour into the meal, I realized how little Beauty appreciated anything, let alone my sacrifice on her behalf, unless appreciation came in the form of loud whining and random complaints.

"Where is that waiter with my drink?" Beauty complained for the fourth time in two minutes. "I'm dying of thirst here." She cleared her throat to emphasize her point.

If only, I thought, but alas, thirst would not be the death of my complaining bride, as the waiter soon arrived with our cocktails.

"About time," Beauty said, snatching the drink from the waiter's hand and gulping it down before letting out a princess-like burp.

I accepted my own drink, taking a fortifying sip before glancing across the table at my fair Beauty, who was dressed in pink flannel floor-length pj's and what appeared to be arm floaties strapped to her flannel-clad biceps. When I raised a questioning eyebrow, her stepfather, the king, responded with, "Just in case."

Next to the king, Beauty's younger sister, Pretty, perched on the edge of her chair, her green eyes brushing over me with desire. I squirmed under her obsession-filled gaze. And really, who could blame her? I was the Frog Prince, after all.

In direct contrast to Pretty's reverence, Handsome, Beauty's stepbrother, who was dressed in a dark blue cop uniform, sat on the other side of the table, glaring at me like I was a child molester. I pictured the next twenty years of my life with Beauty and her odd family and gagged on my glazed ugly duckling appetizer.

Murder didn't seem like such a bad idea anymore.

"So you grew up in New Never City?" Beauty's not-as-annoying sister, Pretty, smiled up at me, batting her eyelashes like a maid a-milking, her green eyes and pale hair as shiny and soft as a newborn unicorn.

Suspicion filled me. No one was that innocent, no matter how cute and perky. I set my fork down and glanced around the expensive restaurant before answering the younger woman. A famous celebrity couple sat a table away, acting annoyed as paparazzi snapped photo after photo. A swarm of B-list celebrities stood at the bar waiting for a table while preening in front of uninterested photographers.

"I did," I answered Pretty. "Mostly. I spent the first few years of my life . . . traveling."

Across the table Beauty let out a snort and a fountain of water spewed from her mouth. I extended an eyebrow. "What?" she yelled, wiping her drool-coated chin. "Take a picture, why don't you? It lasts longer."

"Jean-Michel, you were saying?" Beauty's stepfather glared at his stepdaughter. She responded by letting out a loud belch, and then yawned.

Oh, how I looked forward to our wedding night.

If we had a wedding night.

I almost smiled at the thought.

Dinner with Beauty, while an unmitigated disaster, hadn't changed my mind about our upcoming nuptials. Yes, she was rude, whiny, and generally annoying, but the longer I stared into her grape-colored eyes, the more convinced I became that she was the One.

Mostly because karma was a bitch.

I smirked at my intended. "Mademoiselle, have you ever been to Paris? It is quite beautiful this time of year." Not that I would know. I'd rather not spend eight hours locked in a plane with sniveling kids and equally whiny parents only to wake up in a city that harbored chicks with armpit hair longer than Goldie's famous locks.

"I don't go outside," Beauty answered.

My eyes flew to hers. "Ever?"

"Not for a very long time, not since we moved from New Never City to here when I was four years old." Her eyes bored into mine, reminding me yet again that she was the One. "Nothing's been the same since that day."

"Beauty," the king warned his stepdaughter.

"As I was saying before I was interrupted by dear old Daddy," her lips curved into a wicked smile, "the desert air makes me sleepy."

"Enough," the king growled, and then turned to me. "Beauty's quite the little homemaker. Isn't she, Handsome?"

"Yeah, right," Beauty mumbled loud enough for the table across from us to hear. "I can't sew. I hate cooking. And don't even get me started on how much I hate to clean up after myself. That's what maids are for, or so I keep telling the maids when they whine about steam cleaning my linens four times a day."

The king's smile tightened until I was afraid his face would break. But Handsome, being the good son, smiled and gave a slight nod. True to his name, a lock of black hair fell rakishly across half of his chiseled face in a look that probably cost more to achieve than our waiter made in a year. "No one can compare to Beauty," he said with a glare in my direction.

Our waiter appeared on my right, cutting off the awkward conversation, a steak the size of the big, bad one himself on a plate in his hand. "Your dinner, sir." He set the plate in front of me, and then served the rest of the table.

Handsome and the king had also ordered steaks, each bloodier than the next. Pretty had opted for a salad. And Beauty... well, Beauty had ordered something called *jambes de la grenouille,* which looked suspiciously like fried frog legs.

Maybe we were meant for each other after all.

God help us.

Beauty smiled up at me and then let out another loud belch.

The king glared at his daughter, but said nothing. Beauty shoveled a spoonful of breaded feet into her wide mouth. "Yummy," she said.

"Bon appétit," I said in my best French accent, which in all honesty sounded a bit like the Swedish Chef from the Muppets. Everyone but Beauty, who never looked up from her plate, rewarded me with a devious smile before they dove into their meal.

Ah, the joys of family dining.

Other than the crunch of teeth meeting cow flesh and reptile bones, silence filled the table. Mindlessly I chewed my food, thirty-two times, swallowed, and then took another bite, all the while avoiding any small talk with my future bride and her family.

Halfway through the meal, I glanced up from my plate in time to see a driblet of froggy juice slide down Beauty's chin. Rather than use a napkin to wipe the smear, she stuck out her tongue and lapped it away. But rather than upsetting me, her seemingly deliberate actions amused me. It was almost as if she thought I'd end our engagement if she acted up. As if I could. No matter what Beauty did, I would marry her. My curse gave neither of us much of a choice.

Beauty slurped up another mouthful. I grinned, which forced a frown to her lips. "What's your problem? Didn't your mama tell you it's not polite to stare?" She threw her spoon down; it clattered against her plate, drawing the attention of the other diners as well as a swarm of paparazzi. A flashbulb exploded on my right.

"Beauty!" Her father dropped his own fork to reprimand his stepdaughter. "For once in your life, act like a lady."

"Why would I do that?" Her eyes narrowed as if truly perplexed, or perhaps she was blinded by the sudden splash of camera lights bearing down on us.

The king's face turned bulgy red, and a vein popped out of his forehead, not a look that inspired confidence. "Why must you ruin everything!"

"Whoa." I lifted my hand to quash the budding shouting match, but Beauty's glare quickly changed my mind about interfering. My hand dropped, and I looked to Pretty for help. She winced, but said nothing, and went back to picking at her leafy green plate. Damn vegetarians. They were never any help when you needed them.

The king waggled a finger at his stepdaughter. "You'll push and push until Jean-Michel can't take any more and he ends the engagement. Like all the others."

"Others?" I asked.

Rage burned in Beauty's eyes. "Well then, if you like Jean-Michel so much, why don't you marry him?"

I winced as their arguing escalated to ear-piercing screeches. Angry words flew like killer bluebirds, turning our once-peaceful dinner into an evening with Hansel and Gretel after a sugar fix. Paparazzi circled around us like a mulberry bush. *Pop!* went the flashbulbs.

"Ungrateful little—" the king screamed at Beauty.

"Enough," I yelled. "Let's rewind. What's this about others?"

No one paid me any attention, a relatively new feeling

for me. Years of affluence and servants guaranteed my every need catered to, my every thought treated with reverence. Damn. I actually missed the reverence.

"Spoiled, lazy brat." Spit flew from the king's lips, landing on my steak. "I should've paddled you years—"

I tossed my fork onto my plate with a loud clang. The bickering stopped as the king and his sleepy daughter stared at me as if I'd just kicked a dwarf and his puppy.

"So what's this about 'others'?" I hoisted an eyebrow at Beauty. "Just how many times have you been engaged, madam?"

Pretty answered for my suddenly tongue-tied intended. "Let's see, in the past couple of years, there were ... twenty-eight. If you count Prince Chafing. Which Beauty doesn't. She claims they were never engaged, no matter how many rug burns she had."

Twenty-eight broken engagements? Shit. Now I was sure telling Beauty about my little "indiscretion" would destroy our upcoming wedded bliss, nearly as much as her brains splattered across our wedding cake.

"Twenty-eight?" I repeated.

Beauty had the decency to blush. "I'm selective."

"Not bloody likely." The king snorted. "More like no man will put up with her ... affliction long enough to marry her."

"The sleepy thing?" I tilted my head to the side. All in all, as afflictions went, it wasn't that bad. So she dozed off. Big deal. It wasn't like she "hey diddle diddled" seven filthy dwarfs like another princess of my acquaintance.

"Not that affliction." He brushed his thick fingers over his lips. "The other one."

"What other one?" There were more? And I was only finding out about it now? Stupid fairy godmother. Elly needed to do better research before binding me to a princess for life.

"You know," he said to me and then nodded Beauty's way.

She rolled her eyes and yawned.

Under all that flannel and whining Beauty was quite... well, beautiful. Her long, curly hair shone like golden rays of sun and her eyes sparkled with either insanity or intelligence. I couldn't quite tell which, but the effect was all the same. She wasn't hard on the eyes by any means.

Heaving a heavy sigh, the king said as if admitting a state secret, "She's annoying."

"Oh. That." I nodded. "Yeah, she's pretty annoying. No offense."

"None taken from a guy who smells faintly like my dinner," Beauty replied with a sneer.

"I was talking to Pretty."

"Oh."

"But you're mistaken, sir," I said to the king. While she was annoying, she was also my annoying arm-floatie-wearing *One*. I wasn't about to let her stepfather disparage her in front of a room full of people and cameras. That was a husband's job.

I rose from my seat and came around the table until I was standing over my annoying almost bride. "A man will and does love her enough to marry her." Hundreds of flashbulbs lit the restaurant. I pictured our photo in the front page of the *New Never News* and sighed, hoping they'd get my good side. Not that I had a bad side per se.

"Who? Who loves Beauty?" the king screeched, his eyes darting around the room, a frown on his once handsome, now grizzled face. His jowls sagged nearly to his chest, as did his bushy eyebrows.

"Me." I jabbed my thumb into my chest and winced. "As long as there is breath in my body, I will not break our engagement. Ever."

Leaning down to face my bride, I repeated my statement. Flashbulbs exploded again. Beauty drew in a harsh breath, her face turning a shade of lime I hadn't seen since leaving the pond all those years ago. "Are you demented or just stupid?" she shouted in a harsh whisper.

With a deep breath and the whirl of camera shutters in my ears, I moved closer to my bride. I prayed she wouldn't bite me before I'd made my point. Our lips touched, softly at first. Rather than smack me in the face as I expected, Beauty sat frozen under my kiss. My whole body began to tingle, and not in a normal lusty way.

The tingle grew bigger as a warning bell rang in my head. *She's the One.* Denial was no longer a luxury. This was the girl from the pond. My soul mate.

The drool sealed it.

Did she remember me?

Remember our brief encounter?

Remember trying to *eat me?!*

Angrily, I pulled away to stare into Beauty's grape eyes. Damn her. Damn this curse!

Beauty blinked, as if startled. Her mouth opened and closed. Then with a snort, she dropped headfirst into her half-eaten plate of frog legs and let out a small snore.

I sure had a way with the ladies.

Chapter 11

Two hours later, I sat on the end of my luxurious hotel room bed with its twelve-hundred-dollar pillows and kicked off my highly polished loafers. Dinner had not gone as expected. But I was still engaged.

For the moment.

Karl's voice whispered in the back of my head, "Tell Beauty the truth." Generally, I ignored all advice given by any servant, especially the short, balding ones with a much-too-creepy interest in my sex life.

This time proved no exception.

Telling Beauty the truth would ruin my best-laid plans.

Since my plan included staying in shape, my human shape to be precise, as well as getting laid, telling Beauty anything, especially the truth, ranked up there with getting a magic bean enema by the sadistic chick from this afternoon.

Speaking of sadistic women, I rubbed at a small greasy frog-leg stain on my shirt left by my future wife after her face-plant into her dinner.

Luckily—or not so luckily, depending on your point of view—I'd rescued Beauty before she managed to drown in the congealed frog juice. My soon-to-be father-in-law, the king, seemed properly appreciative, in that he stuck me with the dinner bill.

How I couldn't wait to say "I do"!

My ringing phone interrupted my dire musing. I glanced at my watch. 10:20 P.M. Then I checked the caller ID on my p-Phone. Restricted. I debated not answering, but in the end, cat-murdering curiosity won out, and I said hello.

"Jean-Michel," the voice on the other end huffed. "I'm glad I caught you."

"Georgie?" I said. "Why are you so out of breath? Are you taking a late-night jog?" Weird, since it was after midnight in New Never City, where Georgie lived, but even odder, Georgie's Jell-O like form wasn't built for running of any kind, let alone the exercise variety.

"You could say that," Georgie said through the static. In the background footsteps pounded hard, as if Georgie was being chased by a pack of boys. "Anyway," Georgie yelled over the noise, "I probably won't be around for . . . a while. I have some . . . business to take care of . . ."—he panted—"but I wanted to get in touch regarding that certain matter Karl e-mailed me about this afternoon."

Right. Lollie Bliss. "And?"

"Keep your distance."

I raised my eyebrow. "Why's that?"

"She's bad news." As Georgie finished his statement, shouts erupted through the phone line. The pounding of feet grew louder, as did a string of swear words from Georgie's mouth.

"Georgie?" I called. "You still there?"

A few seconds later he returned to the line. "Yeah, sorry about that. I don't have much time," he huffed out, "but this can't wait."

"All right," I said slowly.

"Lollie Bliss doesn't exist."

I shook my head, stopping when I realized Georgie couldn't see me through the phone. "Not true. I met her. This afternoon, in fact. Karl saw her too."

Georgie giggled, which quickly turned into a wheezing cough. "I meant she doesn't exist in the figurative sense."

"Oh."

"There's no record of Lollie Bliss until two years ago, when she suddenly appeared in Cin City."

Hell, if one did a search for Jean-Michel La Grenouille they'd find much the same. Until the age of eight, I hadn't officially existed, not in the human sense. Since then I'd sure made up for it. A bunch. "That doesn't necessarily make her bad news."

"Hang on," Georgie said as the rattle of chain link echoed through the line. A loud rip followed. "Fudge."

"Are you all right?"

"Yeah. Tore my favorite pants on a fence post." Georgie let out a sigh. "Damn girls. They never just let things go. I mean, you kiss one little . . ."

"Um . . . Georgie? Can we get back to my problem now?"

"Right." Georgie sucked in a deep breath. "So, this Lollie chick. Is she hot?"

I stopped, considering Ms. Bliss. "Hot" wasn't quite a strong enough word to describe the woman. "Smoking hot" came closer, but still didn't do her plump lips and the smart slant of her mouth justice. "She's all right," I answered quietly, unwilling to share anything about Ms. Bliss with a pervert like Georgie. The guy had a collection of pornography as high as the top of old spaghetti, even with the mountain of cheese.

"That's what I thought." He exhaled again, his voice wheezy and weak. "Just be careful. She runs with a bad crowd."

"How bad?"

"Bad enough that the cops have her under surveillance."

"Really?" I bit my lip. "For what?"

"Murder for hire."

I swallowed hard. "Lollie's a hit man . . . I mean, woman?"

"No. No. Not her." Georgie paused. "From what I

heard, her boyfriend's the killer. The cops think he's murdered at least seven people."

Well, that answered that question. Lollie had lied to me in order to protect her lover. A noble gesture, one I could even appreciate given different circumstances, but Beauty's life was at stake. How did her boyfriend get away with seven murders without arrest? I asked as much.

"Lack of evidence, I guess." He let out a long wheeze. "All the murders looked like accidents."

"Accidents?"

"Yeah," Georgie said, his voice raspy like the soles of a glass-slippered princess. "The cops might've never caught on, but he likes to leave a small memento of his crimes."

"What kind of memento?"

"A single long-stem rose."

My mind flashed to the article in yesterday's newspaper, the one about the Cin City assassin with a flower fetish. The assassin called Spindle. A shiver ran up my spine.

"No one knows why he leaves a rose," Georgie said. "But in every case the cops found one somewhere at the scene."

I had a pretty good idea why, and she was brunette, beautiful, and covered in ink. The roses were some sort of sick "I love you" note left by a crazed assassin. One I'd hired to kill my future wife. Shit.

Georgie wasn't finished. "The guy is good. He ran one victim over with a pumpkin."

"A pumpkin?"

"A really big pumpkin." Georgie gave a wet laugh and then quickly sobered.

A man's voice crackled through the phone, sounding highly annoyed. "Stop right there, Georgie."

"She was asking for it!" Georgie screamed. "I swear."

The sound of fist meeting flesh followed and then the phone clicked once and went dead.

"Georgie?" I ventured.

Nothing but static greeted me. I hung up my p-Phone and stared at the desert landscape painted on the wall. Why a hotel in the middle of the sandpit went with a desert motif was beyond me. It was like a princess buying a glass slipper factory.

Speaking of princesses . . . I needed to stop Lollie's boy toy from murdering my lazy bride and soon. But how? A well-placed bribe? And if that didn't work, I could buy a gun and force Lollie to take me to her boyfriend, Clint Easterbunny style.

A good way to get shot, but what other options did I have? I needed to find this Spindle guy and fast.

I wondered if Ms. Bliss, like her boyfriend, packed heat. Probably not. It was hard to hide panty lines in black leather pants. Imagine trying to disguise a pistol.

Unfortunately, a few hours later I learned that, like princesses, weapons came in many varieties.

Chapter 12

Following my phone call with Georgie, I did what any man facing the possible murder of his future wife would do. I squeezed a fair amount of hand sanitizer on my hands and then plopped down on my bed and fell fast asleep.

In my defense, Beauty was probably fast asleep too.

Or not.

The ringing of my p-Phone woke me ten minutes later. "What?" I grumbled at whoever was rude enough to disrupt my slumber.

"Jean-Michel?" Beauty's sleepy voice echoed through the phone. "Did I wake you?"

I stifled a yawn. "Not at all. Is something wrong, my lady?"

Beauty inhaled deeply. "I . . . ah . . . about tonight," she began. "I wanted to say . . ."

"Say what, my lady?" I prompted when the silence lengthened. My mind raced with possible scenarios, most of which left me with olive-colored legs. Damn it, I didn't want to turn back into a frog. Not now. Not when a French restaurant recently opened up on my block.

"Thank you," she whispered as if the words tasted unpleasant.

"No problem."

"No, I mean it," she added, as if the words tasted unpleasant in her mouth. "Thank you."

Damn, I'd only bought her dinner. What sort of appreciation would I get for a full six-course meal? Oddly, I found myself very much wanting to find out. "You are quite welcome, my lady. I'd be happy to buy you dinner again tomorrow evening."

She let out a snort. "I wasn't thanking you for dinner, idiot."

"Oh," I said with a frown. "What exactly did you thank me for, then?" I pictured our kiss. It wasn't the best. Maybe a six on the hotness scale. Maybe the poor dear wasn't as experienced with men, twenty-eight former fiancés aside. She did wear a lot of flannel. . . .

"Not that," she said, reading my mind. "I wanted to thank you for standing up for me. Not many men would argue with their future father-in-law, let alone embarrass a king in public eight days before a marriage the king orchestrated."

When she put it like that . . .

"I mean, my stepfather wanted to boil you in oil after we left." Beauty let out a half yawn, half laugh, and then sneered, "You'll be happy to know Pretty managed to talk him out of ending our engagement."

"Not you, madam? You didn't stand up for your man?"

This time her snort of laughter rang through loud and clear. "Not bloody likely."

Her words slammed into me, shaking the tendrils of sleep instantly from my mind. Did my future bride hate me? What'd I do to her? Well, besides the whole hiring a killer to smother her with a pillow. "Excuse me?"

"What?"

"You said, not bloody likely."

"Did I?" Her yawn traveled through the phone line.

"Yes, madam, you did. Are you averse to marriage in

general or just marriage to me?" Twenty-eight other fiancées suggested the latter to be true. Damn.

"I don't know what you're talking about," she said with another yawn. "I can't wait to become Mrs. Jean-Michel La Gray . . . La Gro . . . Mrs. Frog Prince. Isn't that every girl's dream?"

My eyes narrowed. Was my intended being a wee bit sarcastic or did she truly mean what she said? I couldn't tell, and neither reaction boded well.

But before I could question her further, my bride's soft snores echoed through the phone line.

Following my phone conversation with Beauty, I couldn't fall back to sleep. Guilt tickled in the back of my throat like leftover puddin' and pie. The poor chit seemed to think I was some sort of hero for standing up to her father, but the opposite was true. I was a coward, too afraid of turning back into a frog to warn her of her impending death by an assassin I'd "accidentally" hired. Her snide face floated in my mind's eye as the light faded from her grape-lollipop eyes. Dead, unfocused eyes stared back. I swallowed hard.

I'd make this up to her, somehow.

Maybe buy her a nice fluffy pillow or new Prada pj's.

Since sleep had deserted me, I decided to start my campaign to force Ms. Bliss to take me to her boyfriend. Jumping out of bed, I tossed on a pair of jeans, a baseball cap, and a sweatshirt.

Once I was properly disguised as a commoner slash peasant, I dialed Karl's hotel room. The phone rang once, twice, and a third time. The mechanical voice of the hotel messaging center whirled to life. "The guest you have dialed is unable to answer. Please leave a message at the beep."

I scowled at the receiver. Where the hell was Karl? Normally, my faithful manservant answered on the first ring, no matter what the time. Was he still pouting from our earlier argument? I'd said I was sorry...well, I'd said something to the effect of he'd be sorry, but really it was close enough.

At the time, our argument hadn't seemed like much of one, just two friends disagreeing over my lack of moral fiber. Karl insisted, even after my disaster of a dinner with Beauty's family, that I tell her the truth. I, on the other hand, insisted Karl keep his big, bald mouth shut. In the end, after threatening Karl with a pair of shears, I'd won the argument. Beauty would never know the truth.

Unless Spindle killed her.

Then she might suspect something was amiss.

Or not.

Beauty didn't strike me as the sharpest princess in the kingdom. With a sigh, I hung up and dialed Karl's room again; this time when the recorder kicked on I left a rambling message about honor, loyalty, and my need of a ride to the Rose. Then I sat on the edge of the bed to wait.

And wait.

And wait some more.

Three and a half minutes later Karl still hadn't called back. Frog it. And frog him. I didn't need him or anyone, for that matter. I had the number for Higglety Pigglety Cab Company on speed dial. Of course I had to wait, sometimes nine, and sometimes ten minutes for someone to answer. When someone answered with a squawk, I ordered a taxi to meet me downstairs.

With one last glance around my hotel room I closed the door and headed into Cin City, searching for a killer, or at the very least, his tattooed girlfriend, in order to save the life of a woman who, I suspected, would prefer to have me boiled in oil.

Probably not the smartest move.

Apparently Beauty and I were meant for each other after all.

Chapter 13

Cin City was a different place at night. Not literally, of course. It was still crammed full of cheesy theme hotels and casinos. It still sported a million blazing, retina-burning lights. Greed and lust still oozed from the sidewalks and into even the noblest of hearts. But after midnight the air turned a bit cooler, the people a bit shadier, and the risk a bit greater. Not to mention the increased odds of taking a glass slipper to the forehead from an annoyed prince in drag.

God how I loved Cin City after midnight.

My cab sped down the strip, a dreadlocked hen in a Rastafarian cap at the wheel. I waved away a cloud of questionable smoke hovering around me and grinned as we passed a gaggle of Cinderella impersonators and the occasional fairy dust–addicted princess selling her wares on the street corner. Millions of multicolored lights reflected off the taxi's windows.

The deeper we went into the city, the more dangerous the streets became. Casinos and motels still filled the avenue, but the themes had changed. Gone were the fairytale wonder worlds of New Never City, France, and Egypt, replaced by phallic skyscrapers and cheesy circus tents.

Here, the storefronts offered ten-dollar T-shirts and barred windows. Paint peeled off the sides of the sun-baked buildings, leaving exposed cement and brick. Run-down motels with no vacancy signs blinked: "No can."

Fitting somehow.

At Eighth and Fairily Way, the cab slowed, finally stop-ping in front of the brick-and-mortar storefront of the Rose. Lights blazed inside the tattoo shop. Once again, my mind flashed to the image of a rose covered in blood and barbed wire. The petals faded slowly, replaced with a pic-ture of Lollie Bliss, her blue-black hair and nose ring shim-mering in the fluorescent light, her onyx eyes mirroring my own intense blue ones.

I was inexplicably drawn to her. Probably a latent death wish. Made sense if one considered I'd be married soon.

"Keep the meter running," I said, tossing the cabbie my last hundred-dollar bill. She glanced around nervously, but finally agreed.

Tugging on the sleeve of my sweatshirt, I exited the taxi. The night air smelled of sand and heat with a ting of piss. Ah, Cin City at its finest. Up the block, a police siren whooped and then went quiet. Rats in tiny felt hats scur-ried from the sewer, their manicured claws scraping the pavement in a hypnotic rhythm.

No sooner had I walked two steps away than the cab screeched from the curb, smoke billowing from its tires as it shot down the street, narrowly missing a guy on a magic carpet.

I jogged to the front door of the Rose. A part of me prayed I'd find Spindle inside and end this whole charade. The other, dumber side, hoped for something along the lines of Lollie Bliss naked and waiting for any prince to come.

I was disappointed on both counts.

I opened the front door and bells rang overhead, caus-ing every eye, three in all, to swing my way. A big guy with one eye in the center of his forehead, tattoos up and down his arms, and a blank expression on his face glanced up from his plastic waiting room seat. The red-haired midget lifted an eyebrow, but said nothing. Instead she focused on the tiny, fat, and very dead mouse in her hands. A naked Lollie Bliss was disappointingly absent from the scene.

"Hi," I said to the receptionist. "Remember me?"

She grunted in response.

"I'll take that as a yes." I took a step closer to her small desk. A growl rumbled from her lips. Plastering on my best princely smile, I said, "Spindle around?"

The midget finally glanced up, a frown on her small face. "Who?"

I grinned, keeping my voice low and tight. "Spindle. The guy fucking your boss. Kills people for a living. Strike any midnights now?"

Like a specter, Lollie Bliss materialized in front of me, her hand on her curvy hip and a dark smile upon her plump maroon lips. She wore an outfit similar to the one she had on the day before—black leather pants, a white tank top, pink bra strap peeking through. An outfit selected to showcase the artwork covering her arms, back, and chest. But it did far more than that. My mouth went dry as I pictured running my hands over her soft, inked skin.

"Oh, you struck something all right." Lollie's words shook the fantasy from my mind. "Now get out of here before it strikes you back."

"Ms. Bliss, a pleasure to see you again." I held out my hand, wondering if she'd shake or break it. She did neither, much to my disappointment. I wanted to touch her, even if it was nothing more than a quick handshake. I wanted to feel the heat of her skin, the softness of her fingers, the indentations of ink and flesh. Instead she ignored me and turned to the big biker. "Okay, Tweedle, I'm ready for you."

The biker nodded, hefting his large body from the seat. The chair creaked in relief. Lollie motioned to the purple curtain hanging across the room, and the biker slowly lumbered toward it. Lollie glared at me. "You still here, Kermit?"

Swallowing a sharp retort, I shot her a charming smile. "I need to speak with you, mademoiselle. It's quite urgent."

"Sorry," she said sounding anything but, "I only have time for my customers. Paying customers, that is. A girl's got to make a living." Turning on her boot heel, she headed for the curtain.

Got ya, I thought as I pulled out my wallet, which held a stock photo of some creepy male model I kept forgetting to toss out and a sad lack of funds. Frog! Karl had taken all my petty cash to the dry cleaners. Perhaps Lollie would take credit? "Three hundred dollars for five minutes of your time."

She didn't stop or slow down, for that matter.

I tried again. "Five hundred."

Nothing.

"A grand."

That seemed to get her attention. Slowly she turned around to face me, her eyes on my wallet. Greed was a hell of a motivator. I waved my wallet in front of her like a matador.

Here kitty, kitty.

"I only talk while I work." She crossed her arms under her breasts, her eyes boring into mine as if daring me.

"What's that supposed to mean?"

Her smile widened. "It means, pretty boy, if you want to talk, we talk," she lingered on her words as if savoring the moment, "while I tattoo you."

"I . . . ah . . ."

"That's what I thought." Once again, she spun on her heel and headed toward the curtain, pausing long enough to call over her shoulder, "You know the way out."

Shit. So far my plan for winning Lollie over had failed, and in a big way.

"Wait," I said.

She stopped.

"I'll do it."

She swung around to face me, her mouth curving into an appealing "O." "Really?"

No, I wanted to say, but nodded instead. "Yeah. Let's get it over with."

Lollie grinned, flashing teeth as white as Mary's Little Lamb. "Okay, Kermit. Money up front."

I pulled out a wrinkled piece of paper, wrote "one thousand" on it, and quickly signed my name before shoving it her way.

"What's this?"

"IOU."

"Are you kidding me?"

"Hey, I'm good for it." I straightened to my full six-foot height. "You have the word of Jean-Michel—"

"Yippee for me."

"Mademoiselle, I assure you—"

"Save it," she said, folding the IOU and stuffing it into her bra. She nodded to the midget. "Red," Lollie said, fingering the small diamond on the side of her nose. "Would you finish Tweedle up while I take care of his lordship over here?"

Red grinned her agreement.

"Okay, pretty boy," she said, gesturing to the myriad of tattoo designs on the wall—anything from a cat with a fiddle to three tiny mouse skulls with flames shooting from their empty eye sockets. "Pick your poison."

I studied the wall. While all the designs were expertly drawn and imaginative, I felt overwhelmed by the sheer number, as well as the thought of receiving yet another unwanted tattoo. In less than two days. Worse, the thought of a needle stabbing my skin over and over again had me breaking into a cold sweat.

Picturing Beauty's cold, fixed eyes, I threw my hands in the air. "It doesn't matter. You pick something, and let's get this over with."

"Wrong answer, Kermit." Lollie grinned. "A tattoo isn't like picking out a wife."

"What—" I began.

"A tattoo's forever. It can't simply be erased. No matter how *tired* you get of it."

My eyes narrowed. Was she making a veiled reference to my relationship with Sleeping Beauty? Or perhaps the fact I'd hired her boyfriend to erase my future wife? Either way, I wasn't in the mood, not to mention my nuptials were not a damn bit of her business.

We stared at each other.

Minutes ticked by.

"That one." Tweedle, the one-eyed tattooed biker, broke the silence. "Get that one."

Without taking my eyes off Lollie I nodded, hoping I hadn't just agreed to get a skull and crossbones riding a mermaid with the word "mom" scrawled over her boobs. Not that I had anything against mermaids or boobs, for that matter. Actually, when I considered the flowers already stamped on the small of my back, a mermaid might butch me up some.

"Good choice," she said, a small smile on her plump lips.

I looked up at the wall, surprised to see Tweedle pointing at a small, fluffy bunny tattoo with a red ribbon tied around her ears. "Really?" I glanced at the biker.

"I like bunnies," he said, his eye narrowing to a slit.

"Of course you do. Who doesn't?" I said, a grin spreading across my face.

Chapter 14

Before I could reassess my life choices and/or get my ass kicked by a one-eyed biker with a bunny fetish, Lollie grabbed the string of my sweatshirt and dragged me across the room. She opened a door and practically tossed me inside. She flipped on an overhead light and gestured to a dentist chair in the center of the room. "Have a seat."

I did, taking time to glance around, checking for the closest emergency exit. A mirror hung on the ceiling, giving me a clear view down Lollie's tank top. No wonder Tweedle had so many tattoos. Hell, if it wasn't for my fear of needles, I might return for a few more myself. Miss Bliss was one hell of a beautiful, stacked woman.

Lollie caught me staring and yanked up her top. I sighed, returning my attention to the rest of the space, which was tidy if not a bit cluttered. Art in various tribal designs with flaming dragons, black knights, and swords filled the walls. A machine about the size of a tuffet sat next to the dentist chair, a bunch of levers and cords attached at random intervals. Lollie played with various dials and smiled as the machine responded to her touch.

The phone on the wall next to the tattoo machine started to ring. Lollie held up a finger. "I have to get this."

I motioned for her to answer, not in any great hurry to

have a needle jabbed into my skin again and again, even by a woman as beautiful as Ms. Bliss.

"The Rose. Lollie speaking," she said into the mouthpiece. "Yeah, he is.... No ..." She paused to listen. "I said no!" she added with greater emphasis. "Fine, whatever." She hung up with a sigh.

"Problem?" I asked.

"Not really." She shifted from foot to foot. "My sister. She's getting married soon, and she's a little nervous."

"Understandable," I said.

"I guess." She cracked her knuckles, one by one, sounding like mini-gunshots in the silent room. "So where do you want it?" she asked, almost as if we were discussing something as unimportant as the weather instead of the placement of a very real and permanent design branded on my flesh with a super-large and sharp needle.

Have I mentioned the extremely large size of the needle?

"Beauty better give great head," I muttered under my breath.

"What?" Lollie tilted her head to the side, showing off the soft white skin of her throat. "I didn't quite catch that."

"Nothing ... How about here?" I pointed at the left side of my chest, right above my heart, where a large birthmark that looked remarkably like the letter "B" marred my otherwise flawless skin.

Lollie nodded. "Take off your shirt and let's get started."

Slowly, as if locked in a nightmare, I peeled off my sweatshirt and lay back against the cold leather of the high-backed chair. My face flushed and my stomach clenched.

Lollie moved her chair next to me, a large, pink tattoo gun in her hand. Except it didn't look much like a gun, not in the "blow your brains out" sense. Rather it resembled a futuristic torture device with interchangeable vials.

"No. No. No. It can't be," she mumbled to herself, her eyes locked on the birthmark.

"What'd you say?" I struggled to sit.

"Nothing," she said, pushing her hand against my chest. "Lie back." Her foot pressed a pedal and the tattoo gun whirled to life.

I let it go, my full attention on the gun in her hand. "Shouldn't you...um...disinfect my skin or something...?"

"Naw," Lollie said with a smile. "What's the worst that could happen?" She started forward, the gun looming larger and larger.

I shrank back in the chair. "Maybe this isn't a good idea...."

"Shh..." Her finger pressed to my lips. "It will be over before you know it."

My heart thundered in my chest and my breath came in short gasps. Visions of long, pointed needles danced through my vision, growing larger and larger. Squeezing my eyes shut to ward off the image, I tried not to hyperventilate.

The gun touched my flesh.

"Nooooo!" I lurched up, knocking the tattoo instrument from her hand. It clattered to the floor. Blood-red ink leaked from the chamber, pooling in a circle on the shiny tiled floor.

"I can't do this," I said, scrambling from the chair and holding my arms in front of me to ward off her and her super-large needle.

"Relax, Kermit." Lollie gave a small laugh. "No needle." She picked up the empty gun and jabbed it toward me. "See? Now get out of here before you do get hurt."

Rage boiled in my gut. "That was your idea of a joke? Funny. But we're far from done, mademoiselle." Grabbing her arm, I yanked her to her feet, accidentally knocking over the tattoo machine next to her. It hit the ground with a crash. Broken bits flew off in all directions. I winced at the damage, but rage kept my mind on my mission. "I'm done playing around. Where's your boyfriend? Where's Spindle?"

Her eyes narrowed, moving from the busted machine on the floor to my face. "Let me go. Now!"

Rather than obey her order, I tightened my grip, feeling her delicate skin bruise under my fingertips. "I give the orders now, Ms. Bliss. Tell me what I want to know...."

The fight suddenly left her and she trembled in my arms. I dropped her arm and shoved her away, disgusted with myself. This wasn't me. I didn't manhandle semi-innocent maidens, unless they asked nicely. Even then I used the safe words "Rub-a-dub-dub, hands off my nub."

Lollie snorted with laughter, easing any feelings of lingering guilt I experienced. "Give it up, Kermit. You're not the physical type. Now get out of here and you might live to see your next birthday."

Not much of a consolation when one considered I'd be spending it waist-deep in flies and murky pond water. I glared at Lollie. "You don't understand, madam—"

"Oh, I understand perfectly," Lollie said, her tone soft. "I'm sorry, Kermit. Maybe you're confused. Pre-wedding jitters or something. I don't know. But you're barking up the wrong rose bush."

I frowned, suddenly unsure. Was Lollie right? Was I just suffering from cold feet about my upcoming wedding? "Wait." I held up my hand in question. "How'd you know that I'm getting married?"

Her thin shoulders lifted in a shrug. "You must've mentioned it earlier."

"No, I didn't."

"Then your servant did."

"I don't think so." I took a step toward her, our bodies mere inches apart. Her scent, a combination of ink and strawberries, rose up, tickling my senses. I wanted nothing more than to give into my primal urge and take all that she offered. But I resisted. After all, I was a soon-to-be-married man. Not to mention, Ms. Bliss would likely geld me with the tattoo gun in her hand. "So if I didn't mention my upcoming nuptials and my manservant surely didn't, that leaves only one option." I lifted Lollie's chin with my hand. Her eyes met mine and she swallowed. "Spindle," I said. "Where is he, Lollie?"

"How many times do I have to say it? I don't know anyone by that name." Her eyes flashed with true anger. Shit. Unless she was a first-class actress, and I'd dated a few, Lollie Bliss was telling the truth. So where did that leave me? One step closer to a pair of frog legs, that much was true.

Lollie pushed me away. "I think it's time for you to leave."

"But I—"

"Now," she added, shoving me toward the door. I allowed her to prod me along, pausing at the threshold of the shop. Her hand pushed at my chest, but I didn't budge. Rather, I grabbed her arm and yanked her body against mine. Her nipples hardened under the fabric of her tank top. An inferno of passion swept through me. There was something between us. Something dark and dangerous. I leaned down to take possession of her mouth. She responded in kind, lifting her lips to meet mine.

"Ow!" I yelped, spinning to face my attacker, a tiny red-headed woman with an extremely large and sharp needle in her doll-like hand. "What the hell—"

Red tilted her head to the side and batted her oddly long eyelashes. "What?"

"You stabbed me," I said, pointing to the needle and then to the pin-sized hole in the side of my sweatshirt.

The midget scowled. "Did not."

"You did so!"

She shook her small head.

"Damn it." I turned back to Lollie. "She stabbed me. You saw . . ." I looked around only to find Lollie Bliss had vanished. When I turned to question Red, she had disappeared as well.

There I stood, alone, in the doorway of an empty tattoo shop, a pinprick of blood seeping into the elastic of my boxer shorts.

As first dates went, I'd had worse.

I strolled out of the Rose a few minutes later, my mind filled with questions. Questions like, was Lollie telling the truth about Spindle, and if so, who had I hired to kill my bride? And more importantly, just how much mead would it take to get Ms. Bliss into bed? Sleeping with Lollie wasn't cheating until I said "I do," right? I made a note to ask Karl, if he ever bothered to make an appearance.

Boots scraped against the sidewalk, dragging me from my fantasy. A down-on-his-luck woodsman carrying a bottle of whiskey and a rusted ax approached. "Hey, buddy," he slurred. "You got a light?" He waved a bent cigarette in my direction.

"Yeah." I dug in my pockets, pulling out a pack of matches, and lit his cigarette. The tip flared to life, illuminating the woodsman's eerie jade eyes. Familiar eyes. "Do I know you?" I asked.

"Don't think so," he said. "You in the union?"

I shook my head.

He preened, tossing his hair back like Neverland's Top Model. "Maybe you saw my spread in *Woodland Animals Weekly*." He flexed his biceps under his flannel shirt.

Again I shook my head. "Sorry. I missed that one."

His smile dropped. "Oh. Well . . . thanks." He lifted the lit cigarette. "You're a prince," he said and stumbled away. *Not for long, my good man.* Not unless I found whoever I'd hired to kill my bride and soon.

I fingered the matchbook in my hand. The same one from the other night at Old Mother Hubbard's All Bare Cupboard. A flash of ink caught my eye. There, on the inside cover, behind the unlit matches was a scrawled phone number.

(702) 555-1212.

Frog! All this time I'd had the answer to my problem tucked away in my pants. Sadly, the opposite was usually true. I pulled out my p-Phone and quickly punched in Spindle's number. My luck was changing. I could feel it. The phone rang once. Twice. Then a voice answered. A very familiar voice.

"The Rose. This is Lollie. How can I help you?"

Chapter 15

"Frogging bitch!" I stabbed the End button on my phone and turned toward the Rose, intent on doing Ms. Bliss incredible amounts of bodily harm.

A noise clattered behind me. I swung around to face the sound. Yet before my eyes could adjust to the darkened night, something heavy whacked me in the back of the head. I hoisted my arms to ward off another brutal hit to my noggin, but my feet tangled in a discarded newspaper.

I was falling, grasping at anything to steady myself. My fingers caught something. Something silky. Something soft.

A flash of metal caught my eye a few seconds before it also caught the side of my head. I dropped to the sidewalk, my vision growing gray and then black.

"Sir? Sir!" a voice patty-caked through my head.

I winced, trying to focus on the sound, struggling through layers of darkness to reach the words. I knew they were words, formed by tongue, lips, and vocal cords. Words with meaning. Even if, at that moment, I had no concept of anything other than pain. It tore at my sense, ripping me from the soothing blackness of unconsciousness.

Something cold touched my face, forcing me to jerk my eyes open, a task that took a great deal of willpower. Every movement hurt from my eyebrows to the tips of my littlest piggy. I vowed never to take blinking for granted again.

Like a cartoon, bluebirds with extremely large teeth flew in a circle above my head. A huge pink orb loomed in and out of my vision, growing slowly into focus. Karl. My manservant. And his really big, bald head.

What was he doing here?

And where exactly was here?

I couldn't remember anything, let alone how I'd ended up in a garbage-strewn alley with my head pounding like a diddled fiddle. My last memory was of arriving at the Rose. I raised my hand, glared at the piece of torn black leather fabric in it, and then gently stroked the teacup-sized lump on my temple.

A fuzzy memory surfaced.

Someone had hit me!

I said, "Someone hit me," to Karl.

"What did you do to deserve it?"

"What!?" I nearly shouted, causing my head to throb even more than the bright sun burning overhead. I considered puking on Karl's shoes, mostly out of revenge.

Yet my malicious manservant was far from finished. Crossing his arms over his chest, he made tsk, tsk sounds through his teeth. "Well, sir, it's not surprising when one considers your personality. Heck, I'm amazed it doesn't happen much more often."

"Hey," I protested.

"If you lie with sleeping dogs—"

"What'd you say?" I grabbed Karl's arm and he helped me to my feet. The world spun and then righted itself.

Karl's lips thinned. "I said, if you lie—"

"That's it!" Without waiting for my manservant, I rushed forward. Everything came back to me in a flash. Ms. Lying Bliss. The matchbook. A flash of metal. Pain and finally blackness.

"Sir," Karl shouted from behind me. "Wait."

I didn't slow. I had to find Lollie. She was the key to this whole sordid thing. When I located her, I'd force her to call Spindle off, thereby saving my bride. If she refused, well, I'd call on a power greater than myself, Elly, my all-knowing and all-seeing fairy godmother, as long as you caught her before happy hour—otherwise she was just a gin-soaked bar slut with wings.

"Sir," Karl yelled again.

"I don't have time for a lecture right now." I kept walking, weaving back and forth like the drunken woodsman from last night. Something stirred in the back of my brain. Something about the woodsman . . .

"But, sir," Karl insisted.

I stopped and spun to face my argumentative servant. "What?"

Karl lowered his gaze.

I stomped my foot. "What is it?"

"Um . . . sir . . . ," he started.

"Spit it out already."

"Your pants," he said.

"Frog it, Karl, this is hardly the time to discuss my wardrobe." I pulled at my sweatshirt. "We have to save Sleeping Beauty from a certain death."

"But, sir," he said. "You're not wearing any."

I looked down, and sure enough, my pants had vanished, along with my wallet and my p-Phone, as well as the only piece of evidence against Lollie Bliss, the matchbook. "Shit!"

Karl motioned toward the black limo at the edge of the alley and sighed, as if my lack of pants was a foregone conclusion. "Don't worry, sir. I always carry extras in the car."

After pulling on a pair of Levi's from Karl's secret stash of trousers, I explained how Lollie had lied, manipulated, and ultimately tried to murder me last night.

"Maybe we should see a doctor about your head injury," he said, waving two fingers in front of my face. Apparently not satisfied by my growl of warning, he poked at the lump on my head.

I pushed him away. "I'm serious. Lollie played me. I bet she was the one who hit me too."

"Didn't you say she was inside the building at the time?" His lips puckered as if he didn't believe a word I said. "How could she possibly strike you, sir?"

Fucking Karl and his use of logic. I rubbed the back of my neck. "I don't know. Maybe she slipped outside after our..." I stopped. The less Karl knew about my attraction to Lollie and our botched kiss, the less time I'd have to listen to him lecture me about my lack of moral fiber. I ate a bran muffin for breakfast each morning, what more did Karl want?

"After your what, sir?"

"Never mind." I waved him off. "Just trust me on this. Lollie Bliss is the spawn of a wicked witch. I'm sure of it. If she didn't smash my head in, she damn well knows who did." My guess was Spindle.

I was really starting to hate that supposedly imaginary guy.

Karl patted my hand. "Sure, sir. That's what happened. Now, why don't you have a nice lie-down on the leather seat?" He motioned to the backseat of the limo.

While the soft, plush seat looked mighty inviting, I couldn't give up now. "Forget it." I closed my eyes and gathered my strength. "I'm fine."

"You don't look fine," Karl said.

I glanced in the rearview mirror, noting the Humpty-shaped lump on my forehead and the greenish bruise surrounding it. Thankfully, rather than detract from my good looks, it merely gave me a more rakish, rapscallion sort of appeal that played well with the demented princess crowd.

"I'll live," I told my concerned servant. "Now, take me to the Rose. And hurry."

Karl elevated an eyebrow, but didn't comment. Instead, he hefted his pudgy frame into the driver's seat and took off, throwing me against the sun-warmed leather of the backseat. Two seconds later, the limo screeched to the curb. I flew forward, mashing my face against the privacy screen.

"We're here." Karl hopped out of the vehicle and opened my door. "Watch your step, sir," he said with much too much glee.

Stifling a few choice curses, I staggered from the car, wiping away a trail of blood leaking from my nostril. "You might've mentioned we were across the street."

He nodded. "I might've."

I ignored him in favor of far better game. My sights were set on Lollie Bliss. Nothing could deter me, except, apparently, the locked front door of the Rose. I knocked on the glass. "Hey! Open up."

On the other side of the glass the red-haired midget, looking much too chipper for eight in the morning, beamed and waved. Ever the idiot, Karl waved back. I pounded harder, rattling the door frame.

The midget tilted her head to one side and cupped her hand over her ear as if she couldn't hear me.

"I said open the damn door."

Rather than do what I asked, she closed the blinds in my face.

"Shit!"

"I believe the establishment is closed, sir."

"Really?" I glowered at Karl. "And what gave you that bright idea?"

Rather than shrink under my sarcasm, he grinned. "The sign, sir." His finger pointed to a red and white Closed sign hanging in the window.

Before I could pummel Karl for his mockery, Tweedle, the overgrown biker from last night, came around the corner. He stopped when he saw me, his eye darting back and forth. "Hey," he said as if just recognizing me, "you're that guy."

I nodded.

"Man, you pissed Red off bad last night," Tweedle said, shivering in the burning-hot sun. "After you left, she called you all sorts of names."

"Charming."

"That ain't one of them."

No doubt. In all fairness, I'd called her employer much worse, and I'd meant every utterance. I focused my attention back on Tweedle. "Have you seen Ms. Bliss today?"

"What's it to you?"

Plastering a sincere smile on my face, I took a step forward, all unassuming frog prince. "We were supposed to meet. Here. A few minutes ago...to...ah...finish my tattoo." I tapped my chest for show. "I guess I missed her."

Tweedle nodded, his triple chins bobbing with every movement. "Yeah, Lollie met with some guy and then took off on a bike."

Spindle, I bet. "How long ago?"

"Like, an hour ago."

"Any idea where she went?"

He shrugged his massive shoulders. "She said something about a job in that gated community on the hill."

A lump of fear formed in the back of my throat. Beauty lived in the Old MacDonald gated community; her palace overlooked his farm to be precise. Prime Cin City real estate, if one could stand the stench of heated baa baa black sheep shit all summer. "Did she say what the job was?"

"Nope," he paused to scratch his blubbery chin, "but she brought her gun."

Chapter 16

"Are you sure?" I asked Beauty's butler, Marvin, for the tenth time in the last thirty seconds of our phone conversation. "Sleeping can look a lot like dead."

"Yes, sir," Marvin again reassured me as to Beauty's continued breathing. "I checked the lady myself. She is fast asleep. No need for worry."

"Are you sure?" I asked one more time, my heartbeat finally slowing to normal. Marvin answered by disconnecting the call, leaving me listening to the harsh buzz of a dial tone.

"So what did the butler say?" Karl asked, wringing his hands against the steering wheel as we flew through the streets of Cin City on our way to save Sleeping Beauty.

Not that she'd appreciate it.

I took a deep breath. "Beauty's fine. She's been fast asleep since she called me last night." Apparently, Marvin was under strict orders not to disturb her, so he'd flatly refused to let me speak with her to verify that she wasn't worm food. Yet.

"Thank God," Karl said.

"Karl," I said to my faithful servant, "we have to hurry. If anything happens to her . . ."

"Don't fret, sir," Karl said. "Sleeping Beauty will live a long, happy life."

I grunted. As long as she said "I do," and I didn't revert to my froglike state, I couldn't care less about Sleeping Beauty's happiness. In fact, once we were officially married, I'd send her off to live out her sleepy days locked in the tower.

Just like dear old Dad had done.

Hell, give her a blanket and a pea-less mattress and Beauty would probably be as happy as a clam.

A few minutes later the limo pulled up the yellow winding brick driveway that led to Beauty's palace. The hot desert wind whipped along the valley below, and an eerie sound, almost like E-I-E-I-O, reverberated around us.

Groundskeepers and gardeners tended to the overgrown bushes lining the drive to Beauty's home. Roses, gardenias, and lilac bushes spouted from the landscape like a plague of wicked witches. Oddly, there wasn't a cactus in sight. The lush, emerald grass mocked the dry heat. Thank God I wasn't the shmuck paying the water bill.

"Sir, we're here," Karl, manservant of the obvious, said from the driver's seat.

"I can see that," I said, not moving.

"Shouldn't you rescue Princess Beauty now?"

"Right." I nodded, but still didn't move an inch. What the hell was I going to say to Beauty? If I told her the truth, she was bound to break our engagement. Even the king wouldn't stand for his future son-in-law plotting the murder of his bride.

Karl cleared his throat. "So . . ."

"I'm going." I rolled my eyes, pulling open the passenger-side door. The hot desert air blasted my face. I blinked, trying to restore moisture to my now-sandpaper-like eyeballs. Slowly, like a condemned man, I headed up the golden walkway and knocked on the diamond-encrusted front door.

Marvin answered quickly enough, barely sparing me a glance; instead he nodded up the staircase and then disappeared down the hall, his boots clicking on the highly polished floor.

I stepped through the door, struck again by the opulence surrounding me. Gold and jewels sparkled from every surface. Million-dollar pieces of art hung along the walls, lit by the glow of fairy butts. From the wealth around me, one thing was clear; the Vaniteuse family loved money. I had my doubts the same could be said for each other.

And the bastard king had stuck me with the dinner check.

I supposed that explained the king's desire to marry Sleeping Beauty off to the highest bidder, sight unseen. After all, the La Grenouille name resembled an unlimited credit card. You could buy anything, anywhere. No questions or credit check required.

Sometimes I hated having gazillions of dollars.

Not often, mind you.

Really only on tax day. All those forms to sign. It was exhausting.

"Jean-Michel." Pretty, her olive eyes and blond hair sparkling in the sunlight, appeared in front of me. "What're you doing here?"

"I'm here to see your sister, of course. I've missed her." I forced a smile to my lips.

Pretty shook her head and curls danced around like Old King Cole on a fairy-dust binge. "I don't think so." Apparently the sisters shared rudeness as well as their looks.

I tilted my head. "Excuse me?"

"Oh, I didn't mean it like that." Color stained Pretty's pretty cheeks. "It's just . . . Can I ask you a question?" She took a fortifying breath after I nodded my agreement. "Why Beauty? I mean, I love my half sister . . ."

"But?"

"Well, she's not," her voice turned as silken as whey, "exactly queen material." The "unlike me" part of her statement hung in the air between us.

True enough, but for some reason Pretty's words annoyed me more than I cared to admit. Beauty wasn't that bad. I'm sure, under all that flannel, there lurked the heart of a queen. A really annoying and tired queen, but a queen nonetheless. "Yes, well," I began. "Beauty is special."

"So the psychiatrists say," she said.

"Be that as it may." My tone grew cold. "Mademoiselle, if you'll excuse me, my bride and I have much to discuss about our upcoming nuptials."

"Of course," she said quickly. "I apologize for my rudeness. It's just . . . you're so . . . perfect, and Beauty's so . . ."

"Sleepy?"

"Exactly."

"I understand." I bowed slightly. Poor Pretty, she was another victim of my frog prince charm. Eventually, after a few years of therapy, she would be all right. I patted her shoulder, wincing as she stared up at me, her heart in her bright eyes. "Yes, well . . . I should go find Beauty."

Her face fell, but she managed to utter, "Yes, of course."

Taking a deep breath, I headed up the staircase, Pretty's intense gaze burning into my back.

Once I reached the second floor, I stopped, my eyes fixed on Sleeping Beauty's bedroom door at the end of the corridor. Less than a hundred feet separated me from the woman who could end my curse or damn me for eternity.

Given my luck over the last couple of days, the latter seemed much more likely. With a sigh, I took one step toward my future, my heart thundering in my chest.

"Ow!" I yelped as a sharp pain radiated from my foot. I glanced down, surprised to see Jimmy Cockroach, his top hat askew and the umbrella in his hand bent at an odd angle.

Glaring up at me, he brandished his tiny, bent umbrella at me. "Watch where you're walking, you dolt."

Dolt? Really? Who talked like that? I grimaced, lifting my foot to examine the damage left by his umbrella. A small hole dotted the insole of my shoe, a handmade loafer designed by an old woman who sure knew what to do with shoe leather.

Without further comment or apology, Jimmy Cockroach scurried down the hall, pausing at the top of the stairs to glare at me.

"Nice to see you again too," I said with a wave, which caused him to spin on his tiny heel and murmur something about the sorry state of eligible princes these days.

I shook my head and continued on my path toward the woman I would soon call my wife. Or a corpse. Sadly, I wasn't sure there'd be a really big difference between the two.

A door two rooms away from Beauty's stood open. I peeked inside as I passed. The room was empty with the exception of an industrial-sized sewing machine with an extremely long needle threaded with yarn, yarn the same golden color as Beauty's hair. Murky sunlight crept in through a fogged window. Cobwebs covered the sewing machine, yet the rest of the room looked freshly dusted. I sniffed the air. It smelled faintly of decay, as well as something sweet and familiar, something I couldn't place. A shiver ran down my spine.

The sooner I got Beauty away from this place and tucked safely away in a tower somewhere, the better.

Chapter 17

I tapped lightly on Beauty's bedroom door. The soft sound of snoring greeted my knock. Well, she was still alive. That counted for something, right?

Sighing, I took a step into the bedroom, my eyes sweeping the shadows for any sign of danger. On the far side of the room sat a window with cheerless curtains pulled tight against the afternoon sunlight. I squinted as my eyes adjusted to the darkness.

My bride lay on her back, her kinky blond hair spilling across her pillow and framing her pale face. Silken sheets were pulled past her chin, obscuring most of her face. Her breathing sounded harsh, as if she'd run a great distance. A soft snore escaped her lips, followed by a louder snort.

Dark eyelashes flickered in her sleep, sort of like a hushed little baby swinging from a treetop. I stopped just inside the doorway, my heart in my throat. This was the woman I would marry. The One. My one. The woman I would spend the rest of my days with. Lying there, against the silken sheets of her bed, Beauty looked as innocent as freshly fallen snow.

I never liked the snow.

My eyes locked on the nightstand by Beauty's bed. A half-empty box of nighttime cold medicine sat next to a vase filled with wilted flowers. No wonder she slept a lot. FairyQuil was known to knock out an elephant.

On the opposite side of the room stood a dresser with a large jewelry chest and an array of framed photographs on top. I tiptoed my way toward the dresser, careful not to wake the princess sleeping mere feet away.

"Frog!" I yelped as my little piggy, the anorexic one, caught the edge of the dresser. I jumped around on one foot until the pain went from blow your house down to merely a huff and a puff.

Marvin, the butler, burst into the bedroom, a bat in his hand. He glanced around as if searching for a threat. "Sir? Did Princess Beauty call out?"

I blinked away unshed tears.

"But I heard a loud girlish scream."

"Manly," I corrected.

"What?"

I exhaled loudly. "A manly scream. You heard a masculine scream. Sort of like a wild beast."

"No, sir." His eyes darted around the room. "The scream I heard resembled that of a little girl."

My fists clenched, but my voice stayed calm. "Whatever. As you can see, Lady Beauty is just fine." I rubbed my toe through the leather confines of my shoe. The throbbing eased a bit.

Marvin glanced at my future wife and then to me, his forehead wrinkled. "Well, then, since Lady Beauty is in no immediate danger," he stressed the word "immediate," "I will return to my duties."

My eyes narrowed. Was Marvin referring to Spindle? Or was Beauty in more danger than I suspected? Before I could question Marvin, he tipped his bat my way and left the room. When the door closed behind him, I glanced at Sleeping Beauty. A string of drool slid from her lips, dribbling down her silken sheet.

I rubbed the back of my neck. I was being paranoid. Because, really, how many assassins could one tiny and tired princess have? The number twenty-eight popped into my head, the number of jilted fiancés, to be precise.

Speaking of fiancés, I noticed the sparkle of diamonds winking out from the wooden jewelry crate on the dresser. Since I'd yet to slip a ring or anything else on my intended's finger, again my cat-killing curiosity got the best of me.

Sitting among piles of gold chains, strands of roping pearls, and expensive jewels in a rainbow of colors shiny enough to make Ali Baba and his contingent of thieves jealous were rows and rows of engagement rings in various shapes and colors. Forty-carat diamonds mixed with emeralds and the occasional ruby, each tagged with a handwritten number. One through twenty-eight.

I picked up a ring labeled with the number seven. A big diamond encrusted with sapphires. Pretty perhaps, but not Beauty's style. In fact, none of the rings in the box seemed right for my future wife. One was too big, another too small. None fit her just right. No wonder she'd never married any of those guys. Not that I was husband material either, but I wasn't nearly as clueless as fiancés one through twenty-eight.

"Fools," I whispered.

"You got that right," someone said, the voice too soft to pinpoint its location, let alone the gender of the speaker. The hair on the back of my neck rose.

I spun toward the bed. My bride looked as peaceful as she had when I first entered the room. Her eyes closed, her breathing even and deep. My eyes scanned the rest of the room, finding no one other than my sleeping bride. Maybe I was losing my mind like Lollie had predicted.

Turning back to the jewelry box, I set number seven's ring back in its rightful place and closed the lid. My eyes

locked on a framed photograph sitting next to the jewelry
box. A picture of Beauty, age seven or eight. She smirked
at the camera, a toothless grin, as if she didn't have a care
in the world, and yet, her lollipop eyes told a far different
tale, one of loneliness and longing. In the background,
Handsome stood next to his father, the king, and a fresh-
faced four-year-old Pretty as well as a shadowy figure
barely in the frame.

I peered closer at the picture, unable to make out anything other than the outline of a child. Was this a long-lost
Vaniteuse relative? Not that it mattered. The picture was
worth a thousand tales, none of them the happily-ever-
after kind. All the children held ice cream cones in their
hands, while Beauty's hand was suspiciously empty. Perhaps my bride was lactose intolerant? But I had my
doubts.

In another picture, one with a thumbprint obscuring the
left half of the frame, the family sat at a long table, each
smiling and happy expect for Beauty. She sat a few seats
away, her head in her hands, her sad eyes locked on her
happy siblings.

For a kid who grew up without much in the way of
parental love and with a pair of frog legs to boot, I understood the yearning in her gaze, the need to be a part of
something, to be loved. For all Beauty's faults, and apparently there were quite a few, she deserved better. What the
hell was wrong with me? I was the Frog Prince. A man
women loved to love. Hell, I'd kissed more princesses than
Rapunzel had split ends.

The stress of the wedding was getting to me. That was
all this sudden girly, emotional crap was. I didn't care one
iota about Beauty or her upbringing, as long as she said
"I do."

I set the photograph down on the dresser. A speck of
paper on the back of the frame caught my eye. I peered
closer. Someone had tucked a piece of paper between the

picture and the frame. Carefully, I tugged at the note, inching it until the paper worked its way free. Thick block letters formed the words:

A pin-pricked finger
Will sleep eternal
Until his true heart Be

"What the frog does that mean?" I said, but deep down I knew the answer. I rubbed at the B-shaped birthmark on my chest. "B" for "Beauty." One more sign that Beauty was my One. My fate was sealed by a benign, disfiguring lesion. Figured.

My sleeping bride mumbled something in response, something I couldn't quite make out. I moved across the room, to her bed, and leaned in. Beauty's breath tickled the ten-in-the-morning stubble hugging my chin.

Pop. Pop. Pop.

The vase next to the bedside, an inch or two from Beauty's head, exploded, showering us in glass, water, and flower shrapnel. Velvety petals flew in all directions.

Beauty shot straight up, her eyes wide. Without thinking, I yanked her from the bed and onto the floor, covering her body with my own. My heart slammed wildly in my chest. Frog! Spindle and, very likely, the lying Lollie Bliss were outside, waiting for a chance to blow Beauty's tiny little brains out.

Silence reigned in the large room. Water from the fatally injured vase pooled on the floor around us, soaking into my pants, water that could've just as easily have been my intended's blood.

Anger exploded inside me. That damn Spindle. I vowed to stop him. Any way I could. No more Mr. Nice Frog Prince.

I glanced down at Beauty. Her hands covered her face in an expression of surprise. She stared up at me for a long moment. "Jean-Michel?" she said, her voice husky with sleep.

I brushed her hair out of her grape-colored eyes. Tenderness and something quite foreign, almost like decency, rose inside me. Twenty-two years ago, Sleeping Beauty had saved me from my curse, albeit accidentally, now it was my turn to return the favor and save her from a killer, albeit one I'd accidentally hired to kill her. "It's all right, sweetheart. I won't let anyone hurt you," I vowed.

Sleeping Beauty's lips curled into a frown. "In that case," she said, "get off me, you're crushing my spleen."

Chapter 18

Ten minutes later, Beauty safely tucked back in bed, her curtains drawn, and Marvin standing guard outside her door, I slowly walked down the hall, a litany of complaints following me.

"Great. Now my room smells like hair products and musty amphibian, thanks to you, Jean-Michel," Beauty called out.

I rolled my eyes and kept walking. My mind swirled with a jumble of emotions. Until a few minutes ago the threat to Sleeping Beauty hadn't seemed real. Not truly. Yet, as a bullet flew past my head, the reality of what I'd done slammed into me with the velocity of a sniper's shot. This was my fault. All of it.

Well, three-fourths at least.

Half if you considered I was drunk at the time.

Okay, one-third seemed more realistic. After all, I'd tried to stop Spindle. Now that I thought about it, this was far more the responsibility of Ms. Lollie Bliss. Damn her and her sexy, ink-covered body. When I got my hands on her . . .

"What are you doing here?" Handsome, Beauty's stepbrother, growled from the top of the stairs. A lock of dark hair fell over one of his dark eyes, giving him a rakish appeal that drove princesses crazy. His muscles were gym sculpted for much the same reason, as were the strategic bulges in his freshly pressed uniform, the tin star on his shirt nearly blinding in the sunlight.

What a tool. I could out-handsome Handsome any day.

"What's it to you?" I said, my tone as cold as Jack Frost's frigid wife.

"Beauty's too good for the likes of you," he sneered.

"Good" wasn't exactly the word I'd have used. "Listen, I get it. You've got a thing for your stepsister. Creepy, sure. But it's not going to happen. Beauty will be my wife. So give it up."

Handsome's handsome face crumpled a bit, but he quickly recovered. "I don't have a thing, as you put it, for Beauty. I love her. Truly love her. Can you say the same?"

"Of course," I lied.

"Then say it!" He smashed his fist on the banister.

I tried to form the words in my mouth, but no sound emerged. What was wrong with me? I'd said "I love you" a million times to a million different women. Granted, I was now telling it to some guy with perfectly waxed eyebrows, but still. . . .

"That's what I thought," Handsome said with a sneer. "If you know what's just, you'll leave her alone."

I grinned. "Is that a threat?"

"No," he said, his eyes blazing with fire. My nose wrinkled. The overwhelming scent of Old Spice and pissed-off stepbrother filled the corridor between us. "It's a promise," he said. "You will never marry Sleeping Beauty. I'll see her in hell first."

"Did you tell Sleeping Beauty the truth?" Karl asked as we drove away from the palace and down the winding canyon road. Hot desert air and the smell of day-old prince wafted throughout the limo. I shut my eyes, allowing fear to surface for the first time since Beauty's shooting. I'd almost lost her, and therefore, my only chance to end my curse once and for all.

"Sir?" Karl prompted. "Did you tell Princess Beauty her life is in danger?"

"Of course I did," I lied.

In the rearview mirror, I watched as Karl's eyebrow rose.

I rolled my eyes in response. "Okay, maybe those weren't my exact words." I grinned, picturing Beauty's startled face as a barrage of bullets slammed into the wall above her bed. "But I'm sure she got the gist."

"But, sir—"

"I was about to tell her when . . . well . . . the shooting started."

"What?!" Karl's face paled. "Shooting? Is the princess all right?"

"Seemed to be," I said. In fact, five minutes after nearly dying, not to mention cursing me out, Sleeping Beauty had fallen right back to sleep without a care in the world, leaving Marvin and me to station two guards outside her room, and two more below her window, as well as an hourly patrol around the perimeter of the palace.

Killing Beauty wouldn't be easy. I'd make sure of it.

I stared out the window of the limo, noting the swirl of orange and red in the sky as dusk fell on the desert. Our limo sped down the valley toward the city, the sun glinting off the windows like the reflection in a pond.

We flew past palace after palace as their occupants prepared for nightfall. Lights came on. Kids came home after a long day playing hopscotch. Old couples walked hand in hand. On the side of the road a lone woman leaned against a motorbike.

"Stop the limo!" I yelled.

Karl did, with amazing speed. The limo skidded to a halt, tires screaming against the pavement. I leapt from the vehicle and ran down the street toward the woman leaning so innocently against hundreds of pounds of steel and chrome.

"You!" I pointed an accusing finger in the direction of Ms. Murderous Bliss. She looked as good as, if not hotter, than the last time I'd seen her. Her hair was twisted up on top of her head, leaving small curls to frame her face. Her dark eyes softened in the twilight, appearing almost amber in color.

Attempted murder seemed to agree with her.

I swallowed a wave of lust, disgusted with my reaction. Less than an hour ago, she and her lover had nearly killed Beauty, I reminded my penis. Unfortunately, that failed to cool my ardor. However, her next words worked wonders for my rising libido.

"Sorry I missed you, Kermit."

"What?" I grabbed Lollie's arm, jerking her from the bike. She tried to pull away, but I held tight, resulting in a human tug-of-war. In the end, Lollie won, after kicking me in the shin with her biker boot.

"Ow!" I yelped, rubbing at the fresh, very large bruise growing on my leg. For her smallish size, she had extremely big feet. Which came as a sort of surprise, but then again on our last two encounters, I'd paid far more attention to other areas of Lollie's anatomy.

"What's your problem?" she screeched, her face pinched with anger. "I apologize for missing you at my shop this morning, and you manhandle me? What do you do when someone offers to buy you dinner, punch them in the nose?"

I straightened. "What?"

"Don't you ever listen to anyone but yourself?" She blew out a harsh breath. "I said, I was sorry about not being at the Rose this morning when you came by." She stopped, the annoyance on her face replaced by relief. "But I'm glad I caught you. I have something for you."

"Perhaps an apology for bashing me in the head?" I took a menacing step toward her. "Or maybe you'd like to say you're sorry for trying to kill my fiancée?"

"Are you crazy?" She tried to push me away, but I stayed firmly in front of her. "Why would I try to kill your fiancée? I don't even know her. If anything, I feel sorry for the poor girl."

"What about your lover, Lollie?" My tone grew soft. "Are you helping him? Is that why you're here?"

She chuckled. "I'm here, as you put it, because I had a job to do." When my eyes narrowed, she added, "A tattoo job. Up the canyon. Hence the ink stains on my tank top." She pointed to a red splotch right below her breast.

I wasn't sure if I believed her. Her words sounded right, and the ink stain was real enough, but I'd fallen for her innocent act before, and it had cost me, namely my favorite pair of pants. Not to mention a lump on the head the size of Wee Willie Winkie after a dose of Viagra.

"Well, Kermit," her lips curled into a smirk, "don't you want to know what it is I have for you?"

I nodded, slowly, unsure.

"Are you sure?" she asked, her tone filled with laughter.

I nodded again.

Lollie reached into the black leather saddlebag behind her.

A gun emerged.

A gun aimed at my heart.

Her finger flexed on the trigger.

Chapter 19

A stain of red spread across my chest, growing larger and darker as seconds passed. Lollie dropped the gun, the smile leaving her face. "Oh God, I'm so sorry," she said, dabbing at my sweatshirt.

"What the frog?" I glared down at the cherry-colored ink on my now-ruined sweatshirt, and then back at Lollie. "What'd you do that for?"

"I . . . ah . . . it was an accident," she said, motioning to the tattoo gun on the ground. "I meant to grab these." She reached into her black saddlebags again. I took a step back, my hands out in front of me to ward off another inky attack. But rather than another tattoo gun, Lollie removed a pair of grimy Levi's from the leather tote, the same pair I'd worn last night.

"Here," she said, holding the Levis out to me.

Taking the jeans from her ink-stained hand, I quickly checked the pockets. My wallet and p-Phone sat tucked where I'd left them, but the matchbook as well as the rose petal, my only pieces of evidence against Lollie, was missing.

I thrust the jeans her way. "Where are they?"

"What?" she repeated, her black eyes staring innocently up at me. "I don't have a clue what you're talking about."

My eyes narrowed. "Really? I find that hard to believe."

She gave me an eye roll.

I decided to let it go, for now, and focus on a more important issue, like why Lollie had my jeans in the first place. So I asked a question I'd never expected to ask a woman in this lifetime. "How'd you get my pants?"

"I did not smash you in the head!" Lollie yelled.

I raised my eyebrow. "Then who did?"

"How should I know?" Her eyes smoldered, turning jet black in color. "You probably have a hundred people willing to smash in your head. Mostly women would be my guess."

"Perhaps," I acknowledged with a nod, "but they all live a couple thousand miles away. Which leaves only you, Ms. Bliss."

She laughed. "What about your sweet fiancée?"

"Funny," I said without humor. But my mind flashed to my fiancée as well as her overly protective stepbrother. Had Handsome smashed in my head? I shook said wounded noggin and focused on the tattooed lady. "Beauty wouldn't hurt a fly." It might take too much energy. On the other hand, she could complain so much that the fly flew into the bright blue light of a bug zapper to make it stop.

Lollie raised a disbelieving eyebrow.

"Let's just ignore my upcoming wedded bliss, Ms. Bliss, and focus on the important stuff, namely . . ." I motioned to my jeans.

"Can't you think of anything but your crotch for even a second?" She picked up the tattoo gun, shoved it her bag, and then straddled the motorcycle, her long legs squeezing the chassis like a vise. She stared at me for a moment, as if debating, and then held out a black motorcycle helmet. "Coming?"

I pondered her and then her offer. On one hand, the idea of going anywhere with Ms. Bliss seemed demented.

Perhaps a bit suicidal.

Masochistic at the very least.

Now I knew how the fly felt.

"No head smashing?" I pointed at her. "Poison? Or tattoo guns?"

She crossed her fingers over her heart. "Cross my heart and hope you die."

"What?"

She smiled, innocently. "I said, cross my heart, hope to die. Now get on the bike."

My eyes narrowed on her sculpted face. Her head tilted to one side, revealing the subtle slope of her neck. I wanted to run my fingers down her throat, to feel the inky designs underneath the pads of my fingertips. "Come on, Kermit. You're in Cin City, take a gamble," she ordered with a grin.

I glanced from the motorcycle to Karl and my limo, and then to Lollie's face. Her dark eyes dared me to defy my survival instincts and ride away into the sunset with a wicked tattooed woman.

"Sir?" Karl called from the window of the limo.

Against my better judgment, I threw my leg over the back of Lollie's bike and wrapped my arms around her waist. Her breath quickened under the palms of my hands. Her skin felt so warm, and she smelled like the desert and strawberries, hot, deadly, and deliciously juicy. I wondered if she tasted as dangerous as she smelled. A thought a soon-to-be-married frog prince was better off not thinking. Not when his bride's life was on the line.

Lollie revved the engine.

Karl opened the limo door. "Sir! Wait!"

I gave Karl a small wave. Lollie gunned the large motor. The bike buzzed to life. The back tire spun. Gravel flew up. And then we were gone, flying down the canyon, the wind ripping across our bodies. The only sound was of the chrome and steel engine between our thighs.

Well, that and the occasional manly scream of "Fuck, I think I swallowed a fly."

Lollie parked the bike in a narrow alleyway. A sign above the door of the brick building in front of us read, "The Biggest, Baddest BBQ in Town." I assumed it meant the food, not the door. Yet as hungry as I was, given enough BBQ sauce, the door didn't sound half-bad either.

Pulling off her helmet, Lollie's black hair spilled down her back like an oil slick. "Hope you like BBQ." She leapt off the bike and motioned to the run-down building. "This place is a Cin City icon. It makes the *New Never News* three or four times a year."

From the looks of the cracked windows and crumbling brick, I suspected those news articles often started with "three dead," but decided not to voice my concern.

I held the BBQ-stained front door open and waved Lollie in. She shot me a smile and sashayed inside. My eyes locked on her nicely shaped bottom as I followed her through the door, wondering about her sudden invitation to dinner. Was she yet another victim of my frog prince charm? Or was there something far more sinister to her invitation? From the look of the place, death by salmonella seemed like a possibility. Perhaps Spindle had run out of bullets? I grabbed her arm and spun her to face me. "Why did you bring me here?"

"Why do you think?" She sighed. "I was hungry."

"And?"

"And when I'm hungry I eat. It's not rocket science, Kermit."

I stared into her eyes, debating if she was telling the truth. Her nostrils flared under my assessment, a sure sign that Ms. Bliss was being less than truthful. "You're lying. You want something from me." People, women especially, usually did. Money, houses, cars, paternity tests. Everyone wanted a piece of the prince. "What is it?"

"Fine." She crossed her arms over her breasts. "I'm flat broke since I had to buy a whole new set of knuckle busters and clip cords after you destroyed my equipment last night. The least you can do is be a good Kermit and buy a girl dinner." She paused to lick her lips. "I promise I'll make it worth every cent."

I nodded my agreement and released her arm, once again enjoying the view of her backside as I followed her inside the restaurant. Unlike Lollie's butt, the interior of the joint was sadly lacking in beauty, let alone anything remotely nice. Straw covered the floor where two sets of empty picnic tables sat. A bar ran along the far wall filled with a flock of bikers dressed in leather. They turned to stare as we entered. Their eyes looked Lollie up and down like a lollipop. A low growl, almost like the engine of a motorcycle, reverberated around the small room.

I stepped in front of Lollie.

She giggled, pushing me aside, and grabbed the table closest to the doorway. "Sit down, Kermit. You're making Bo Peep nervous," she said, gesturing to a very large, very hairy biker dressed in a bonnet and carrying a sheep-herding staff.

The biker growled again.

I quickly sat down. A little piggy wearing a blemished apron approached our table. "Can I take your order?"

Without glancing down at the BBQ-stained menu stuck to the wooden table, Lollie said, "We'll have two of the BBQ chicken platters. Extra sauce. And two beers." She added loud enough only for me to hear, "And a nice poisoned apple strudel for dessert."

"Funny," I said, my eyes locked on hers. "But I'll have the ribs. Full rack."

The pig swallowed hard. "Would you like beef or . . . p-p-ork ribs?"

"Which do you recommend?"

"Beef!"

"Yeah, maybe," I said. "Doc says I should watch my intake of red meat, though . . ."

The little piggy whimpered.

"What the hell, you only live once, right?" I hesitated. "Beef it is. Well done."

"Thank you, sir." He grinned from ear to curly piggy ear.

"No . . . Not that you're not doing a bang-up job . . . but I meant, that's how I'd like my ribs cooked. Well done."

"Oh," he said, his face crumpling. "Can I get you anything else?" Lollie smiled and shook her head. The waiter turned to leave, but I stopped him. "Do you guys have any pork rinds?"

The piggy squealed wee, wee, wee all the way back to the kitchen. Good help was so hard to find. Leaning back in the metal chair I contemplated the enigmatic and alluring Lollie Bliss and wondered just what kind of help she'd be to me.

She lifted up one dark eyebrow, followed by the other.

"What?" I asked.

"Nothing," she said.

I scowled. I hated when women did that. "Nothing" was girl code for "the guy next to me is an idiot," which nine out of ten times proved to be completely true.

Silence grew between us, thick and heavy, much like the smoke curling through the restaurant. I cleared my throat. "Care to explain how you got my pants?"

"I found them on the doorstep when I opened the shop this morning. I remembered you wearing them last night, so I figured I'd bring them with me and drop them off at your hotel this evening," Lollie said with a smile. "My good deed of the day."

Her words seemed plausible enough, but I still had my doubts. Lollie was a liar, a pretty damn good one at that.

But she was no match for a frog prince. Besides, someone had shot at my princess. "How kind of you."

"I do try," she said, an innocent smile on her plump lips.

Before I could devise an appropriate response, our waiter appeared at the table. "For my lady," he said, placing a plate piled high with food in front of Lollie. The chicken was perfectly cooked and slathered in BBQ sauce. My mouth watered just looking at her looking at the food on her plate.

My own platter came next. Smoke curled around the burnt remains of what looked like a mouse that ran up a clock, was electrocuted and then drowned in sauce to finish the poor bastard off, served with a side of wilted coleslaw.

"Bon appétit," the piggy said.

"Um . . . wait a second," I said. "My ribs are a tad bit overcooked." I forked the tiny, charred entrée, which crumbled into a pile of ash.

The pig's eyes widened as if shocked by my statement.

Lollie made a slashing motion across her throat.

"Overcooked, you say?" the pig whispered, his piggy eyes darting from me to the kitchen door and back again.

The restaurant went quiet. Deadly silent, in fact.

I glanced at Lollie. But before she could say a word the room shook with a gale-force wind strong enough to topple Biker Bo Peep and all her equally hairy leather-clad flock. Mugs full of mead flew in all direction. Glass shattered as the ferocious wind battered the restaurant.

Lollie wavered on her chair and then crashed into my arms. I caught her, folding her against my body, and waited for the sudden windstorm to end. A loud howl sounded from the kitchen, followed by a crack of wood, and a shower of thousands of toothpicks rained down on us.

As suddenly as the windstorm came, it stopped, leaving a path of debris in its wake. BBQ sauce coated everything, from the straw on the floor to the fan slowly twirling overhead. The smell of charred pig flesh hung in the heated air. Yet there wasn't any serious damage to the restaurant or its assortment of oddball patrons.

Lollie was still pressed against me, her mouth buried in the crook of my neck. Warm, sweet breath teased my skin, sending the blood in my brain far south. My body tensed, and all I could think about was kissing Ms. Lying Lollie Bliss's plump pink lips. Her lips parted, drawing me in like a fairy to applause.

I bent down, stealing a kiss before Lollie had time to regain her senses. My lips settled on hers. Rather than fight me as I'd expected, she wrapped her hands around my neck and pulled me closer. The brief stolen kiss twisted into something much darker, dangerous, and infinitely more appealing.

All thoughts of my future bride, Lollie's assassin lover, and my possible return to frogitude vanished under the heat of Lollie's body. This was the One, my penis stated in no uncertain terms.

And in that perfect moment, she was—until reality, or rather, a hairy paw, smashed me in the back of the head.

Chapter 20

"Get your hands off her and face me like a man, you . . . toad!" a voice growled above me.

I leapt up, knocking Lollie off the bench and onto the floor. Neither I nor the guy I assumed was her assassin boyfriend, Spindle, spared her a glance, each of us bent on sizing the other up.

The guy wasn't anything like I'd thought Spindle would be. Not even a little bit. The guy was furry, for frog sakes. Everywhere. From his claws to the tip of his elongated nose. What could Lollie possibly see in him? I glared down at Lollie, who was trying to get up off the straw coated floor without much luck.

"So you're the guy," I said, stabbing my finger in Spindle's direction. Anger vibrated through my body. Not only had he attempted to kill my bride, but he'd ruined my very first indiscretion as a soon-to-be-married frog prince.

Spindle grabbed my offending appendage and shoved me away from him. "Don't you dare point your finger at me."

Our waiter squealed again, ducking under the table next to the bar. The rest of the patrons looked on with something akin to excited horror, like the look on Miss Muffet's face when along came a spider that sat down beside her and said, "Hey, baby, whatcha got in the bowl?"

Taking a steady breath, I considered my options. As much as I wanted to pound Spindle into a puddle of mush, I needed his cooperation in not murdering my fiancée more. On the other hand, beating him into a pulpy mush appealed to my sense of fair play, if not my designs on his girlfriend's body.

Sometimes it was so hard being a noble prince like me.

Before I decided whether or not to act, the matter was settled for me. Lollie jumped between us, jamming her hand into her lover's sternum. "Damn it, Oliver," she said. "We've been through this time and again."

Oliver? Who the hell was Oliver? With as many lovers as Ms. Bliss had, she was bound to live up to her name. "Wait a minute. He's not Spindle?" I yelled once my fantasies involving Lollie settled. "You're not Spindle?" I faced the wolf-man Lollie called Oliver. "What the hell's going on?"

Lollie answered, her glare fixed on the hairy guy in front of me. "Oliver is the proud owner of this restaurant," she began, only to be cut off by the wolf.

"Five-star restaurant," he corrected.

She nodded. "And sometimes he takes offense to certain criticisms offered by clients at this fine dining establishment."

"Pedestrian criticisms by unrefined palates like yours," Oliver said, motioning my way. His tone suggested that I ate flies or something, which I had, but not for many years, if one didn't count the motorcycle ride over.

I laughed without humor. "Are you kidding me? All this," I gestured around the wind damaged room, "was because of a few burnt ribs?"

"Burnt?" He took a threatening step forward, his claws scratching against the stained floor. "Why you . . . I trained with Gram-mam-me, one of the finest pastry chefs in the world—"

Lollie gave Oliver a shove, sending him falling back a

step. "In all fairness, Kermit, you did order them well done."

The little piggy stuck his head out from beneath the table. "He certainly did."

"There goes your tip."

The piggy flipped me off.

"Listen," I said to the wolf growing bigger and madder before my eyes, "I didn't mean to upset you. I'm sure you're a hell of a cook—"

"Chef!"

"Fine. Chef." I grinned, sneaking a quick glance at Lollie. She winced as if she knew what I planned to say next. "But come on, how hard is it to BBQ a rack of ribs?" I asked. "It's not like it's architecture or something."

Lollie groaned. But the sound was lost to the crazed growl emanating from Oliver. He started with a huff, which quickly turned into a puff, and then the restaurant exploded around us.

Chapter 21

Picking straw and barbecued little piggy out of my hair, I staggered from the elevator to my hotel suite, images of Ms. Bliss, who'd just dropped me off at the hotel, flickering through my mind. She was a distraction I didn't need. I wanted her. A lot. But I wasn't quite ready to jump into full-on frogitude for thirty seconds of Ms. Bliss.

Besides, I'd made a commitment to Sleeping Beauty. Yeah, I'd also hired someone to kill her, but princes made mistakes. After all, she was my One. Nothing could or would stand in the way of our union, barring her death at Spindle's hands, of course.

I unlocked the door to my suite and shoved it wide. Exhaustion hung on me like the emperor's hand-me-downs. And what did I have to show for it? Nothing. I hadn't found Spindle, and I had a pounding headache the size of London's bridge, and to make matters worse I think Lollie's friend Oliver gave me fleas.

What else could go wrong?

A cloud of smoke materialized in front of me, followed by the telltale form of my irritating fairy godmother. "Yoo-hoo, Johnny," Elly called, stumbling forward. "I've been looking all over the place for you." She punctuated her statement with a loud belch.

I bowed low. "As you can see, madam, I am here. At your service."

Her wand lashed out catching me on the back of the head. "Don't be smart with me, Johnny." She hiccupped. "We've got trouble."

Rubbing at my head, I glared at the woman entrusted with my happily-ever-after, if not my life. Her dress was stained with gin, her silver hair a mess, and her stockings hung around her bulging ankles. *You get what you pay for,* I thought, cursing my father and his penny-pinching ways.

Elly conked me with her wand again. "Are you paying attention?"

I yanked the wand from her hand and jabbed it in her direction. "If you hit me with this one more time . . ."

Her icy eyes narrowed. "You'll what?"

Taking my time, I sauntered to the balcony, pushed open the window, and causally tossed the wand out of the window. For a second it hung in the air before spiraling downward and smashing on the Cin City strip below.

Elly gasped. Her hand clutched at her heart. Her pudgy face grew as pale as Snow White after the pregnancy test turned pink. She staggered a few feet and then fell to her knees, wheezing for breath.

I rushed over. "Oh God, Elly," I said catching her in my arms. "I'm so sorry. I didn't mean—"

Whap! Her fist smashed into my nose followed by the edge of a shorter, stubbier wand with a glittery tassel on the end. "You think that's my only wand?" She patted her silvery hair. "You're so naïve."

I staggered to my feet, poking at the wound on my noggin. A small bump formed underneath my silken locks. I sat down heavily on the bed. "Listen, Elly, I have enough problems as it is without having you buzzing around. So what is it that you want? Cash?" I pulled out my wallet, only to realize Karl hadn't returned my freshly laundered funds yet. "I'm tapped out at the moment, but I can call the concierge for a loan."

Elly cleared her throat loud enough to rattle the windows. "I don't want your money, Johnny." Her eyes locked on my wallet with blatant greed in direct contrast to her words. "How is the wedding planning going? I can't wait to walk you down the aisle. I bought the perfect dress this afternoon. Cost you ten grand, but it's well worth it, you'll see. It's made of the finest troll hair—"

I winced, hating to disappoint the only motherly figure I'd ever known. "Better save the receipt," I said.

Elly's eyes narrowed to slits. "What did you do, Johnny?"

I blinked up innocently. "Whatever do you mean?"

"Don't go all charming on me, mister." She stomped across the room, stopping a few inches away, and glared down at me. "I repeat, what did you do?"

I patted the seat next to me. She rolled her eyes, but sat down, waiting for my tale to begin. For a long moment I said nothing. The air conditioner cooled the stale hotel room as hundreds of people gambled away their futures in the casino below.

"Well," she prompted when I stayed silent.

Taking a deep breath, I took a gamble of my own. "Remember my friend RJ . . ."

Chapter 22

"What am I going to do with you?" Elly paced in front of me, yet her tiny fairy godmother feet never touched the ground. Rage kept her afloat. "How could you let this happen? I mean, really, you're a frog prince."

"I know." I hid a small smile.

"How many times have we been through this?" she asked. "A hundred? Two?"

"I know," I repeated, louder this time.

She crossed her arms over her chest. "Hiring a non-union killer is like playing pinochle naked with a semi-erect fairy."

I swallowed the bile pooling in the back of my throat at her graphic picture. "I think you mean playing Russian roulette with a semiautomatic weapon."

"You wish." She tapped my ear with her wand before resuming her pacing along the plush carpet. Elly twirled in my direction, sending a bolt of static electricity shooting from her wand. I ducked, narrowly avoiding being barbecued by the errant strike.

"I never liked that girl," said the fairy godmother banned from forty-five out of fifty states, barring a pending hearing in MaryHadALittleLand.

"What girl? Sleeping Beauty?"

"No. Not her. The other one." She tugged at the collar

of her gown. "The one you're playing hide the tadpole with."

"What?" I swung to face Elly. My chest burned with righteous anger. How dare she? Damn it, I'd stayed faithful to my intended. So far. "I'm not fucking anyone, let alone Lollie Bliss." I counted to five to calm down before I lost control and said something I'd regret. "You old drunken crone!" Oops. Should've counted a little higher.

Elly gasped as if I'd struck her with her own stupid wand. "How dare you, Johnny. After all I've done for you."

"Done for me?" I gave a hollow laugh. "Done to me is more like it. Do you remember my first boy girl dance in the seventh grade?"

"Of course." Her hands went to her face. "You looked so handsome in your—"

"Dress, madam." My fingers curled into a tight fist. "You and your magic wand dressed me in a dress." I blew out a harsh breath. "I was the laughingstock of the entire school. They called me the Frog Princess until my senior year."

"Which made you the frog prince you are today," Elly declared with a hiccup. "God help us all."

After a long hot shower, I toweled off, Elly's words festering in my mind. What exactly did she know about my relationship with Ms. Bliss and, more importantly, how the hell had she found out? A name popped into my head, but I shook it away. Karl wouldn't betray me. Not to Elly. The two rarely got along, except when they joined forces to stop me from "doing something stupid."

Shit!

I grabbed the hotel phone and quickly dialed Karl's room. The phone rang and rang, finally clicking over to the hotel messaging center. "Call me," I ordered, tossing the phone back in the cradle.

Just where the hell was Karl? Two nights in a row my supposedly "at your beck and call" servant was suspiciously absent from both my beck and my call.

Pulling on a pair of clean Dockers and a button-down shirt, I contemplated heading to the hotel bar for a light snack and a really large bottle of whiskey, but ultimately decided against it. I hated eating alone, which probably had something to do with my early tadpole development. I'd spent nearly eight years eating every fly-crusted meal alone.

I didn't want to be alone.

Not anymore.

Reaching for my p-Phone, I dialed Lollie's number, even though a voice said, "Bad idea, Johnny." I kicked the bathroom door closed, silencing Elly.

The phone rang once.

"Vaniteuse residence," a familiar voice answered.

My eyes narrowed. "Marvin? Is that you?"

"Yes, sir," Sleeping Beauty's butler said. "Did you call to speak with Princess Beauty?"

"Um...I..." Shit. What the frog was wrong with me? How could I have dialed Beauty by mistake? Talk about your Freudian slipper. I heaved a sigh. "Yeah, I guess so."

"Glad you're still alive."

"What?"

"What?" Marvin echoed.

"You said, you're glad I'm still alive. What's that supposed to—"

He cut me off. "I said no such thing."

"Marvin? Is that you?" Beauty jumped on the phone line, her voice husky from sleep. "Who are you talking to? I warned you about calling those 900 numbers on my phone."

"I know, my lady," he said.

"Beauty," I said to gain her attention. "It's Jean-Michel."

Silence.

"Beauty?" I repeated, afraid she'd fallen to sleep.

"Who?"

"Your fiancé," I yelled.

"Number twenty-nine? What do you want?" She paused. "Are you calling to end our engagement?"

"No."

"Oh," she said, sounding shocked and a wee bit disappointed, but I might've been projecting. "Well, what is it you want, then?"

Stay calm, I told myself. After all, the poor princess had almost died that afternoon. It was bound to make her a wee bit irritable, if not downright bitchy. I cleared my throat. "Marvin," I said. "I'll take it from here."

"As you wish, sir," he said, hanging up the phone.

Once he cleared the line, I growled. "Mademoiselle, in the future you will refrain from speaking to me like a servant in front of . . . well . . . the servants."

I could picture her eye roll, but she sounded contrite when she said, "I apologize. You woke me, and I'm always a bit . . . cranky when I don't get enough sleep."

"I see."

Silence grew between us until Beauty broke it. "So, did you call for something?"

"I . . ." Shit. It wasn't like I could admit the truth, that I'd dialed her number on accident while trying to make a date with a woman whose boyfriend I'd accidentally hired to kill her. *Think, damn it!* I ordered my brain, but low blood sugar and lack of sleep had taken its toll. Not to mention the dent in my forehead.

"Well, thanks for calling," Beauty said. "I look forward to your next pearl of conversational wisdom. I do hope it's soon," she said sweetly. Before I could response, she hung up the phone, leaving me staring at the receiver, a small smile on my lips.

Chapter 23

The next morning, I woke up around ten to the scent of fresh coffee and Candi, as in the stripper from Old Mother Hubbard's All Bare Cupboard. Not her exactly, just her scent, smothered all over my manservant like a cheap Dalmatian fur coat.

"Karl, what the hell? You smell like a stripper," I said as I tossed on the pair of Dockers from last night and a freshly pressed oxford shirt.

My manservant stepped back. "I . . . ah . . . ," he stuttered. "I most certainly do not." He finished with as much dignity as a guy with lipstick stains on his trousers could muster.

I raised an eyebrow. When he turned a nice shade of crimson I decided to let him off the hook. For now. At least about his latest candy-coated conquest. "Talk to Elly lately?"

His skin turned from pink to chalk white. "Elly?"

"Yeah, you know." I held up my hand chest high. "Fairy godmother. About yea high. Usually smells like gin."

Karl gave an exaggerated laugh. "You're very funny, sir. You should consider a career in comedy. Fans would come from all over—"

I cut him off with a shove. The back of his knees hit the

bed, and he tumbled backward across a mound of pillows. "Don't try and change the subject. You told Elly about my taking off with Lollie yesterday."

He swallowed hard. "I did not."

"Don't lie to me." I leaned over the bed, menacing my manservant. For a few seconds I enjoyed the power, but it quickly faded under Karl's whimpering. I dropped down on the bed next to him. "Why, Karl? I thought I could trust you," I said, laying it on thick.

"I'm so very sorry, sir." He scrambled off the bed, his face wrinkled with guilt. "I didn't mean to make you angry."

"So why did you?"

He swallowed, his throat bobbing. "I fear that you are making a grave mistake in trusting Ms. Bliss. One that might cost you your very future, if not your life. Lady Beauty is your One."

"I know that." Better than anyone. Without Beauty I would return to being a frog, something I relished less and less as the days passed. But that wasn't the point. "Don't be such a drama servant," I said, crossing my legs at the ankle, and leaned back to survey my manservant. "I can take care of myself. I've done so for thirty years without grave injury." At least nothing a shot of penicillin didn't cure.

"What about that time—"

"Okay then," I said, leaping from the bed and crossing the room in two strides. "We really should get a move on. Places to go. Princesses to save."

"But, sir," Karl said. "I really am concerned—"

"As long as you wore a condom, everything will be fine." I smirked, closing the door on Karl's flaming face.

Twenty minutes later, my stomach full of casino buffet Humpty hearts and fried little piggy, I slumped against the backseat of the limo, once again on my way to encourage

Lollie Bliss to reveal her dirty little secret . . . boyfriend. And if she revealed a bit more, like her naked body, well, who was I to argue?

The thought of a naked Lollie excited me much more than it should. After all, I'd be a married frog prince in less than seven days. One hundred and sixty-eight little hours between me and wedded bliss. Too bad I couldn't get the thought of pre-un-wedded Bliss from my head.

I lowered the privacy screen between Karl and myself. "So how was it?" I asked to take my mind off my own fantasies. "Did you blow her mind? Make her beg for more? Cause her to laugh uncontrollably when she saw that your mommy stitched your name on your under-wear?"

Karl's hands tightened on the wheel, probably imagin-ing my neck, but he didn't say a word, a sure sign that I was getting under his pale pink skin. Good. He owed me for tattling to Elly. Because of him I now had a drunken wand-happy fairy watching my every move.

Karl turned the limo onto Fairily Way, stopping briefly at a red light. Silence filled the vehicle.

"Well?" I tapped him on the shoulder. "Are you going to tell me all about your evening of debauchery?"

Karl exhaled noisily. "For the last time, sir, I do not know what you're talking about. I spent last night alone, asleep in my room."

"Uh-huh," I said as we pulled into a parking space a block from the Rose. Not waiting for Karl to open my door, I leapt from the limo and into the street. A blast of heated air sucked the moisture from my skin like a wicked witch invited to Hansel's house for dinner. God, I hated the desert. What kind of idiot built a city in a forsaken pile of sand? And then decided to build a lush emerald golf course on top of it? I couldn't wait to return to the rainy weather and rude citizens of New Never City. Home sweat-less home.

Deciding to share my increasingly lousy mood, I turned to tease Karl a bit more when the whirl of a car engine grabbed my attention. I glanced over my shoulder and spotted a black Ford Unicorn riding low to the ground, the sun reflecting off the tiny unicorn emblem on the hood.

I squinted at the car, unable to make out the driver through the tinted windshield.

Tires squealed.

The vehicle headed straight at me.

Time slowed.

My heart leapt into my throat, cutting off my screams as my life flashed before my eyes. Sunny afternoons by the pond playing games of live-action leapfrog all by myself. Nights spent on a lily pad. Alone.

Always alone.

Until the day she came into my life—a golden-haired girl with grape-lollipop eyes and a sloppy wet kiss.

My eyes locked on the car less than ten feet away.

A sloppy wet kiss wouldn't save me now.

Chapter 24

Drool-coated lips hovered an inch from mine. Hot, fetid breath assaulted my senses. My stomach rolled, but not from the putrid breath of my unwashed whore of a manservant who leaned over me. Nope, the bile rising into my throat had much more to do with the fact that I was nearly kabobbed by a unicorn horn a few seconds ago.

"Sir," Karl dropped to his knees, "are you all right?"

"That idiot almost killed me." I sat up, brushing bits of shattered glass and dirt from my shirt. At this rate I'd need a new wardrobe by my wedding day.

"Yes, but are you hurt?"

"You saved my life," I whispered to my concerned servant. He blushed, but didn't comment. I staggered to my feet, my knee nearly giving way. "Ow! Ow! Ow!"

Karl caught me before I fell to the ground. "Um . . . sir," he said, trying to hold me upright while I hopped around. "People are staring."

I stopped my acrobatic tricks long enough to glance around. Other than a pied piper and a pack of brainwashed rats, the street appeared deserted. "I don't see anyone."

Karl exhaled loudly. "Very well. But still, this just isn't dignified. For frog sakes, you're a prince, and I'm . . ."

"Bald?" I suggested.

Karl scowled. "Well yes, but that wasn't what I meant."

"Oh." I stopped jumping around and gazed at my long-time friend and servant. I owed him my life. He'd swooped in to save me from certain death like some sort of pudgy, pink-headed superhero. "How can I ever repay you for saving me?" I grabbed his face in my hands, squishing his pudgy cheeks until his lips disappeared beneath. "I'll give you anything. Name it."

His eyes narrowed. "Well, I wouldn't mind having a couple of days off next week. . . ."

I released his puffy cheeks with genuine regret. "Next week's not good. You know, with the honeymoon and all. Bags to pack, unpack . . . carry." I tapped my bottom lip, thinking. "How about the first week of July? You can watch the fireworks from a beach somewhere."

"July?" His voice increased an octave. Not an attractive sound, sort of like squawks coming from Peter Piper's bathroom after a peck of jalapeño peppers. "I'm already on vacation that week," he whined.

I scratched my chin. "Oh . . . July's not good for me. I was thinking about going to West Wickedginia for Maple Fest. Maybe we should reschedule your vacation for November."

Karl's face turned a shade of pink not found outside the imagination of a crayon company. "You pompous, selfish as—"

I wagged my finger in his face. "You can thank me later."

A block later, Karl yanked the front door of the Rose open with a growl. What a baby. It wasn't like I asked him to break up with my ninth-grade girlfriend . . . again. What an ordeal that was. I spent four long hours at the hospital while a gaggle of doctors removed a #2 pencil from Karl's testicle.

As I entered the shop, bells overhead jangled in greeting,

but no one came to welcome us. The buzz of a tattoo gun echoed through the room. I limped farther inside, nodding to the back room where Lollie usually worked. "She must be with a client." The accompanying scream clinched it.

"Lovely," Karl said, picking up a dog-eared magazine titled *Tramp Stamps: The Art of Tattooing Hobos* from the waiting room table.

I sat down in the red office chair behind the tiny reception desk that Red normally manned. A stuffed mouse dressed in a small pair of Dockers and a white button-down shirt sat on the desktop, tiny tire tracks across its chest.

My eyes narrowed on the stuffed mouse and the letter "B" burned into its small chest. A frown puckered over my brow. I hefted the rodent up and held it to the light. Karl glanced up, his eyes widening as he pondered the mouse. "Oh my God. Sir, that's—"

"Sure, it's not everyone's cup of tea...." My thought trailed off as the buzz of Lollie's tattoo gun stopped, as did the agonized screams of Lollie's client.

A minute later Lollie stepped out of the back room, a pair of thick rubber gloves, the kind worn by electricians and firefighters, covering her slender hands.

I dropped the mouse and beamed at the beautiful ink-covered woman in front of me. She stood, as regal as a princess in black leather pants, looking at me as if I was a bug about to be squashed. Lollie Bliss appeared as fickle as lady luck. One minute she was sucking on my tonsils, and the next she was staring at me like I was toe jam left in the bottom of a glass slipper.

"What's with the gloves?" I asked, for lack of anything better to say.

"What's with your face?" she returned.

"Ha. Ha."

Her skin went white. "I'm not joking. You look a little ...

green. And there's blood on your pants. What the hell happened to you?"

Oh, right. The accident. I'd almost forgotten about that in my haste to see Lollie. A bad sign. I didn't want to like her, and I wasn't exactly sure I did, but we had some sort of connection, other than the obvious one about her lover wanting my bride dead and all.

Karl spoke up. "My lordship was nearly run down outside your establishment." The censure in his tone was clear. He blamed Ms. Bliss, if not for the accident, for the fact we were on our way to see her when it occurred.

Her gloved hands hovered over her abundant chest. "Are you all right? Did you get a look at the driver? The license plate?"

"I'm fine." I gave her a wilted smile, designed for optimum pity. "Karl exaggerates. It's nothing more than a scratch."

"Let me see." She rushed over and knelt down in front of me, the swell of her breasts peeking through the scoop of her tank top. I tried not to look. I really did. But, alas, my libido overrode my good intentions. My mouth went dry at the thought of my fingers against her flesh.

Snap out of it, I told myself. I was to be married in less than a week. Now was not the time to covet thy ink-covered neighborly chick. Lollie's fingers on my thigh drew me back to the present. She pulled off her thick rubber gloves and carefully rolled up my pants to expose the wound on my knee. Pain rocketed through my body, but I refused to cry out. Not in front of Lollie. I'd die first.

"Ow! Ow! Ow! Stop!" I whimpered when she prodded my mangled flesh. "Oh, the agony . . ."

"Suck it up, you big baby." She pressed a Band-Aid to the tiny red mark and rolled my pant leg back in place. "It's only a scratch. I've gotten worse cuts shaving my legs."

Her words brought up a wealth of soapy, wet images to my head. I shook them away, trying to focus on what Lollie was saying. "So tell me again how this near-fatal injury happened?" she asked with a grin.

Again Karl answered for me, his voice harsh as if reliving a painful memory. "The prince had just left the limo. I've warned him time and again not to exit street side, but my lord likes to live on the edge."

Lollie heaved her eyebrow upward. "Apparently."

"Anyway," I said. "Long fairytale short, a car sped up the street toward me. I, having the ninja-like reflexes, leapt over the fast-moving vehicle, landing surefooted on the sidewalk where my prone-to-panic manservant," I smirked at Karl, "tackled me in his terrified concern. Hence my injured knee."

"How awful for you." Lollie patted my arm, her voice insistent. "Did you get the license plate number?"

I glanced at Karl. He shook his head. "I believe the license plate was absent from the vehicle, sir." Karl glared at me. "But in my overly melodramatic state I could be wrong."

"If there's some crazed drunk driver out there running people over, shouldn't we call the police?" Lollie asked.

She had a point. If only Handsome wasn't on the Cin City PD. I imagined that if I called to report the incident, I'd find myself in handcuffs instead of the intoxicated driver.

But the driver hadn't appeared drunk. The Unicorn wasn't swerving all over the place. In fact, it maintained a clear, straight line as it sped toward me, almost as if the vehicle was aiming at me.

"Oh, Kermit," Lollie said, her hand over her mouth.

A shiver ran up my spine. Was someone out to get me? Plotting to kill me at this very moment? I rubbed the back of my neck as paranoia like ants at a picnic went marching through my mind. "Let's not jump the gun just yet. It was an accident. Nothing more." I nodded to myself. "The sun was probably in the driver's eyes, and he panicked and hit the gas."

Lollie blew a dark curl from her eyes. "You're probably right."

"Of course, sir," Karl agreed.

"Frog it!" I jumped to my feet, the intense pain in my knee all but forgotten. "Someone tried to kill me."

"Now, sir," Karl began. "We don't know that."

"He's right, Kermit. Besides, who would want you dead?" Lollie grinned, her teeth gleaming in the sunlight. "Except for the poor girl forced to marry you, that is."

"There will be no wedding," a deep voice said from the doorway.

Chapter 25

"Father," I said to the man in the doorway, a man who looked nothing like me. The Frog King stood just over six feet with sandy brown hair tinted gray at the tips. He wore an inexpensive linen suit and loafers with a small scuff on the toe. His chiseled face looked carved in stone. No expression, no happiness or joy at seeing his only son, a son he hadn't bothered to see in over two years.

"Jean-Michel." The Frog King nodded in my direction. "You look . . . well."

"What are you doing here?" I asked, staring into his sapphire eyes. My eyes. The only feature we shared. Admittedly, I should've asked something like, "No wedding? What are you talking about?" but the shock of seeing my father, here, in Lollie's shop after years of absence affected me more than I was willing to admit. The Frog King rarely left his castle, let alone ventured anywhere near his black sheep of a son.

The Frog King cleared his throat. "May we speak in private?"

"Of course, sir." Karl quickly jumped to his feet. "If you need anything. Anything at all. I'll be right outside."

"Thank you, Karl." The Frog King frowned, his nose wrinkling. "What's that smell?"

Karl blushed.

"Hmm." I sniffed the air. "I'm not sure. Smells a little like Candi. What do you think, Karl?"

Karl ran out the door.

We watched as my manservant nearly toppled a newspaper stand on the corner. He righted it in time, and disappeared from view.

Lollie also stood, but at a slower pace, her long, lean legs looking longer and leaner in the gleaming sunlight. I gulped. Lollie stuck out her hand. "Hi. I'm Lollie. Lollie Bliss." The king glanced down at her outstretched hand, his wrinkled brow wrinkling more. Her smile grew as she added, "This is my shop."

The king lifted his sandy-colored eyebrow. "A pleasure, Ms. . . . Bliss, was it?"

Lollie nodded, her smile slipping a bit under the king's obvious disapproval. Having been on the receiving end of the king's censure more often than not, I knew exactly how Lollie felt. With one harsh word the Frog King could turn a mere mortal to quivering mush. Not that Lollie was mere, nor mortal.

"Forgive my rudeness, Father," I said, gaining the old man's attention. "But I repeat, why are you here?"

The king sighed. "I heard a rumor."

"I can explain!"

"That you are engaged to Princess Vaniteuse," my father finished with a frown.

"Oh," I said. "That one? Yes, I am engaged to Beauty. Now, if that's all, I'll show you the way out. . . ."

The Frog King's eyes narrowed, but before he could question my outburst, Lollie spoke. "You must forgive Kermit." At the nickname, my father raised a sandy-colored eyebrow. Lollie grinned, adding, "He recently suffered a grave injury and hasn't quite recovered." Lollie motioned to a red plastic chair. "Please have a seat. You must be tired after your long journey. Can I get you a drink? Bottled water? Coke?"

"Arsenic?" I mumbled under my breath like a petulant child, which, given our relationship was an apt description.

Glancing between Lollie and me, the king did as she suggested, sitting down gingerly on the hard plastic. "Tap water. Ice. Three cubes."

Figured. The penny-pinching Frog King loved to save a buck, be it drinking tap water rather than Perrier, or sending his only son to the Row, Row, Row a Borrowed Boat with a Cracked Hull summer camp instead of the more expensive and safe version.

"Right. Three cubes. And you, Jean-Michel?" she asked, sneering my name. "Would you like something?"

"No thanks. I'm good." I crossed my arms over my chest.

"Why don't you take a seat next to your dad?" She gestured for me to sit. "I'm sure you have plenty to talk about."

"Not really."

Lollie smiled.

I shook my head.

Her grin grew wider, exposing her teeth in an almost threatening manner. I dropped into a chair next to my father. Lollie nodded, apparently satisfied by my obedience. "I'll be back in a minute," she said. "Please make yourself at home." With those parting words, Lollie strolled from the room, her hips hypnotically swaying back and forth.

"She seems . . . nice," my father said with only a hint of disapproval.

"She's not," I said. "In fact, I think she'd like nothing more than for me to croak."

My father frowned, as if my sense of humor left a lot to be desired. "I see."

Anger burned in my chest. Like my father saw anything beyond his pile of money. He'd spent all my life locked away in his castle, counting his pennies. He knew nothing about my life, about my relationship with Ms. Bliss. About me. Sometimes I hated him for it. But more often than not, I hated myself for the years I wasted seeking his approval.

"Let's get this over with," I said. "You don't want me to marry Beauty. Good to know. Now, if you'll excuse me, I have a wedding to plan. A very expensive wedding, I might add. . . ."

"You can't marry Sleeping Beauty," he said, harshly. "I forbid it."

"What objection could you possibly have to Beauty?" I gave a bitter laugh. "She's a rich princess with an unblemished pedigree, for frog sakes."

"Not for long, son."

"What are you talking about?"

"Your princess is mortgaged to the hilt."

Chapter 26

Before I could question my father further, Lollie strolled back into the room, a glass smudged with ink in her hand. A small chip ran down the side of the glass. "Here you go," she said, handing the glass to my father.

He took it, his mouth twisting with disgust. Lollie tapped her finger to her lips, waiting, until the Frog King grudgingly drank a sip. "Thank you," he said, clearing his throat.

Lollie nodded, and then turned to me, her dark eyes glowing. "So what'd I miss?"

I was pretty sure she didn't miss much. Ever. But Lollie was the least of my concerns at the moment. "Father," I said, "do you have a shred of evidence to support your ridiculous claim? Or are you making this up to avoid buying a tuxedo for my wedding?"

"I am not making this up. Besides, it's much cheaper to rent a tuxedo by the hour." He pounded his fist into his palm. "But that's not the point. Jean-Michel," he began, ignoring Lollie, "I order you to break off your engagement and return to New Never City to find a more appropriate bride."

"I'm sorry, Father." I took a deep breath. "But I can't." Even though I wanted nothing more than to do just that.

But Beauty was my One. Forever. Until death did us part. I cleared my throat. "Beauty will be my wife."

My father slowly rose to his feet. "Then you leave me with no choice."

I nodded, knowing exactly where he was going. "So be it," I said with a calm I didn't feel. The Frog King closed his eyes, as if in pain, nodded once, and left the shop.

Lollie stared after him, confusion etched on every tiny line of her face. "What was that all about?"

"Not much," I said, carefully rising to my feet. "My father just disowned me."

Chapter 27

After my father's announcement, I left a confused Lollie at the tattoo shop and headed for the limo, my father's words ringing in my ears. Disowned. Alone. And no closer to finding Spindle, or getting Lollie naked. My visit to Lollie's had accomplished nothing. I closed my eyes and let the full weight of my upcoming nuptials wash over me. Karl opened the door of the limo, his face full of concern. "Sir?" he ventured.

I shook my head.

He swallowed and closed the door, leaving me alone in the car. I pulled out my p-Phone and dialed a number I hadn't called in over three years. A number I'd promised to never to dial again, or so I told the judge.

Three rings later, a woman answered. "Detective Locks."

"Hey, Goldie," I said, my tone infused with princely charm. "Been a while."

She groaned. "What do you want, Jean-Michel?"

"I've missed you. Remember all the good times we had together?"

"We went on two dates," she said. "The second one ended . . . badly."

I rubbed at my chest where Goldie had tased me after a small misunderstanding involving her roommate and a can of whipped cream. "Good times," I said with a smile. "Good times."

"I'm busy here, Jean-Michel." She huffed. "Just tell me what you want so I can say no, and we can both get on with our lives."

I winced, but got to the point. "I need your help—"

"I can't fix another ticket." She paused. "No matter how many times you deny it, indecent exposure is a real crime."

"Funny, but you know as well as I do that those charges were trumped up. I still had my boxers on. I don't care what that Contrary Mary said." I gave a small laugh. "But that's not why I called. Today I need a little information. About a princess."

Now it was Goldie's turn to laugh. "Tell me she's not pressing charges."

I winced, realizing too late that Goldie, while the best detective in New Never City, couldn't see through the phone line. "Nothing like that. I just need some financials for a woman named Beauty Vaniteuse."

Goldie chuckled again, this time with real humor. "Jean-Michel, I'm a homicide detective with a stack of case files a mile high. Not an accountant."

"Please," I said, mustering up all of my French charm.

"Fine," she said, hurriedly. "I'll see what I can come up with."

"Thank you," I said and hung up. A sudden wistfulness came over me. Perhaps I should've tried harder to win Goldie's heart. Then I considered the fact that she was pretty picky, had a bit of a temper, and carried a gun, one that fired real bullets instead of ink, and my regret instantly evaporated. I had enough women wanting me dead already.

Speaking of which, I cranked the window down. "Karl?"

"Where to, sir?" he said, snapping to attention.

"Vaniteuse Palace," I said, my eyes locking on Lollie's face in the window of the tattoo shop. "It's time I had a little talk with my bride."

Twenty minutes later, we arrived at the Vaniteuse palace. Surprisingly, it looked much like it had the day before, when Beauty was just a sleepy chick, and not the woman who'd just destroyed the lifestyle I'd become very accustomed to. Yet being poor felt remarkably like being rich. Of course, I still had seventy million dollars in my trust fund, which, if I was frugal, would keep me from having to rub-a-dub-dub guys on the street corner for Armani.

Workers watered beds of roses, trimmed hedges, and mowed the jade-colored lawn into impressively straight rows for less money than I spent on a pair of shoes.

Out of the corner of my eye, I caught sight of a shiny black vehicle parked in the palace driveway. A very familiar, shiny black car complete with a large, almost phallic horn attached to the hood. "Son of a bitch," I whispered. "She really did try and kill me. What did I ever do to her?" I asked Karl.

"You hired an assassin to kill her."

Oh yeah. I'd almost forgotten about that. All my anger at being run down vanished, replaced by an odd sense of relief. "Guess we're even, then."

"The foundation of many a great marriage," he said.

My eyes narrowed. Was he mocking me? His blank expression suggested he wasn't, but the gleam in his eyes spoke volumes. "Like you know anything about women or marriage. Your last girlfriend was made from recycled Tupperware."

Without waiting for his comeback, I jumped from the limo and stormed up the sidewalk. Stupid Karl, like he knew anything about what made relationships work. Well, I'd show him. Beauty and I would live happily ever after, even if it killed her. I pounded on the diamond-encrusted door. "Open up."

The door swung wide. The butler, Marvin, stood to the side, a frown on his block-like face. "Prince La Grenouille, whatever are you doing here?"

"I'm here to chat with my loving bride," I sneered, glancing at my watch. A little past noon. Just in time for Beauty's naptime. "If you'd be so kind as to wake her."

"But, sir—"

"Wake her," I repeated. "Now."

Marvin jumped to attention and all but flew up the staircase. I grinned; years of torturing my own servant had finally paid off.

From down the hallway, the king's voice boomed. "I will not!" A door opened and then slammed shut. I caught sight of a flash of pink before it disappeared around the corner. The scent of gin floated down the hallway. A few seconds later, Jimmy Cockroach appeared in front of me, his top hat askew.

"Hey," I said in greeting.

The cockroach looked up, his lips curled with disgust. "Oh goody, it's you again. The Frog Prince. Whoopee."

"What's the supposed to mean?"

"It means," he glared at me, "not everyone is overjoyed by whatever crap falls from your stupid mouth."

Was I just insulted? By a roach? I took a step back. "Whoa. Ease back on the hostility a little. We've only just met." It usually took years, okay months, occasionally a few hours, for someone to genuinely hate me. Since I'd exchanged no more than ten words with the cricket wannabe in the last couple of days, I wasn't quite sure what was going on. Not that it mattered. If I wanted to I could squash him like a . . .

"Bug! The word you are looking for, you moron, is bug!" he yelled. "You're all alike." He smashed his stick-like leg against the ground. "Think you're a fairy's wet dream, but you're not." He clasped his tiny hands behind his back. "And who will pay the price when your true colors emerge? Poor Princess Beauty. That's who."

I gave a bitter laugh. "I'm sure Beauty will survive." "Poor" was an interesting choice of words, though. Did the roach know about Beauty's recent money trouble? If so, that explained twenty-eight broken engagements. What prince wanted to marry a pauper? Other than a cursed prince with little choice in the matter.

"How I wish that was true," he said, dragging me back to the conversation at hand. "Unfortunately, Beauty is doomed as soon as she says 'I do' to the likes of you."

"Doomed? Aren't you being a tad melodramatic? Marrying me isn't the worst thing in the world." The black plague still existed, right? If not, *Fairyland's Ugliest Stepsister* was just picked up for a fourth season. That show had to be worse than a wedding night with me.

"Doomed!" he repeated, tapping his tiny walking stick against the hardwood floor. "If Sleeping Beauty marries you, she will suffer a fate far worse than death."

"Oh yeah? What's that?"

"Marriage to a moron."

"Hey, let's not bring religion into this." I folded my arms over my chest. "Besides, I'm agnostic."

"Idiot." With that insult hanging in the air between us, Jimmy Cockroach spun on his tiny heel, and slipped through the crack under the front door.

"Wait," I called after him, but he had vanished. A feeling of dread washed over me. Was the roach right? Would marrying me literally ruin my bride? I rubbed the B-shaped birthmark over my heart and shook my head. Nonsense. She was my One. That was all that mattered.

What was taking Marvin so long? I glanced at my watch. I'd been waiting in the hallway for five minutes now. Time was money, or so poor people often said. To me, time was just time, but maybe that would change now that I was on my own. Or not. I yawned and checked my watch again.

"Jean-Michel!" Sleeping Beauty's stepfather materialized in front of me. "No use standing by the door. Come in, son. Come in."

Son? Really? Hell, my own father rarely called me by name, let alone used the term "son." Of course, he'd just disowned me, but that was a moot point. "Thanks, but I'm waiting for your daughter."

"Pretty?"

"No. Princess Beauty. We have . . . something to discuss." Something like the little matter of wanting me dead, I thought.

"Yes, well," he said, "don't be too hasty, son. Beauty meant well."

Yeah, I'm sure she had my well-being utmost in mind when she tried to kill me. "So you know what she did?" I asked, my blood heating. What was wrong with this family? They discussed outright murder like others did the weather.

The king nodded. "Don't get too upset. Her dear mother did the same thing to me a couple of days before our wedding."

"And you still married her?"

"Let's have a drink and I'll tell you all about it." The king grabbed my arm and pulled me inside his "library," which consisted of a collection of unread literary classics and dog-eared fairy-on-fairy pornography. "Have a seat, son. Have a seat." He motioned to an empty recliner on the far side of a faux fireplace.

"Nice room," I said, glancing around. Every surface spoke of wealth and privilege, like a commercial for Viagra and overcompensation. The rug alone must've cost a hundred thousand, not to mention the ivory fireplace and diamond-covered lampshade. Ali Baba and his forty light-fingered friends would've loved to spend five minutes alone in this palace. Hell, even I was tempted to pocket the ruby paperweight the size of an oversized little lamb on the coffee table. All this extravagance explained the king's current financial woes. I wondered if Beauty knew the king was selling her to anyone willing to pay for her hand in marriage. It gave her one hell of a motive for murder.

"Can I get you a drink?" the king asked. "I have a fine eighty-year-old scotch from my private stock with your name on it."

Private stock. If he hadn't stuck me with the dinner check, his words would've told me all that I needed to know about Sleeping Beauty's stepfather. The greedy bastard. "Why not," I said.

The king beamed as he poured two fingers of scotch into a crystal glass. "This bottle," he held the liquor bottle to the light, "cost me ten thousand dollars at auction last year. But what's a few dollars when it comes to family." He handed me the drink and poured three fingers for himself. "To the great institution of marriage," he said in salute.

I hoisted my glass and then downed the smooth amber liquid in one gulp. Wiping my mouth with the back of my sleeve, I bowed to the king, enjoying the flash of anger that crossed his face. "Hit me again," I said, hoisting my glass.

Had his stepdaughter not been about to marry me, I'm pretty sure the king would've done just that. Instead, he smiled tightly and poured a half inch of scotch from his "private stock" into my highball glass.

Taking pity on the poor guy, I took a small sip first before knocking back the rest. "Not bad. Not bad at all."

"I'm glad you approve," he paused, sneering the word, "son."

He wanted something badly. Badly enough to share his ten-thousand-dollar bottle of scotch with a guy he'd only days ago wanted to boil in oil. I wondered if his newfound friendliness had something to do with Sleeping Beauty's recent attempt on my life.

"So?" I began when silence descended over the room.

"So," he repeated as his eyes misted. "Beauty is very special." So I'd heard, numerous times. But the king wasn't finished. "She's been like a daughter to me since her father, rest his soul, was killed in a freak climbing accident."

"Rock climbing?"

The king's eyes grew damp, almost amphibian-like. "Scaling Rapunzel's palace wall. The rope he was using just gave way mid-climb. The coroner declared it an accidental death by split ends." He stopped, tilting his head to one side as he stared at me. I grew increasingly uncomfortable under his gaze until he finally spoke again. "You remind me of Beauty's father in a lot of ways."

"Really? How so?"

"He loved his family. Wanted the best for them and would do anything to reach his goals. A prince among men. That he was." The king's eyes grew moist with unshed tears. "Sadly, he left little in the way of support for his wife and young daughter. Just this dinky, run-down palace in the middle of nowhere and a small dowry, pennies really."

Run-down? Dinky? Mind you, my collection of shoes had a palace twice this size, but this castle was far from being either dinky or rundown. The bastard king had likely squandered away Beauty's dowry on his hundred-thousand-dollar rugs, three-thousand-dollar shoes, and ten-thousand-dollar bottles of scotch.

I could see it now. He'd homed in on a grief-stricken queen and her semi-orphaned and sleepy child and set himself up in the lap of luxury. But I'd be damned if he'd continue to pick Sleeping Beauty's bones clean. Once Goldie came through with Beauty's financial picture, I'd devise a plan to rid her of the greedy king for life. Neither the king nor his offspring would ever touch another dime of Sleeping Beauty's money.

It was time for King Vaniteuse to pay the piper, by which I meant Phil, the piper the king had hired for the wedding ceremony. The guy cost a fortune.

The king was saying, "So you can see why this day means so much to me," he jabbed his finger into his chest, "her dear stepdaddy."

"Oh, I see." I patted his shoulder hard enough to leave a mark. "I see everything."

Not that any of this mattered. I wasn't here to chitchat with the king. I'd come to see my future bride. Not that I had a clue as to what I'd say to her when she honored me with her presence. 'What the fuck?' held a certain dignified appeal. I glanced at my watch. "Listen, sir," I said. "I really do need to speak with Sleeping Beauty, so if you'll exc—"

"Don't break up with Beauty." The king grabbed my hand. "Please." He paused, increasing his grip. "She didn't mean anything by it. I promise. It was a test. Nothing more."

"Whoa," I said, peeling each of his fingers off of my sleeve. "A test, you say? Trying to kill me was a *test?*"

"What?!" He bolted upright, spilling his scotch all over the hundred-thousand-dollar rug beneath our feet. I winced. That would leave a stain. The king frowned and then broke into a fit of giggles. "Good one, son. You had me going for a minute there."

"I'm not joking."

"While I'll admit Beauty is a wee bit annoying," he said, "she would never hurt anyone, let alone attempt to murder the man she's come to adore."

"Who's that?"

The king's brow wrinkled. "Why, you, son."

"Of course." Because nothing says "I love you" like a speeding car. I started to say as much, but the king cut me off. "Please, son. You must believe me." He leaned forward, his eyes intent. "Under the bitchiness, Beauty's as sweet as they come."

"Sweet" wasn't the term I'd apply to my pajama-wearing princess, but then again, I wasn't her stepfather, a man intent on selling his ward to the highest bidder. I scratched my chin, taking a moment to study the king. "If Beauty had nothing to do with the attempt on my life, what was all that about her testing me?"

His sigh filled the room. "The colors."

"What colors?"

"The wedding colors." The king swallowed. "Beauty changed the color scheme for the wedding. She wants everything to be green. Frog green."

Ten minutes and a half a bottle of private-stock scotch later, I patted the king's arm and assured him, for the tenth time, that Beauty and I would marry in less than seven days, her poor color choice, and possible homicidal tendencies, aside. What marriage didn't have its ups and downs?

Speaking of ups, a flash of color in the window caught my eye. I squinted, making out the well-endowed breasts of Ms. Lollie Bliss squished against the glass. What the hell was she doing? I stood, excusing myself from the king's company to investigate what now appeared to be Lollie's ankle slithering upward.

I headed out the front door and around the side of the palace, nearly tripping over a worker who sat in a corner, eating a pie with his fingers. I nodded as I passed. He gave me a sticky purple thumbs-up. "What a good boy am I," he said before again losing himself in his afternoon treat.

"Um, sure," I said, quickening my pace. I rounded another corner, this one thankfully empty with the exception of an ink-sleeved woman tangled in a rose trellis about six feet off the ground. Leaves and rose petals mixed with

long, jet-black strands of hair as Lollie Bliss fought to escape her flowery prison, unaware of my presence or the
fact that her leather pants had slipped dangerously close to
revealing her bliss.

My blood suddenly flowed south, and my body hardened. Turned on by a chick stuck in a tree, what a sick frog
prince I was. Scratch that. Since the Frog King had disowned me, I was merely some pervy guy with a fly fetish.

"Achoo." Lollie sneezed, sending a shower of rose
petals raining down on me. I brushed off a few leaves, and
stared up at the beautiful woman above me.

"Gesundheit," I said.

"Ahhh," she screamed, twisting on the trellis until her
body faced mine. Her eyes shot daggers at me. "Well,
don't just stand there. Help me down."

I scratched my chin. "How about we start with 'Hi,
Jean-Michel, good to see you again'?" My eyes roamed
over her tangled limbs with both appreciation and concern. The damn trellis was covered in thorns. "And then
maybe you could explain why you're climbing my fiancée's rose trellis?"

"You bas . . . achoo . . . ta—"

I raised an eyebrow.

"Fine," she spat. "Hi, Jean-Michel. Now help me down
before I sneeze and impale myself on a thorn." To emphasize her point, she let out a string of sneezes. I ducked a
particularly wet one. A loud crack echoed from the trellis,
followed by a waterfall of splintered wood. Frog! If I didn't
help Lollie down soon, she'd surely break a leg. How
would I explain that to my future bride?

I reached for Lollie's waist. The leather of her pants
scorched my fingertips, but I held tight, hefting her body
from the tangle of rose vines. Beads of sweat dribbled
down my forehead and into my eyes. I blinked away the
sting, completely focused on the task at hand, not to mention the feel of Lollie's skin against my hands.

Once she'd cleared the thorniest of the branches, Lollie used my body like a slide and slithered down until her feet hit the ground. We stood inches apart. The warmth of her body enveloped me, warming parts of me left frozen in the wake of my soon-to-be-married state. My hands curled around her bottom, cupping the softness underneath, dragging her naughty parts closer to mine.

Lollie lowered her gaze to my sudden, semi-erect appendage pressing against her. "Please tell me that's a gun in your pocket," she said, her voice growing husky.

"Best I can do is a roll of Fairy Savers breath mints." A grin broke across my face. "A really big roll."

Taking a ragged breath, Lollie stepped back. "Well . . . I . . ."

"What was that about?" I motioned to the trellis, ignoring the ache in my groin. Sadly, within the last two hours, I'd gone from a frog prince without a care in the world (Beauty's probable assassination aside) to little boy blue balls. Who knew what nightfall might bring? A case of the clap? I shook off that thought and instead tried to focus on Lollie's explanation. It promised to be entertaining, if nothing else. "What are you even doing here? If Beauty catches you . . ." I swallowed hard, my mind racing with scenario after scenario. About half of them ended with me sporting a brand-new pair of frog legs. And those were the happy endings.

"I was in the neighborhood."

My eyebrow rose.

"Fine. I'm here," she sneered, "to stop you from doing something stupid."

Stupid? Me? I snickered. "So what, you decided to break into my bride's palace? How's that for stupid?"

"Would you rather I rang the doorbell?" Her hands fisted on her hips. "Maybe invite your sweet fiancée out to lunch for a little chat?"

My eyes lowered, giving her body a slow, leering once-over. "You're not her type."

"Funny," her smile sparkled with humor, "yet I'm sure we'd find plenty to talk about."

"Are you threatening me?" I leaned in, her minty-fresh breath hot against my neck. "Because I don't scare that easy. Not since my dear bride attempted to run me down this morning."

Lollie took a step back, all the humor gone from her face. "You really think your fiancée tried to kill you? Are you insane?"

My eyes narrowed. "You're the one who suggested it, remember? Today at your shop? I didn't believe it when you first said it, but then I saw the car in the driveway. . . ."

"What car?"

"The black Unicorn Beauty used to try and run me down." I gestured to the front of the palace and the long, yellow brick driveway. "How could you miss it? It's the only vehicle in the driveway with a prince-shaped dent."

Concern lined Lollie's face as she waved two fingers in front of my face. "How many fingers am I holding up?"

"Knock it off," I said, pushing her hand down. "What's gotten into you?"

"There's no Unicorn in the driveway, Kermit." She shot me a sad smile. "Are you sure you saw a black Ford Unicorn? Maybe it was a Chevy Mermaid. They can look a lot alike."

"I know what I saw, damn it!" I started forward. I'd show her. But before I reached the driveway, Marvin stopped me, his pudgy face beet red in color.

"Beg your pardon, sir." Marvin's eyes darted between Lollie and me. I could only imagine how things looked, me with an unbelievable-sized bulge in my trousers, and Lollie, as hot as ever, leaves tangled in her hair.

"Did you wake my bride?" I growled, snapping Marvin's attention from Lollie to me. The less attention Marvin paid Lollie, the better. I was already risking too much having her in the vicinity as my bride, let alone flaunting our . . . relationship to the help.

"That's what I came to tell you, sir." Marvin bowed low, beads of sweat dripping down his face. He mopped them away with the edge of his uniform. "Princess Beauty . . ." His eyes locked on Lollie.

I motioned for him to get on with it.

"Right," he said. "Of course. It's just . . . your bride . . ."

I closed my eyes. Would nothing ever be easy with Beauty? "What's she done now? Added frog legs to the wedding feast? Ordered a hemlock cake? What?"

"Well, sir," Marvin straightened to his full height, "Princess Beauty has disappeared."

Chapter 28

Damn her! Less than seven days until our wedding, and Sleeping Beauty had pulled a runaway bride. I should've seen it coming. She showed all the signs of a flight risk, excessive sleepiness aside. Well, that and the fact she rarely left the palace.

I ran into the palace and rushed up the stairs, taking two at a time in my haste to reach Sleeping Beauty's bedroom. Lollie followed behind, her normally pale face as white as snow. Two guards stood at attention outside the bedroom door. The taller one nodded as I approached.

"No one saw her leave?" I asked.

"No, sir," he said. "Me and Paul here," he gestured to the other shorter and familiar-looking guard, "we've been here the whole time. Nobody came in, and nobody came out."

My eyes narrowed on the second guard's face. "Do I know you?"

"Um...no...sir...," he stuttered, and then suddenly cried out, "*Wolf!*"

I jumped back, nearly flattening Lollie, who stood behind my back. The first guard blushed. "Beg your pardon, sir. Paul...he suffers from Tourette's."

"Oh," I muttered. "Do you remember anything unusual

that might've happened today?" Perhaps Sleeping Beauty slithering down the storm drain?

Both guards shook their heads. "No, sir."

"Did either of you hear anything strange?"

Paul scratched the hair on his chin. "I . . . ah . . . *wolf* . . . didn't hear her . . . snores . . . like I . . . normally do."

"Since when?"

"Maybe . . . *wolf* . . . nine this morning."

Plenty of time for her to sneak away, drive into Cin City, and try to run me down. After all, it was much cheaper for a princess on a budget to murder her fiancé than pay a killer to do it.

"Thanks," I said to the guards. "I'm going to have a look around her bedroom." An idea occurred to me and I grinned. "Why don't you go grab a drink and relax? In fact, the king would love to share a bottle of his finest scotch with you. It's in the library. Go help yourself."

The guards beamed. "Thank you, sir." They headed off, the occasional cry of "wolf" echoing down the hallway.

Once they were gone, I turned to Lollie. "Bitch!"

She smacked me in the face.

I rubbed my stinging cheek. "What the hell was that for?"

"You called me a bitch."

"Not you. Sleeping Beauty."

She smacked me again.

"What was that one for?"

"I felt like it."

I took a calming breath. "Next time try really hard not to feel like it."

"We'll see, Kermit." She winked. "We'll see. So, what's with calling your sweet bride names? It's not her fault that she's being forced to marry the likes of you. Given the circumstances, I'd run away too."

"Good point." I nodded, my fingers hovering above the

door handle to Beauty's lair. "However, my displeasure relates to her attempt on my life. Not her sudden vacation plans."

Color boomed on Lollie's cheek. "What if it wasn't her driving the Unicorn? What if Princess Beauty is innocent as well as sleepy?"

I pointed to my skinned knee. "Someone tried to kill me this morning, remember? And I suspect that someone is a certain princess who's currently on the run."

"Aw, poor baby. But what if you're wrong too? What if it wasn't her? What if it was someone else?"

A smile touched my lips. "Like who, your boyfriend, Spindle?"

Lollie's hand fisted at her side. "I'm serious. I think you're looking at this all wrong."

"We'll see, Lollipop," I said, tossing her words back into her face.

"*Don't. Ever.* Call—"

I laughed and pushed Sleeping Beauty's door open, bending low at the waist. "After you." I waved Lollie inside the room and then followed quickly behind, my eyes glued to the gentle sway of Lollie's hips.

"Holy crap," Lollie said, her mouth dropping open as she gazed around Beauty's bedroom.

Glancing up from Lollie's derriere, I stepped back. In a matter of a day since I'd last entered Beauty's bedroom, someone had wrecked the place. Books, magazines, and clothes lay scattered throughout the room as if a stampede of forest creatures had invaded.

But the destruction of Beauty's bedroom wasn't what shocked me the most. What rocked me to my very perfect toes was the single stem rose, the same blood-red color as the one drying in my pocket, placed gently across Sleeping Beauty's pillow.

Chapter 29

"Where is she?" I grabbed Lollie's shoulders and gave her a hard shake. "Where is Sleeping Beauty?!" Blood pounded in my head, muffling the words pouring from Lollie's plump, lying lips. Sleeping Beauty hadn't run away. That damn Spindle had kidnapped her.

Or worse.

I didn't want to even think about the worst-case scenario. It involved flies and trying to fit a flat-screen TV into a one-bedroom lily pad. I tightened my grip on Lollie's arm.

She punched me in the jaw until I let her go. "What's wrong with you?" She screamed. "I have no idea where your precious bride went."

Picking up the rose petal from the pillow, I shoved it under Lollie's nose. She sneezed in response. "Sorry, allergies," she said, wiping her eyes.

I stared at the wilted rose in my hand. "You're allergic to roses?"

"So?" Her arms crossed over her chest. "It's not like I'm diseased or something. It's an allergy. I take a pill each morning and I don't even notice."

"But Spindle . . ."

"This again?" She rolled her eyes. "How many times do I have to say it? I don't know anyone named Spindle."

"But the roses." I held the rose up again. Lollie backed

away. I dropped the offending flower. "Spindle leaves a rose at his crime scenes."

"So?"

"He leaves them for you."

Lollie gave a high-pitched laugh. "No, he doesn't. Why would this Spindle guy, even if I did know him, leave me flowers? I hate flowers, especially roses."

"Yeah, right." I gestured to the bright blue peonies inked on the inside of her arms. "Tattoos aside, you named your shop the Rose. And you expect me to believe that's just a coincidence? Do I look stupid?" Probably not the best question to ask considering I was standing in my missing fiancée's bedroom, a rose in my hand and a blank look on my face, since I had no idea what to do next.

Lollie grunted, spun around, and headed for the door. Her heels clicked on the hardwood. "Believe what you want, Kermit. I couldn't care less."

I reached for her arm, dragging her back. "Liar." Oh, she cared all right. Why else would she be here? For all Lollie's grumblings, she had fallen for me. Hard. The poor chick was just one more notch on my belt of love.

"For your information, Kermit," she yanked her arm from my grip and glared at me, "I didn't name the shop."

"Then who did?"

"Does it really matter?"

"Yes."

"Fine." She exhaled loudly. "A friend."

"Spindle?"

"No, you jerk. Red." At my blank look, she added, "My receptionist. Red hair. About," she held her hand to her waist, "this high."

"I don't understand."

Lollie exhaled, speaking slowly as if I was the village idiot. Which, given the past few days, I very well might've been. "Red, she's a midget. It's a genetic condition often referred to as dwarfism."

My face burned. "I know what a midget is. I'm talking about the fact Red named your shop." Lollie wasn't the type of woman to leave something as important as the naming of her shop to just anyone.

"Well," Lollie said, her eyes darting away. "It's not exactly my shop. Not totally."

"What?"

She scowled. "Maybe you should get your hearing checked. Perhaps all those years of debauchery, not to mention a strict fly-eating diet, have finally taken a toll."

I took a deep breath. "Mademoiselle, I assure you my hearing is as perfect as the rest of me. And I don't eat flies!" *Not anymore,* I added silently. "Now tell me, what the hell's going on?"

Lollie sat down on Sleeping Beauty's bed, her bottom molding to the mattress as if she belonged there. I felt the slightest twinge of guilt. Yeah, Beauty had likely tried to kill me, not to mention her being really annoying, but she was still my future bride, unless Spindle had already disposed of her.

Then she was probably worm food.

Having Lollie here, on Beauty's bed . . .

"Are you listening to me at all?" Lollie snapped her fingers. "I'm trying to explain how I met Red, and there you are fantasizing about a threesome."

Not quite, but now that she mentioned it . . .

"Damn it, Kermit." She leapt off the bed and stabbed her finger into my chest. "This is important. Red named the shop. I never asked why, but maybe she knows this invisible assassin, Spindle."

Footsteps sounded in the hallway outside Beauty's doorway. Lollie grimaced, her voice turning urgent. "I have an idea how to find your wayward bride." She grabbed my hand, and pulled me to the door. "But you have to come with me to the Rose. Right now."

Chapter 30

Lollie and I headed down the stairs, pausing a few steps from the bottom. Guilt nearly overwhelmed me, not at Sleeping Beauty's kidnapping, even though I felt sort of responsible for that, but for my growing attachment to Lollie Bliss. She had gotten under my skin, slowly, over the past couple of days. But I didn't trust her. Not in the slightest. Lollie had her own agenda, and I doubted my or Sleeping Beauty's continued good health topped the list.

"Karl's parked out front," I began.

"Jean-Michel? Is that you?" a high-pitched voice called from around the corner. The click of high heels followed, rapping against the hardwood floor like the little drummer boy in the gay pride parade.

"Frog! That's Sleeping Beauty's sister, Pretty. Wait for me outside." I turned to face Lollie, but she was already gone, disappearing out the front door in a flash of ink and blue-black hair. I glared after her departing figure. Pretty came around the corner as the front door snapped closed.

I held up my hand. "Don't worry your pretty little head."

"About what?" A wrinkle formed between her eyebrows. Her blank stare met mine and she gave me a small smile.

"Never mind." I decided to keep Sleeping Beauty's disappearance a secret, for now. Why worry her loving family unnecessarily? It was the princely thing to do, I assured myself. "Would you do me a favor?" I asked.

"Of course." She batted her eyes at me. "Your every desire is my command."

"Um. Good to know." I cleared my throat. "For now, could you just show me which bedroom is Sleeping Beauty's?" When she looked at me like I was demented, I quickly added, "From the outside. I need to know which of the windows is hers . . . for a wedding surprise."

Spindle had to get Beauty out of the bedroom somehow. The window seemed like the ideal choice given the guards parked outside her door.

"How sweet." Pretty sneered, but motioned for me to follow her down the hallway and into the garden at the back of the palace. She pushed open a large redwood door. A new world emerged before my eyes. Plants the size of a less-than-jolly-giant swept across the yard. Birds chirped a little too brightly overhead. An array of rainbow-colored stones, which looked suspiciously like gumdrops, lined the walkway.

Pretty stepped onto the yellow brick walkway. "This way," she said. The path was covered with multiple-colored flowers. Blond-haired fairies buzzed around playing tag with baby bumblebees. A pond filled with lily pads sat dead center of the garden, but there wasn't a frog in sight.

Well, except for me, and I didn't exactly count. Not yet. Unless Sleeping Beauty stayed kidnapped—then all bets, as well as my handsome face, were off.

I followed Pretty, half-listening as she pointed out various plant life. Where was Beauty? I wondered. Was she still alive? She had to be. I would know if she wasn't, right?

She was my *One*.

My heart lurched at the thought of a life without her. A life filled with lonely, fly-eating evenings by the pond, a pond much like the one in front of me.

Pausing in her flora lesson, Pretty pointed to a row of thorn-coated roses, almost black in color. The blooms appeared as big as Pretty's head. Petals littered the ground like drops of dried blood.

"Aren't they pretty?" Pretty asked, fingering the closest bloom in a sensual manner. I swallowed hard, pulling my eyes from her deft fingertips, and murmured my agreement. She beamed up at me. "The . . . three of us, Beauty, me, and our mother, we used to come to the garden every afternoon during the summer. Mother would point to each flower and tell us all about them." Pretty's eyes sparkled with unshed tears. "I never enjoyed gardening, but the time with Mother was priceless." She took a shaky breath. "And then she died."

"I'm sorry," I said, meaning every word. Even though my own mother was alive, albeit crazy and locked away in a tower, I understood the hole left by the loss of a parent. Thankfully I'd had a drunken fairy with a sadistic streak to fill a little bit of that void. Yeah, Mother's Day was a bitch.

Who had Beauty had to protect her? To bandage her skinned knees? I pictured the four-year-old menace from the pond. She'd seemed so alive, bratty, sure, but eager to take on the world. Nothing like the bitchy woman I'd met a few days ago.

"Father did his best," Pretty said when the silence grew between us. "But Beauty . . . well, she's Beauty. When she's not asleep, which is maybe an hour out of the day, she spends her time here, in the garden. Father has tried again and again to draw her out of her shell, but Beauty . . . Well, you'll find out soon enough."

"That I will," I said in agreement. Yet I doubted every word falling from Pretty's pink lips. What a thorn the grief-stricken, sort-of-sleepy princess must've been in the king's side. Unlike his private stock and thousand-dollar rugs, Beauty didn't quite fit into his carefully crafted world of wealth and privilege. An embarrassment he'd called her, only hours ago. Hate bubbled inside me. The king had destroyed that precocious child from the pond, turned her into a sleepy, annoying replica. Yet every so often, a spark of that kid surfaced. And maybe, in time, I'd meet the real Sleeping Beauty, unless Spindle smothered her with a pillow.

Damn.

Pretty reached for my hand, pulling it against her beating heart. "I would make a wonderful queen, don't you think?"

"The window," I reminded her.

"Of course." Her sigh was loud enough to fell a lesser man, but I was made of much sturdier stuff, namely the highest quality of snips and snails and puppy-dogs' tails.

Pretty brushed her fingers against her skirt. "Follow me." She took a couple of steps, crushing the petals on the ground. They left little red stains on the yellow concrete.

A half hour later Pretty led me back to the palace. My mind swirled with questions. The trip to Sleeping Beauty's bedroom window had proved uneventful as well as unproductive. The dirt under the window looked untouched, as did the rose trellis winding its way up the side of the palace with the exception of the footprints Lollie and I had left less than an hour ago.

I sighed and scratched my chin. What the hell had the king been thinking, putting in what amounted to a rose-covered ladder up to his stepdaughter's bedroom window? A horny prince would climb anything for a little action.

I should know.

Which brought me to another question: If Spindle hadn't used the window, or the rickety trellis, how had he managed to take Sleeping Beauty from her bed without anyone being the wiser? The palace wasn't exactly empty, and Beauty wasn't quiet. Not by any means.

Had he drugged her? That made the most sense. But even then, he had to remove her from the palace without getting caught. So how had he done it?

Another thought popped into my head. What if Spindle didn't need to drug her? What if she'd left of her own accord? I shook my head. That was crazy. I wasn't just some run-of-the-mill prince easily tossed aside by an annoying princess. Besides, what chick would choose spinsterhood or another thirty broken engagements over yours truly? I knew, deep down, that Sleeping Beauty hadn't run away.

Mostly because leaving would expend too much energy. Spindle had her. I was sure of it.

Ninety percent. Okay, eighty-three percent when factoring in my general lack of evidence. Hell, without the rose on her pillow I was down to the low twenties. Not that any of it mattered. I had to find Sleeping Beauty, kidnapped or not, in less than 158 hours or face a fate worse than death—a ten-millimeter lime-colored penis.

Chapter 31

"Took you long enough," Lollie sneered when I hopped, figuratively, into the backseat of the limo. "What were you doing in there? Or do I even want to know?"

I waggled my eyebrows.

"Pig!" She smacked me in the arm. "She's your fiancée's sister. Your kidnapped fiancée, I might add."

"Mademoiselle," my gaze drifted to the tribal vine tattoo snaking out of her tank top, "are you, perhaps, a wee bit jealous?"

Her snort grated on my ears. "Are you kidding? If anything, I'm trying to protect that young woman from the likes of you. She probably loves her sister too much to tell you to go to hell."

"Not bloody likely."

"What?"

"Nothing." I grabbed Lollie's fist before it met my flesh for a second time. "Forget Pretty. We need to focus on the big picture here."

"Big picture?"

"Sleeping Beauty, of course."

"Of course," she repeated with a sneer.

"Karl," I called to my manservant, who sat behind the privacy screen ready and willing to drive me to wherever I needed to go at a moment's notice. "To the Rose, and step on it."

Nothing happened.

"Karl?"

Again no response. I lowered the privacy screen. As expected, Karl sat behind the steering wheel, his chauffer hat askew. "Hey, Karl," I said.

"Shh!" He pointed to the phone in his hand. "I'm on the phone."

"I can see that." I motioned to the palace and then to Karl's phone. "But this is important."

"Oh, and my call isn't?" Karl glared at me in the rearview mirror. "No, I wasn't talking to you," he said to the person on the other end of the phone. "I was talking to Jean-Michel. Yeah. That he is."

"I'm what? Paying you by the hour? Going to have you beheaded as soon as we get back to the hotel?" I grinned. "If you don't hang up and drive me to the Rose by the time a certain red-haired midget closes shop, I'll pick the option I like best." It was already five minutes to five. The likelihood of us getting to the Rose to confront Red had vanished twenty minutes ago. But it was always fun to torture Karl. He caved so easily.

Or not.

"Hold on," he said to the caller and then spun to face me. "I said I'm on the phone. Now, keep it in your pants until I'm finished. Oh, right. You don't know how."

The privacy screen rose once more, blocking my cry of outrage. "Ungrateful little twerp," I muttered. "After all I've done for—"

"To," Lollie said.

I glared at her. "For. To. What's the difference?"

"I get that you're mad, Kermit." Her hands slid to her ample hips. "But does everything always have to be about you?"

I jerked back as if she'd slapped me. "What? Are you

saying I'm selfish?" Me? Selfish? Was she insane? I spent my life giving to others. Damn it! "I'll show you selfish."

With a day's worth of frustration, both sexual and kidnapped fiancée wise, I yanked Lollie out of her seat and onto my lap. My hand wrapped itself around the back of her neck, and I pulled her to my lips. The kiss was filled with violence and desperation, but sensual too.

Lollie didn't seem to mind the swirl of emotions, if her hand gripping my thigh was any indication. Her tongue swept inside my mouth, teasing mine like a game of ring around the roses that I only hoped would end in someone going down.

She moaned, low and deep in her throat, a sexy noise that drove me to let out my own. "Ribbit," I croaked.

Lollie jerked back. "What was that?"

"What was what? I didn't hear anything." I swallowed and pulled her against me, feeling the heat of her skin on mine. "Now, where were we?"

She frowned, but resumed her position, crushing her mouth to mine. My fingers roamed over her body, running along her tank top and finally slipping inside to trace the creeping vine tattoo. Under the pad of my fingers, her skin felt so soft, no inky outlines, just smooth flesh. I brushed my thumb over a particularly inviting bit of artwork that resembled a distorted number "8" mere centimeters above her nipple. Her pulse leapt under my touch.

Trembling in my arms, Lollie took control, knocking me against the leather seat and straddling my upper thighs. She yanked my shirt over my head; her eyes caught mine and then slowly lowered to the letter "B" above my heart. "True heart," she whispered and then gave a bitter laugh. Rather than question how she knew about the birthmark, I focused on the heat of her touch. My body burned as her fingers stroked my heated flesh. I reached for her, wanting to brand her as she'd done to me, pulling her mouth against mine until flames devoured both of us. Her fingers left my chest and tangled in the top button of my trousers. I gripped the edge of her black lace panties, tugging at the back of the fabric.

"Yes," she moaned, which sent shivers of lust through my body. "Oh yes."

I tugged harder.

She paused to smile down at me. "Will you still respect me in the morning?"

"Doubtful." I winked. "But I will like you a lot better."

"Oh goody," she said before her hand slipped inside my pants. I groaned as her fingers trapped my erection, teasing and tempting me to yield all control. But her efforts were in vain. I would never surrender to her tantalizing torment. Not today. Not any day.

"Oh God," I said, turning to putty in her skilled hands.

My head began to buzz, almost like a mechanical whirl.

"I'm not cleaning up after you." Karl's voice penetrated my brain. Unfortunately, that would be the only penetration for yours truly today. At the sound of Karl's voice, Lollie scrambled off me, her cheeks flushed and red.

"Mind your own business," I said to my manservant, reaching again for Lollie's arm. I missed her scent and the heat of her body against mine. I wanted, near desperate with need, to own her, to mark her like the ink staining her skin.

Lollie glared at me and slapped my hand away. "Behave yourself!" Her eyes met Karl's. "He jumped me."

"Of course, my lady." Karl bowed his head. "Happens all the time. I'm only glad I was here to protect your innocence."

"Really? I jumped you?" I gestured to my swollen lips, battered from her passionate assault. "That's what you're going with?"

She shushed me and smiled at Karl. "Be a good man and take me back to the safety of the Rose."

"If you're finished with your call, that is," I sneered.

Ignoring my comment, he asked, "Shall I raise the privacy screen?"

"Yes!" I shouted.

"No. That won't be necessary." Lollie crossed her arms over her chest, her breasts swelling against the fabric of her tank top, and scooted to the far side of the vehicle. "Thank you for your consideration, though." She added after a pause, "And your silence."

"Whatever you wish, my lady." Karl tipped his chauffer's cap in her direction. *My lady?* Twenty-four hours ago he warned me away from her, and now he was tipping his cap and calling her my lady? What the hell? Karl had obviously been kidnapped by aliens and probed. A lot.

Without sparing a glace in my direction, Karl returned to the driver's seat and started the engine. It roared to life, reflecting my own frustration.

"Beheading it is," I muttered, yanking my shirt back over my head.

"Only if I point out which suitcase holds the travel guillotine." With that insolent remark, Karl put the limo into gear. We slowly drove down the yellow brick driveway to the nearly empty street. No sign of the Ford Unicorn anywhere. I settled back into the soft leather of the backseat as we headed down the canyon, on a mission to save my wayward fiancée, and, if I was lucky, find my way back into Lollie Bliss's panties.

Chapter 32

We arrived at the Rose by fifteen minutes after five. The shop was already closed for the night. I hefted an eyebrow at Lollie. "Odd hours you keep."

"We're a small shop." She crossed her arms defensively across her ample chest. "Most of our business is by appointment only."

"Uh-huh." Something bothered me, but I couldn't place what exactly it was, maybe Lollie's attitude, for one. No longer was she thwarting my every attempt at finding Spindle. In fact, since this morning when someone decided to play a live-action game of Frogger with me, Lollie seemed downright helpful.

"So what now?" I asked.

"I guess we could try Red at home." She smiled, her dark eyes burning into mine. "That is, if you still want to find your fiancée."

What? Stop looking for Sleeping Beauty? Was she crazy? I needed Beauty more now than ever. "What's Red's address?" I said in lieu of a better response. Lollie's lips tightened, but she rattled off a string of numbers not too far away.

Red lived in a neighborhood known as Two Feet Under the Rainbow that catered to a flamboyant, bohemian, and often shorter group of artists, drag queens, and CPAs. An area so liberal that it made West Witchwood look like a Republican National Convention.

"Got that?" I asked Karl when Lollie finished giving us directions to Red's bungalow. Karl rolled his beady eyes in the rearview mirror as he shoved the limo into gear. "Of course, sir. I am neither deaf nor blind," he stopped to add, "unlike another certain someone."

What the hell did that mean? I frowned, but Lollie's sigh drew my attention. "What?" I snapped.

Her cheeks flushed. "Don't snap at me. I didn't lose your fiancée. This is your fault. Not mine."

She had a point, but one I would die before admitting. I should've warned Sleeping Beauty that her life was in danger, and now it was too late. Spindle had her, and who knew what sort of torture he was capable of. I glanced at Lollie. Well, one person knew, and luckily—I popped the door locks—she was now trapped inside my limo.

Her eyes flew to the door locks and then back to me. "Don't even think about it, Kermit. I'm annoyed with you, so you better keep your grubby hands to yourself."

"Don't flatter yourself." I pressed the button to raise the privacy screen. Once Karl's shiny dome disappeared behind the glass, I faced Lollie. "I need you to answer a question for me."

"Yes, those pants make you look fat."

"Funny." I thumped my fingers against the leather seat, implying her comment was anything but. "But tell me this, Lollipop, will Sleeping Beauty be all right?" When she gave me that "are you demented" look, I quickly added, "Yeah, I know, you don't know anyone named Spindle. Got it. But you don't think he'd hurt . . . her, do you?" A hundred blood-soaked images raced through my mind.

The humor in Lollie's eyes vanished. She reached for my hand, our first contact since our interrupted interlude twenty minutes ago. I found myself reassured by her touch, and a little turned on. Okay, a lot turned on, but I was a guy, for frog's sake. A strong breeze in the right place was enough to turn me on.

"Everything will work out. It's meant to be," she said. "You'll see."

I grinned down at her fingers on my hand. "What sort of crap answer is that? I asked you a question and you turn all Zen on me? If I wanted a stupid answer I'd have asked Karl."

The limo took a hard right, smashing me against the door frame. My face hit the window with enough force to rattle my teeth. "Oops. Stupid me," came Karl's voice through the glass.

Amazingly, we arrived at Red's bungalow without further damage to my person. She lived just off the avenue on a quiet street in a row of tiny houses in an array of wild colors. Surprisingly, Red's house wasn't red. It was pink, bright, retina-shearing pink, the kind of pink unknown outside a super-gay rainbow. Jamming on a pair of sunglasses, I nodded to the house. "Not quite what I expected."

From the front seat, Karl whispered, "Never judge a midget by her house color," he paused, "or a princess by her sleeping habits."

"What does that even mean?" My hands clenched at my side. "You're as bad as she is." I pointed at Lollie. "Why doesn't anyone say what they mean anymore?"

Lollie shot us both a glare and carefully picked her way up the yellow brick sidewalk. What was it with Cin City and yellow brick, not to mention the pink flamingo lawn ornaments? Was everyone in the city color-blind? The whole city looked like something Simple Simon threw up after a ride on the Tilt-A-Whirl.

Lollie peered in the front window of Red's bungalow. "No one's home," she said. "Oh, wait."

"What is it?" I scrambled up the pathway to join Lollie

at the window. My eyes scanned the front room, noting an upturned table and some broken dishes on the floor. Either a twister had swept through Red's tiny house or someone had trashed the place, just like Beauty's bedroom. Since we weren't in Kansas anymore, I was betting on the second option. Had the vandal found whatever it was he was after? I scanned the rest of the room for clues.

"Oh my God," I screeched when I noticed a pair of feet encased in ruby red slippers sticking out from under a couch. My heart slammed in my chest. Was that Sleeping Beauty on the floor?

I kicked in the front door and ran to the body. My knees went weak. Up close it was far worse than I could've imagined. My stomach gurgled as bile settled in the back of my throat. What kind of monster would do this?

My answer came in the form of the telltale click of a round being chambered in a 9mm pistol. "Well, well, well, how about a little firepower, scarecrow?"

Chapter 33

"Red," Lollie yelled to the short chick in the doorway with the 9mm pistol in her hand. "There's no need to shoot him. Jean-Michel will pay for a new door. Right, Kermit?"

I nodded, afraid I'd lose my lunch if I dared to open my mouth. Karl ran inside the room, pulling to a stop at the vile sight in front of us. "Is that the Wicked Witch of the East under your couch?" he asked with a frown.

The supposed dead wicked witch leapt up, the minidress wrapped around him like a second skin barely covering his cankles. The small man said, "We're doing a production of *The Wizard of Oz* with a gangster twist for our theater group next month. Red and I were just working on our parts."

"Sick bastards," I said, unable to face another second of their depravity. "You should be locked up."

"What's wrong with you?" Lollie rubbed her chin. "Your precious fiancée isn't dead. No one's hurt. Nothing's going on but a harmless little fun."

Karl answered for me. "My lord is dreadfully fearful of flying monkeys or anything to do with *The Wizard of Oz*, really."

Lollie hooted with laughter and then sobered when she caught sight of my face. "You're not kidding. Are you really afraid of a movie?"

I took a deep breath. "The Wiz damaged a lot of people. You might not realize it, but that movie is nothing more than a Communist-fairy propaganda film." I pumped my fist. "Flying monkeys. Come on, people!"

"Um . . . right," Karl said. "I'll just take my lord outside for a bit of air while you talk to Ms. . . . Red." He grabbed my arm and pulled me from the horrific scene unfolding before my eyes.

"Monkeys, Karl. Flying monkeys," I whispered as he led me out the door.

I recovered from my ordeal soon enough, but decided, for the sake of my mission, to stay in the air-conditioned limo until Lollie returned with some answers. It was the princely thing to do.

Seven minutes later Lollie's perfectly rounded rump plopped down on the seat next to me. She fanned herself with her other hand. "Whew, it's hot out there. We're in for one long summer. And you know what that means. . . ."

"Just spill it." I grabbed her arm. "I'm a big boy. I can take it. What did Red say?"

Lollie grinned. "I'll get you, my pretty, and your little frog too?"

"Funny."

"I thought so."

"Enough of the comedy act." My voice grew cold. "Is Sleeping Beauty still alive?"

Lollie licked her lips. "Yes."

Relief rushed through me. I needed her alive until death did us part and my curse was broken, but after that, she was on her own. Spindle could have her for all I cared. "Whew, that was close."

She didn't appear to share my joy if her frown was any indication. "Don't go celebrating just yet."

My brow furrowed. "Why?"

Wincing, she looked away, out the window, seemingly

lost in thought or plotting my immediate murder, which seemed more her style.

"Why not!?" I demanded.

She took a deep breath. Her chest rose and fell in an appealing manner before she turned back to me. "I'm so sorry," she began. Never words I enjoyed hearing, and yet, coming from Lollie's mouth, I hated them that much more. I wanted her body, not her pity.

"Just tell me," I said, each syllable dripping with frost. "What is it? What happened?" Had Spindle deformed my sleepy bride in some manner? Was she now ugly as well as tired?

Lollie heaved a sigh that nearly cracked the window. "Sleeping Beauty wasn't kidnapped."

"Sure she was." I rubbed my eyes. "We found that rose in her bed. How else would it have gotten there?"

She arched one eyebrow.

I shrugged.

Her other eyebrow followed.

"What!"

This time her eyebrows waggled up and down.

"For God's sake, woman, make sense."

The privacy screen dropped, and my manservant's big bald head appeared through the hole. "What the lady is trying to say is, Princess Beauty and the infamous Spindle were together."

"Yeah," I said. "I know. That's why we need to find them."

"Idiot," Lollie muttered. "In the biblical sense. Your sweet fiancée, who you swear tried to kill you, is sleeping with Spindle."

A stab of pain circled my heart, but I waved it off.

She nodded.

I started to laugh. "Not possible."

"It's true," she said. "Red said—"

"She lied."

"I'm sorry, Kermit." Her fingers brushed my arm. "At least now that you know the truth about your bride, you can move on with your life. Forget about her and find true love."

"Why?"

"Why what?" Her brow furrowed. "Why give yourself a chance to find true love?"

"No, why should I forget Sleeping Beauty? So she doesn't wear white to our wedding." My shoulders rose and fell. "Big deal."

Chapter 34

"Take me home," Lollie ordered, her arms crossed over her chest, her lips pulled into a pout. "Now."

"What's your problem? So I marry Sleeping Beauty. It doesn't mean we," I gestured between us, "can't be... friends."

"That's exactly what it means! I won't be your mistress."

A pain shot through my heart. "Come on, Lollie. Be reasonable."

She struck me instead. Her fist slammed into my arm with enough force to leave an imprint on the sleeve of my shirt. I rubbed my aching muscle.

"Reasonable?" she whispered through clenched teeth. "I'm being unreasonable? You're still planning on marrying a woman who is fucking another guy!"

She had a point. But why was she so pissed? I was the supposed cuckold. If anyone was going to be angry, it should've been me. Yet I couldn't muster even the slightest bit of rage, mostly because Lollie was vibrating with enough for the two of us.

When I didn't respond, she said, "I'll show you reasonable, you... you... prince."

"I look forward to it, mademoiselle," I said with a smirk. "It will be a side of you I haven't seen before."

A low growl reverberated from her vicinity.

"Sir," Karl said from the front seat. "Perhaps you should ride up front with me until we arrive at Ms. Bliss's shop."

By the speed of the cactus flying by my window, I was fairly sure we'd arrive at the Rose in a matter of seconds. Karl was in some hurry. I wondered why.

"I'm good," I said to Karl. "Besides, what's Lollie going to do? Cheat on me like Beauty?" I snorted. "Perhaps she'll try to kill me like my dear bride."

In hindsight, tempting fate wasn't the smartest move on my part. No sooner had the words left my mouth than the window next to my head shattered. I dove across the leather seat, throwing Lollie to the floor. Karl swore as he twisted the wheel.

Three more shots followed. The back window exploded, showering us in glass. Lollie tried to push me off her, but I held fast. As pissed as she was at me right now, she'd be much more annoyed with a bullet in her brain.

"Get off me!" she demanded, trying to scramble from underneath me to grab her large black bag. Since I didn't consider a handful of tampons and a tube of lipstick worth dying for, I tossed her to the floor. Flying bits of debris dug into my back and legs. The pain seemed distant, though, as my body rocketed with adrenaline. My breath came in short gasps as my blood pounded through my veins.

Another shot whizzed by my head, embedding itself in the minibar. A whiskey bottle shattered, spilling amber liquor down my back. Lollie stopped fighting me then, and instead yanked me closer to her. "Stay down," she ordered like a drill instructor.

Like I had other plans.

"Hang on, sir!" Karl yanked the limo into a spin, tires screeching against the pavement. The vehicle skittered and then finally righted itself. Again, Karl slammed his foot on the gas, and we shot forward, playing chicken with the black Ford Unicorn with a prince-shaped dent in its grille.

The driver appeared to be one big black blur as we charged each other. "Karl," I warned as the limo sped up. My hands gripped the driver's leather headrest.

"Not a good time for complaints, sir."

He had a point, so I shut up and pinned Lollie to the floor, protecting her with my own body, which wasn't nearly as altruistic as it sounded, at least not to my semi-stiff penis.

The Unicorn hurtled closer.

Lollie screamed and closed her eyes, her nails digging into my back. Perverse pain and pleasure curled in my stomach. Even though we were about to die a horrific death, her body against mine felt right. Like we belonged together. Forever. Or at least until I tired of her. I gave it a week. Maybe two if I brought along a gag.

Sadly, two weeks would be a record given the length of my prior relationships. Not that I wanted happily ever after. A night of no-strings-attached debauchery was just what the veterinarian ordered, or so I assured myself, lying in bed, alone, in the dead of night.

"Ahhhh!" Karl yelled, bracing his arms in front of his face as the two vehicles came within five feet of each other. The Unicorn swerved out of our path, went into a tailspin, and crashed into a roadside glass slipper stand. Slippers flew into the air, shattering against the Unicorn with a crash.

"Oh my God. We're alive," Karl said, pulling his hands away from his eyes. I helped Lollie from the floor, assessing her for injuries. Besides a few cuts on her forehead and cheek, she appeared unscathed.

The same couldn't be said for the limo, though. Shards of glass littered every surface. Not a single window had survived the attack. The minibar looked like a victim of a giant on a bender, the door hanging on one hinge as various alcohols pooled into deadly concoctions served only at frat parties.

"Nice driving." I patted Karl on the shoulder. "Aren't you glad I taught you how to play chicken?"

"Not especially."

My lips curved into a wide grin. "I said I was sorry. Besides, you were only in the body cast for a couple of weeks."

"Six months, sir." His hands tightened on the wheel, knuckles growing white. "And it still hurts when I pee."

Chapter 35

The limo limped down Fairily Way, a couple of blocks from Lollie's shop. With the exception of the hot desert wind rushing through the missing windows, silence filled the vehicle. My mind fully occupied, sickened by the thought of what could have happened, I glanced at Lollie. She sat rigid in her seat, anger vibrating off her in waves.

We hadn't spoken since the assassination attempt. What could I say? "I'm sorry that I almost got you killed?" Guilt weighed on me, a new and totally unwanted feeling. I didn't like it. Not one bit. How I longed for those shallow, not-a-care-in-the-world frog prince days. But I did care, and more importantly, I wouldn't risk her life again. The farther I stayed away from Lollie Bliss, the better for all of us.

Beauty included.

Lollie interrupted my errant thought. "You're still planning on marrying Sleeping Beauty, even after this." She motioned around the broken limo. "Why, Kermit? Do you love her that much?"

"No." I closed my eyes.

"Then why?"

I wanted to tell Lollie, a practical stranger with a sadistic streak, the truth—about Beauty, about the curse, about the loneliness of watching the world from the confines of a pond. But I couldn't. Not when she looked at me with those big dark eyes. I blew out a breath. "Arranged marriage," I lied.

Karl grunted.

"You're a very bad liar." Lollie gave up. The anger left her face, but sadness remained.

I stared into her eyes. "Thank you for not pushing."

"You're welcome." She paused, as if weighing her words. "We all have our secrets to keep," she said as she opened the door to the limo. It creaked once and then fell to the ground. Lollie winced. "Oops. Sorry."

Karl gave her a sweet smile. "It will be all right, my lady."

"I doubt it, Karl." I motioned to the busted door in the street. "I think the car's totaled. Even All the King's Horses Body Shop won't be able to put it back together again."

Lollie gave Karl a half smile. "Thanks for the ride." Then she turned to face me, our eyes locked, mine icy blue, hers black in color. I wanted to know all Lollie's secrets, the good, the bad, and even the ugly stepsister variety. I wanted to know everything about her. But there was a cost for wanting Lollie, a price I wasn't willing to pay, namely Beauty's life.

"Well, I guess I'll see you tomorrow," Lollie said, standing completely still, as if waiting for a scrap of frog prince wisdom. After a few seconds, she turned to the Rose and started to unlock the front door.

"Lollie, wait," I said, scrambling from the missing doorway. Metal crunched under my feet.

"Yes, Kermit?" She spun to face me, her hands out. Her eyes sparkled in the fading sunlight like rich chocolate ice cream with sprinkles. I was a sucker for sprinkles.

I shook my head to clear my desire. "Um . . ."

"Yes?"

"We can't see each other anymore." I licked my lips. "I'm sorry."

The corner of her upper lip crooked upward. "You're sorry, Kermit?"

"I am." I inhaled sharply. "Listen, you're a wonderful woman, but right now I need to focus on saving Beauty—"

"Try saving your breath instead." Her eyes blazed as she turned away and vanished through the front door of the Rose. A lump formed in the back of my throat. I wanted nothing more than to scream, "Stop. Wait." But I didn't. Instead, I watched as Lollie walked out of my life, forever.

With a heavy heart, I turned to Karl, whose face was twisted with anger. What was his problem? For once I'd taken his advice and dumped Lollie. Now he went all pouty on me?

"That was stupid," he said.

"Forget Lollie." I doubted I'd be able to. Not for a long time. I released a harsh breath. "Let's go back to the palace. See if we can find a clue as to where Beauty is and end this nonsense once and for all."

Karl ducked his head. "I can't play junior detective with you this evening."

"Why?"

"I have other plans."

"Plans, you say?" I tilted my head in question. What was it with Karl lately? He was never around when I needed him. Not that I "needed" him, or anyone. I was the Frog Prince, for frog sakes. "What sort of plans?" I asked, trying to keep the whine from my tone.

His face heated, growing almost as red as the sunburned ring on the top of his head. "I don't see how that's any your of business."

"Fine," I said. If Karl had naked plans with Candi, so be it. I was a big boy. I could handle one night alone, provided room service served forty-year-old scotch. And a lot of it. "Take me back to the hotel."

Karl winced.

"What? You want me to walk to the hotel?"

"I knew you'd understand," he said, jamming the limo into gear and taking off up the street. Smoke billowed from the limo's engine, leaving a trail of exhaust in its wake.

"Frog!" I kicked the lamppost on the street corner. In any other part of the city, I'd simply hail a cab, but finding a taxi down here was as unlikely as baa baa black sheep joining the Klan. "Now what?"

I turned around, catching a glimpse of myself in the window of the Rose. I looked tired and greener than I liked. Dried blood matted my black locks. The bruises left by RJ's beating had faded to an unhealthy yellowish brown. All in all, I was looking a little worse for wear, but nothing a hot shower, an ice-cold beer, and a steak wouldn't cure. Well, those and finding my missing fiancée before the greenish color became permanent.

With a sigh I shoved a pair of sunglasses over my eyes and prepared for a long walk back to the hotel. Darkness hovered on the horizon. The desert at night was no place for a frog prince.

"Hey," a voice called from behind me. "Leaving so soon?"

I turned toward the sound, surprised by the vision in front of me. Lollie Bliss stood behind me, wearing a black sports bra and a pair of jean shorts. While I certainly didn't mind the view, what she had in her hand drew my attention much more—an icy-cold bottle of beer dripping with sweat.

For a second, I lost my mind and considered begging Lollie to run away with me. Luckily I came to my senses in time and managed saying nothing more than "I think I love you."

"How sweet." She held the beer out to me. "But I prefer my princes a little less...Oh, what's the word...engaged."

I took the beer from her fingers and gulped down half the bottle. The alcohol slid down my throat, easing away the aches and pains of today's events. I tilted the bottle in her direction. "Oh well, it probably wouldn't have worked out between us anyway. Great, mind-blowing sex aside."

"How will I ever survive?" She waited a beat. "Well, good night, then."

"Funny," I said with a stiff laugh.

"I thought so." Her smile widened. "It's going to be dark soon."

"Yep."

Her hand fisted on her hip, but her eyes filled with vulnerability. "So do you want to spend the night or not?"

All noble ideas and princely concern about my future bride and Lollie's safety vanished under the sudden rush of blood to my bollocks. Besides, what harm could there be in our spending one night together, other than blown minds and chafed knees?

"Well, are you coming in?" She motioned to the door.

"What do you think?" I shot Lollie a half smile, the one I reserved for special occasions, the one that melted the panties off even the most frigid princess.

"Let's get something straight." Lollie pulled open the front door. "I asked you to stay the night out of pity. It's a very long walk back to your hotel, and I hate to see a prince with blisters."

"Your concern for my feet is sweet."

"Keep your hands to yourself." She glared down at my appendages. All of my appendages. "We are not going to sleep together. Got it?"

"Of course not." I added a dimple to the smile. "Who wants multiple orgasms anyhow?"

Ignoring my sexual prowess, she motioned to the back of the shop where a small spiral staircase stood. "There's an efficiency apartment upstairs."

"After you, my lady," I said, bowing low.

The glare she shot me was enough to ignite the Snow Queen on fire. I frowned, unsure what I'd said wrong this time. Lollie's moods swung like a group of fairy-dust addicts around a mulberry bush. It was hard to keep up. "What?" I asked.

"If you don't know..." She pushed past me, nearly knocking me over in the process, and stomped up the staircase. I followed behind, watching her toned butt under her tight shorts. Shorts designed to display the inky swirls and tribal designs that rose up her legs. Craziness and possible killer boyfriend aside, Lollie Bliss was the kind of woman a frog prince dreamed of.

Nightmares counted as a form of dreaming, right?

"Stop looking at my ass," she ordered when she reached the top of the stairs.

"Me?" My lips curved in affected shock. "I would do no such thing. I'm a prince, mademoiselle, not some commoner."

"Right." She pushed open a door at the top of the stairs. The scent of ink and woman drifted from the apartment. "Well, Kermit, make yourself at home."

Walking into the apartment was like waking up in heaven, literally. White everywhere. The couch. The cabinets. The walls, ceiling, and floors. I half expected to meet Saint Peter at the pearly refrigerator.

For a woman as colorful as Lollie, her apartment lacked any spark, as if a different woman lived there. Yet the place seemed to suit her. She was the splash of color the atmosphere needed. Just being here, with Lollie, in a stark white room, calmed me more than a case full of mead. My missing fiancée, my father's disownment, a killer, all these things faded away.

My finger ran over a white bookcase filled with books on sketching the human form, calligraphy, and even the ancient art of Japanese tattooing known as Hitoppori. No Mother Goose or Grimm's sordid tales here. This was the bookcase of a woman who lived and breathed visual art. "Nice place," I said, gesturing to the mostly empty room.

"I call it home. Would you like another beer?" Walking a few feet into a small but tidy kitchen, she grabbed two bottles of beer and held one out to me.

"Thanks," I said, taking the bottle from her hand. Our fingers touched, and my heart skipped a beat. I cleared my throat, trying not to focus on the fact that I was alone in an apartment with the woman featured in many of my fantasies over the last few days. "So why tattoos? It's kind of an odd profession for a young lady such as yourself." I gave her a wink.

Taking a long drink from her beer bottle, Lollie plopped down on her white couch and touched a button on a remote. Soft violin music filled the room. For a few seconds I thought she hadn't heard me, but then she tipped her bottle in my direction. "Do you really want to know?"

Her fingers stroked the neck of the bottle, and the blood in my head, as well as my good intentions, went south. Since I'd spent most of my teenaged years fighting the same problem, I managed to focus on her odd question. "I asked, didn't I?" I moved from the bookcase to the couch and sat on the edge, far enough away from temptation and her smooth, ink-lined legs.

She took another sip of beer, her eyes never leaving my face. Whatever she saw in my expression relaxed her. "I love to feel the power of the needle in my hands, the way color soaks into the flesh, the beauty of skin and ink. When I finish a tattoo it is a living, breathing opus, a forever reminder of a moment in time, a story for the world to see." Her eyes lit with intense excitement. I wanted to put the same look on her face, but for a far different reason.

"You're very good at what you do." I gestured to the beautiful, colorful, and intricate designs on her body. My fingers itched to caress the number "8" on her breast one more time.

"Thank you," she said with a little laugh. "Yet tattooing bikers, drunken co-eds, and the occasional prince isn't really the Fairymerican dream come true."

I let the prince comment pass. We had the rest of the evening to discuss the pocketful of posies tramp-stamped on my back. "So when did you realize you wanted to be a tattoo artist?" I pictured a little girl in leather and pigtails inking her friends with a ballpoint pen.

"When I was a kid, I spent most of my time alone." She smiled sadly. "While my siblings took piano lessons and played outside with the other kids, I stayed locked inside, daydreaming."

A faraway look entered her eyes. The innocent dreams of youth quickly faded from her gaze. "My stepdaddy wanted me to be a proper lady so I could land a rich husband, but I wanted more." She gave a bitter laugh. "I tried to please him, to make him love me, even a little ...'"

"I'm so sorry." Taking her hand in mine, I gave it a reassuring squeeze. I understood, perhaps more than anyone, what it felt like to crave a father's approval. "He's a fool. You are beautiful and talented."

"Save the fancy compliments for your wife." She snickered, the humor not quite reaching her eyes. "They won't get you laid tonight."

I winced, hating her words and the hurt that settled deep within my chest. "That wasn't—"

She waved me off. "When I turned sixteen, I realized that I could never live up to my stepdaddy's ideals," she said, her eyes glistening with unshed tears. "I would never be a beauty like my sister." Like the bottle clutched so tightly in her hand, she seemed ready to break. "So I vowed to be true to me, and do my own thing."

"You left home?"

"There's nothing left for me there." She drew in a long breath. "I took odd jobs to support myself."

I pictured Lollie flipping burgers at the Pease Porridge Hot Diner. The image brought a smile to my lips, until she spoke her next words.

"One day, broke, desperate, living in a tent shaped like a shoe and having no idea what to do," her eyes locked on mine, "I met someone who taught me how to tattoo."

I closed my eyes.

"That's the day," she paused, as if weighing the effect of her words, "Spindle saved my life."

Chapter 36

Frog! Blood pounded in my ears, drowning out everything but Lollie's betrayal. I grabbed her arm and yanked her to her feet. "You lied to me." I gave her a small shake, my mind filled with anger at her duplicity.

Lollie pulled back. "Yes, but not about what you think."

"Then what?" A sudden, terrifying thought occurred to me. "Please don't tell me that you're really a man." Been there, thankfully I'd realized the lump in the "princess's" bathing suit was probably not a tail before I'd done that.

Lollie raised her eyebrow.

I waved her question off. "I'm not the one on trial here. You've lied to me for the past four days. For what?" My fingers dug into her arm, leaving red welts against the jade leaves tattooed into her skin.

Slowly she sank back down on the couch, tucking her feet under her like a child seeking comfort. My rage cooled a bit. Whatever lies she'd told, Lollie was not at fault.

Spindle deserved my rage.

And yet, he'd also saved Lollie's life. Knowing this, I couldn't muster up a really good hate for the guy anymore. However, he had probably abducted and was fucking my future wife and perhaps ruining my only chance to save myself from my curse. A chicken-or-the-egg argument if

I'd ever heard one. Not that I'd ever heard one. Everyone with half a brain knew eggs came from rabbits.

I heaved a long, drawn-out sigh. "I won't kill Spindle."

Lollie burst out laughing, spitting beer foam halfway across the room. When she finally stopped cackling like a wicked witch, she wiped her mouth with the back of her hand. "What makes you think, even for a second, you could take Spindle, a professional killer?"

I tried not to take offense at her tone. After all, she'd never seen me lose my self-control. Normally I was a lover, a really good one, and not a fighter, but I'd been in my fair share of scrapes. Hell, thanks to Elly, I'd worn a dress to a seventh-grade dance and lived to tell about it. That didn't happen unless you could hold your own. "It isn't me you should be so worried about, Lollipop."

"Last warning." She crossed and uncrossed her long, luscious legs. "Stop calling me Lollipop or else I'll be the one to kick your ass."

"Fine," I said. "No more Lollipop. But it's time to come clean. I need the truth, Lollie. Tell me where I can find Spindle." I slid down on the couch next to Lollie, our bodies close but not touching.

She bit her bottom lip. "I'm sorry. I wasn't lying. I don't know where Spindle is. It's been years since we last... spoke." Her hand reached for mine. "You have to believe me."

I grunted.

Her grip grew insistent. "Please, Kermit. I haven't seen him for years, not since the night I came home and found a red rose on my pillow." She paused, her eyes locking on mine. "And a bloodstain on the floor that spelled my name."

Later that night, I stretched out on Lollie's couch, my belly full of hops and a pizza from a local pizzeria with the motto "We probably won't deliver in thirty minutes or less." In her bedroom, a few feet away, Lollie prepared for bed. A drawer opened and closed. I wondered what she wore to sleep. Was it something slinky and silky? Or was she the sweatpants and T-shirt type? Or better yet, did she sleep in the nude? I imagined her ink-covered body naked against white cotton sheets and groaned.

My mind drifted back to our earlier conversation, and the look of genuine fear in Lollie's eyes. She had lied to me about Spindle, but for a far different reason than I'd first assumed. Fear was a powerful motivator.

I vowed, in that moment, that I wouldn't let anyone hurt her, including a cursed frog prince with a target on his back. Sadly, I'd made much the same promise to another, albeit sleepier, woman a few days earlier. And we all know how well that turned out.

The scent of fresh coffee woke me a few hours later. I groaned, my head aching from a long, sleepless night of couch-surfing. Lollie puttered around in the kitchen singing a tuneless melody. She poked her head around the corner, looking beautiful but tired, deep bags under her mud-colored eyes. "Coffee?"

"Yeah," I growled, staggering from the couch. Sunlight spilled from the windows, exaggerating the whiteness of the room until I thought for sure I'd go blind. "Curtains," I muttered.

"What?"

"I'm buying you curtains. Bright red ones."

She yawned and then took a sip of coffee from the cup in her hand. "Why?"

"The appropriate response is, 'Thank you, Jean-Michel.' "

She rolled her eyes. "Thank you, Jean-Michel."

"Better." I grinned. "Mind if I grab a shower?"

"I'd prefer it," she said, motioning to her bedroom and the adjoining bathroom. "Towels are in the top cupboard. New razor's in the bottom shelf of the medicine cabinet."

"Thanks." I grabbed the cup of coffee from her hand and took a drink. "I like mine black," I said, but carried her milky mixture of coffee, sugar, and cream into the bathroom with me.

"Hey—"

I closed the door on her protest. Whistling "The Alphabet Song"—I used to sing "The Song That Never Ends" but the water always grew cold before the last verse—I stripped off my boxer shorts and adjusted the faucet. *Oops, too hot.* I twisted the knob the other way. *Damn, too cold.* One more turn, and everything was just right. I stepped into the shower and groaned as the water pounded away my sleepless night.

A bottle of pink-colored shampoo sat on the edge of the tub. I picked it up, inhaling the scent of strawberries. Kind of girly, but my natural masculine scent would overpower it soon enough. Dumping a handful into my palm, I scrubbed my body until it shone a healthy ruddy color. The shallow cuts on my backside from yesterday's attack stung, but by the time I toweled off, I felt better than I had in days.

Things were looking up.

Clean and dry, a towel wrapped around my waist, I headed into Lollie's bedroom. Perhaps Spindle had left some clothes when he disappeared all those years ago, I told myself. I wasn't snooping. Not really.

I opened the first dresser drawer. Black lace met my eyes. I quickly slammed the drawer shut and closed my eyes, picturing Lollie with a tattoo snaking down into said panties.

The next drawer held rows of tank tops and an empty contact lens case. I pictured Lollie wearing geeky thick, black glasses and smiled. The next drawer after that offered T-shirts and sweaters in a variety of shades of black and white. All in all, the dresser held nothing overly suspicious, but noting very personal either. I moved on to the closet.

"Kermit?" Lollie called.

"Be right out," I said, wrenching the closet open. An avalanche of shoes and the occasional glass slipper tumbled forth, nearly clobbering me in the head. I quickly slammed the doors shut.

"You okay in there?" Her voice floated through the door. "Your cell phone's ringing."

"Okay, I'll be out in a second," I said. My eyes scanned the rest of the room, falling on a small nightstand next to her bed.

I made my way across the room, sinking down on her soft bed. A picture sat on the nightstand next to a bottle of prescription sleeping pills and a heart-shaped box. I picked up the black-and-white photograph stuffed into an expensive silver frame. The image was of a tall, dark-haired man. He looked vaguely familiar, his avocado-colored eyes burning into mine.

Was this Spindle, the guy who'd taken my bride and possibly my future? The guy looked rugged, as if he spent most of his time outdoors without a care rather than attending to important princely duties, like yours truly.

My fingers curled around the picture frame as anger burned inside me. I wasn't sure what bothered me most, the fact that Lollie kept a picture of a guy who'd threatened her or that she kept it on the table next to her bed. "I'm coming, Spindle." I tapped the tip of my finger against the glass. "That's a promise I will keep."

Following my shower and a hot bowl of curds and whey minus the arachnid companionship, I checked the messages on my p-Phone. Six missed calls. All from the same number. Taking a deep breath, I punched in the digits with dread. My hands started to sweat as the phone began to ring.

"Locks," Goldie answered, sounding distracted and a little frazzled, not to mention smoking hot in a dirty librarian way. "I said black, two sugars," she said to someone on the other end of the line before returning her attention to my call.

"Hey, Goldie," I began.

"Jean-Michel," she interrupted. "Whatever it is you're involved in, get out now before you wind up dead."

"What do you mean?"

Her sigh reverberated through the line. "Your Beauty, well, she's not quite the upstanding citizen one would expect. In fact, she's one bad princess. Hold on a second," she said. Paper rustled in the background. I hummed a tuneless song in my head. "Did you check the beanstalk for prints?" Goldie asked someone in the background. "Fine. Bag it, and then get the meat wagon in here to pick up the body." Goldie soon returned to the matter at hand. "Sorry about that, Jean-Michel. I'm in the middle of a case. Wife called nine-one-one when she discovered her husband a lot less green and jolly, and full of bullet holes."

"A tragedy. Really." I rolled my eyes. "But back to Beauty. I asked you to check into her finances, and now she's at the top of *Fairymerica's Most Wanted*? What the frog happened?"

Goldie laughed. "Twenty-eight missing fiancés. That's what happened. The Cin City PD suspects Beauty is a serial killer known as the Black Window. But every time they gather enough evidence to arrest her, the evidence disappears."

"Black Window?" I asked in disbelief.

Goldie sighed. "The Cin City chief of police is dyslexic."

Chapter 37

"Where to, sir?" Karl asked as I folded myself into the front seat of our replacement vehicle, a banana yellow four-door Ford Princess. Zero to twenty-five in the amount of time it took a mouse to run up a clock (thirty-eight seconds on those stubby legs).

My head scraped the ceiling of the front passenger seat, leaving a trail of black hair and blood along the interior. "Ow! Damn it, Karl. What the hell kind of medieval torture is this? I'm a prince. I can't be seen riding an ugly Princess."

Karl's eyebrow slowly rose until it reached his bald head.

"You know what I meant." I pulled the passenger-side door closed, nearly gelding myself in the process. With the rest of the way my day was headed, a good old-fashioned neutering was looking good.

"I'm sorry, sir." Karl ducked his head. "This was all the rental company had left." He motioned around the cramped vehicle. "Apparently there's a wicked drag queen convention in town and all the limousines are booked."

I caught a flash of blue-black hair and leather out of the corner of my eye and winced, feeling a tad bit guilty for giving Lollie the slip a few minutes ago. But I wasn't up to another argument.

The last hour of my life had consisted of a steady barrage of sharp-tongued female. First Goldie and her insane warning about my apparently crazy, ax-wielding, and sleepy bride, and then Lollie, who'd insisted, quite forcefully, on joining me on my quest for my aforementioned lazy, murderous soon-to-be wife.

Normally I would've jumped at the chance to get Lollie into the backseat of any vehicle. But yesterday's near-death experience, not to mention Goldie's dire admonition, had me rethinking letting her tag along. I didn't want to see Lollie hurt. The very thought had me breaking into a cold sweat in the 104-degree heat. So I'd done what any frog prince in my situation would've done. I snuck out of the apartment like a rabid one-night stand.

"I can call around," Karl was saying, "see if any other limousines are available." He pulled out his BlackFerry and began to dial. Lollie's face appeared in the window of the Rose. She glared at me and shoved the shop's door wide.

"Forget the car," I yelled to Karl. "Just drive." Without waiting for his reply, I slammed my foot on the gas pedal, sending the car screeching into traffic. Karl swerved to miss an oncoming pumpkin carriage, overcorrected, sending us barreling toward a light pole, and then straightened the wheel.

In the rearview mirror, I watched as Lollie stood in the middle of the street, cursing my name. I winced as a particularly loud string of swear words drifted through the ugly Princess.

Damn, Lollie looked beautiful when she was pissed enough to kill someone. Her hair shone like coal in the harsh glare of the sunlight. And her eyes flashed black with violence. A part of me, namely my libido, wanted to stop the car and forget I'd ever heard the name Sleeping Beauty, let alone had to marry the serial-killing chit. Oh, the things one did for clean, clear, and ungreen skin. My p-Phone rang. I quickly looked at the caller ID and winced. "Hello?" I answered, innocently.

"Damn you, Kermit!" Lollie's screech cut through the line, nearly puncturing my eardrum. "You're going to get yourself killed. Stay away from—"

"I think it's for you," I said and shoved the phone at Karl. He shook his head. "Fine," I heaved, sticking the phone back to my ear, wincing as Lollie's screeching continued. After a particularly brutal outburst about the size of my brain, I interrupted, "Going in a tunnel. Gonna lose you," I said and then promptly hung up.

Karl sighed. "Shall I send Ms. Bliss the standard flowers and a note of apology? Or is this more of a STD test and fifty bucks scenario?"

Twenty minutes later, we arrived at Sleeping Beauty's palace sans ink-covered distraction. Without Lollie around, my mind stayed focused on my mission, which was to find Sleeping Beauty, at any cost. Proving she wasn't some sort of deranged serial murderer would be nice too, but beggars couldn't whine when I "accidentally" ran over their feet with my Jag. On the bright side, one-legged pants were all the fashion rave this year.

With a sigh, I knocked on the front door of the palace, Karl at my side. He shifted from foot to foot. "Stop it," I ordered. "You look like a little kid who has to pee."

He stilled, but only for a second. "Sir, is this really a good idea? What if," he lowered his voice, "Beauty is waiting nearby for a chance to . . . ?" He made a slashing gesture under his chin. My manservant had been on edge since I first told him about Goldie's warning. My own feelings were more ambivalent in nature. Even if what Goldie said was true, it hardly mattered in the scheme of things. Give me frog legs or give me death, either way the next day sucked.

"What? Give me a shave?"

"No, sir." He gulped. "Kill you. What if she's waiting inside to kill you?"

"Don't worry so much." I rubbed my chin. "I have a plan."

"You do?"

"Of course." I nodded. "If Beauty tries anything, I'll just use you as a shield."

Karl sucked in a sharp breath.

I grinned. "I'm kidding. You're too short to make a good shield."

"How considerate," he said.

The door opened before I could respond. Marvin stood in the entrance, his beefy body stuffed into a ghastly jade suit with a wide lapel. I winced and took a step back. "My God, man. What the hell are you wearing?"

Marvin glared down at his outfit. "It's for the wedding. Princess Beauty ordered these suits for all the staff." He lowered his voice. "Before she . . . left . . ."

That bitch. Attempting to add me to her twenty-eight kills wasn't enough for Her Majesty, she had to torture me with the emerald abomination in front of me to boot. What was wrong with her? I closed my eyes, mostly to avoid the glare of green. "No one's suspicious of her disappearance, then?"

"I did as you said, sir." Marvin's eyes darted around. "I told the king that Sleeping Beauty needed her beauty rest for the big day, so he and the rest of the family should stay away."

"Good man." I patted his shoulder. "Now, please show me to Sleeping Beauty's bedroom."

"Of course, sir. Right away." He motioned up the hardwood staircase decorated in sea green and orange ribbons for the wedding. I scowled at the puke-inducing color scheme and quickly dashed up the steps, Karl on my heels.

At the top of the stairs, I pulled to a stop. Handsome,

Beauty's lovesick stepbrother, stood in front of the room a few doors down from Beauty's bedroom, the eerie room with the sewing machine, if memory served.

But it wasn't the sight of Handsome that stopped me. Rather, it was the long straight pin in his hand. He looked up as I approached. "Why couldn't you just leave her alone?" he whispered. "She was happy. Happy."

I tilted my head. It was hard to find fault with his statement. After all, have you ever met an unhappy serial killer? However, his creepy tone sent Mother Goosebumps up and down my arms. Was there something going on between stepbrother and sister? Something less one-sided and more demented than I'd first presumed? Was he the reason the Cin City PD's evidence of Beauty's serial killing kept vanishing into thin air?

I shook my head. For a chick who rarely left her bed, Sleeping Beauty sure had a lot of suitors. Or maybe it had something to do with the fact that she never left her bed.

"I hate you. Hate you. Hate you," Handsome muttered. "You'll pay for what you've done. You'll all pay."

Chapter 38

Handsome charged past me, nearly knocking me over in his haste. "Nice talking to you too," I called after him. "I'll be sure to give Beauty your regards." Once I found her.

"Sir," Karl said, staring after Handsome's not-so-handsome backside. "I fear Princess Beauty's stepbrother is dangerous."

"Really? You think?" I winced when Karl's face fell. "Sorry," I said. "I'm a little frustrated at the moment."

Karl's face wrinkled with disgust. "Not sexually, you moron," I said. For a guy in his thirties, Karl was a terrible prude. Just mention the word "sex" and his face flamed red. "By the way, how was your date?" I grinned at my manservant. "Did you get any?"

"I . . . ah . . . ," he choked out.

I watched him squirm, enjoying every second. Served him right for leaving me at Lollie's yesterday, not that I minded all that much, spine-crushing couch and little boy blue balls aside.

Karl ducked his flaming face. "Ah . . . um . . ."

Before Karl stroked out, I took pity on him. "My God, Karl. Enough with the smut chitchat. I'm going to be a married man soon. I don't need to hear that kind of talk," I ordered, crossing my arms over my chest. "Now, we have a job to do. Sleeping Beauty's not going to find herself, you know."

"Yes, sir." He rolled his eyes. "I'll try to control myself in the future."

"See that you do." I nodded to the two guards standing at Sleeping Beauty's bedroom door and entered the room. Stale air swirled to life, tickling the back of my throat. I sneezed.

"Bless you," Karl said, closing the door behind us. He glanced around, his eyes filled with guilt. "Are you sure we should be in here? Won't Princess Beauty be upset at the intrusion?"

"Probably." I snickered. "But she's already attempted to kill me. What else can she do? Send me to bed without supper?"

"Refuse to wed you," Karl muttered.

He had a point. But, I assured myself, once I found my wayward bride, convincing her to marry me would be as easy as selling a bag of magic beans to a ten-year-old. I was the Frog Prince. What woman in her right mind wouldn't want me for a husband. . . .

Right, Sleeping Beauty. Damn.

I guess I'd cross that troll-infested bridge when I came to it. My fingers brushed the wallpaper, looking for any sign of a secret passageway or other clue as to how my wayward bride and Spindle had made their escape. "I'll search here." I motioned across the room. "You check over there."

"As you wish, sir." He hesitated. "But can't we just—"

"As far as wishes go, Karl," I said, cutting him off, "standing in the room of my missing fiancée and searching for clues to where she'd disappeared to in order to stop her from murdering me in my sleep doesn't make my top-ten list."

Sadly, the top three wishes on my list today revolved around getting Lollie naked, keeping her that way, and a medium-rare steak. Not a mutually exclusive list, mind you. I wasn't some kind of perv.

"Sir!" Karl shouted, drawing me from my musing. "I found it. I found a passageway." He leapt up and down like a manservant on a pogo stick.

"Nice work." I crossed the room to where he excitedly pointed. "Where is it?" I asked, motioning to what appeared not to be a passageway, but a solid wall.

"There, sir." He again indicated the rock-solid wall. "Look at the wallpaper."

I strained to get a closer look. Sure enough, the strip on the wallpaper didn't line up. A fraction of a centimeter separated the two. "How do we get it open?" I pressed my fingers along the crack.

"You only asked me to find it, sir."

I closed my eyes and prayed for patience, or, barring that, a really big hammer. When neither appeared in front of me, I asked for the next best thing. "Elly!" I shouted.

Poof!

My alcoholic fairy godmother materialized. Her dress hung off her shoulder, exposing her bedazzled bra. "What?" she yelled, burped once, which smelled faintly like ten-thousand-dollar scotch, and then crashed to the floor.

"Damn it, Elly!"

Karl winced. "Perhaps a cup of coffee."

Elly let out a loud string of snores.

"Perhaps not," I said, stepping over the puddle of godmother on the floor. "There has to be a secret lever that opens the passage."

"Or we could try—"

"Hush, Karl. I'm thinking." My eyes scanned the room, noting the high ceilings and fancy furniture, not to mention a bed big enough for an ogre orgy. If I was a demented, albeit sleepy princess, where would I install a lever?

Again, my eyes fell upon the bed. I frowned, trying to

remember some urban legend about a princess, a mattress, and split pea soup. Or was that a porno?

Taking my time, I studied Sleeping Beauty's pretty pretty princess bed. Everything seemed normal. The bed wasn't too hard, nor too soft, but fit my butt just right. So I sat down, letting the fluffy pink comforter swallow me. After a minute I kicked my legs up, lay back against the feathery pillows, and closed my eyes.

Where the hell was the lever?

"Sir, this is no time for a nap." Karl leaned over me, his breath hot on my face. "Why don't you forget the passage-way and we can—"

"Quiet." I cracked one eye open. "How many times do I have to say it? I can't think with your yammering on and on about absolutely nothing. I have a bride to save."

"Sorry." He let out a drawn-out sigh. "I couldn't hear the rusted squeak of your brain from across the room."

"Funny." I opened my other eye. "If you were Princess Beauty—"

"I'd buy some No-Doz and head for less-green princes."

Leaping off the bed, I stubbed my toe on the bed frame. "Ow! Damn it." I rubbed at my throbbing appendage. "Are you making fun of me in this most dire of times?"

He hung his head, nearly blinding me with the sheen from his bald head. "My apologies, sir. I am a terrible person."

"And?"

"I don't deserve to live."

"Bravo." I clapped my hands.

A second later, a groaning filled the room. I glanced at Elly, but she was still fast asleep, a string of drool slipped down her chin. The stale air inside the bedroom grew mustier as the wall next to Karl opened up. A concrete staircase disappeared into the darkened passageway.

Karl and I stared at the passageway, neither of us saying a word. I looked at my manservant and grinned. "After you."

Chapter 39

I carefully maneuvered my way down the narrow passageway, pausing every few steps to squint past the circle of light illuminated by my p-Phone fairylight app. At best I could see a few feet in front of me. The air smelled like Old Spice and mildew, sort of like Beauty's stepbrother. My face wrinkled at the thought of Handsome lurking in the passageway, watching my missing bride sleep.

"Damn it, Karl," I yelled to my manservant, who'd refused to aid me in my, as he put it, "asinine quest." Instead, he valiantly offered to wait right there until I, or rather if I, found my way out.

At the time, I'd chalked his reluctance up to pure cowardliness. After all, commoners were known for their weak minds and tiny bladders. Or was that the littlest piggy? Either way, wee, wee, wee stains were hard to get out of silk, so I'd let Karl off the hook and ventured into the darkness alone.

Twenty minutes and a face full of what I only hoped was spiderwebs minus the spiders later, I was lost somewhere inside the castle walls.

Dark, dank places like this were no place for a prince. Damn Karl. A buzzing sound echoing from somewhere mid-prince worried me until I realized I wasn't losing my mind, but rather, my p-Phone was set to vibrate.

"Hello," I answered.

"...me...and...try," a female voice crackled through the speaker. I bent my head, hoping to get better reception, but only managed to smash my noggin on the brick wall.

Rubbing at my head, I said, "Lollie? Is that you? I can't hear you."

Suddenly the static stopped.

"Lollie? Who the hell is Lollie?" Sleeping Beauty's voice screeched through the now-crystal-clear connection. Damn P-Mobile had it in for me.

I cleared my throat. "Mademoiselle, you misunderstood me." I touched the end of my nose to make sure it hadn't grown before adding, "You are the only princess for me."

Unfortunately.

"Oh," she said. "Well, that's...um...nice?"

"Mademoiselle, where are you?" I asked.

"I can't say," she whispered. "But you have to stop..."

The phone cut out, garbling her words in an explosion of static. "Beauty?" I yelled into the mouthpiece. "Tell me where you are!"

"...No...Hurt...Wedding..."

"Beauty!" I screamed louder, but to no avail. The phone line went dead. I stared at my p-Phone, watching as Beauty's phone number blinked, mocking me, and finally went black. I'd lost her. Again. A lump formed in my chest, directly under my B-shaped birthmark.

Serial killer or not, I'd made a vow to keep her safe, and I'd failed. Spindle would kill her, eventually, unless my sleepy bride killed him first. For a second I almost felt sorry for the fiancée-stealing assassin. Then I pictured Lollie's face and something green and completely unfroglike filled me, something that felt a lot like jealousy, which was ridiculous. I was the Frog Prince. There wasn't a chastity belt made that could stop me.

"Sir?" Karl's voice called from somewhere above me. "Are you enjoying your adventure?"

"Oh, it's tons of fun. Why don't you come down and join me?" I yelled back, nearly tripping over my own feet as I staggered along, using the brick wall as a guide. Something that sounded suspiciously like bones crunched underfoot.

"Have you located Princess Beauty's whereabouts yet?" He waited a beat. "Or should we just use the GPS to track her phone like I've been trying to suggest for the past hour?"

"Hey, Karl?"

"Yes, sir?"

"Once we find Sleeping Beauty, remind me to beat you to death with my shoe."

He gasped. "Not the Ferragamos."

"Princess Beauty should be just on the other side of this building." Karl gestured to a towering red brick building with small gargoyle statues guarding the rooftop. I bit my lip. The neighborhood looked vaguely familiar, but so did a lot of Cin City streets. Tiny rows of houses with postage-stamp lawns sat on crumbling foundations of sand intermixed with run-down businesses and random degenerates. A merry old homeless soul carrying a pipe and a bowl staggered past.

I glanced at the device in Karl's hand; a red dot blinked furiously. "Are you sure that's Sleeping Beauty?"

"Sir," he began, "as I've told you ten times already, it is Princess Beauty's mobile phone, not the lady herself. If she still has her phone, we will find her."

We'd been hot on Beauty's trail for the last thirty minutes, ever since I'd squeezed my way out of the passageway and into the rose-covered garden. We were close. I could feel Sleeping Beauty's annoyingness like a noose around my neck. "What happened to my life?"

"Buck up, sir." Karl pulled his eyes off the GPS to meet mine. "All will be well. You'll see."

I snorted. "I have to marry a girl who wants me dead in order to stop a curse that started before I was even born. I'll have to wear Kevlar on our wedding night. How will all be well, Karl? How?" Slumping down in my seat, or as far down as one could get in a Ford Princess, I bemoaned my soon-to-be-married fate.

"That can't be right."

"Oh, but it is. I have no choice, remember?" I rubbed my eyes. "You really need to pay better attention."

Karl scowled as we turned the corner, checked his GPS again, and frowned some more. "Sir, not your situation. The GPS coordinates."

"What are you talking about?" I glanced up to see what he meant. His finger pointed to an overly familiar two-story brick building complete with a barbed-wire rose on the front window. I glanced from the building to Karl and back again. "What the frog? Why is Beauty at the Rose?"

Karl waggled the GPS in his hand. "Perhaps the princess wanted a tattoo?"

Yeah, right. I started to say as much when the Rose exploded into a ball of flames that reached high into the desert sky.

Chapter 40

"No!" I screamed, leaping from the car and running toward the burning building. Smoke billowed from the structure, but the flames for the most part had faded after the initial explosion, leaving a wake of broken glass and charred debris. The air tasted thick with grit and smoke.

"Sir," Karl yelled from behind me. "Wait! Don't—"

I ignored his warning and pushed my way through the shattered front door. Black smoke blinded me, choking the sunlight and leaving only darkness inside the building. "Lollie?" I screamed, my heart in my throat.

A faint cough sounded from overhead.

I ran toward the spiral staircase, or what was left of it, carefully picking my way up the steps. They groaned and creaked underfoot, threatening to send me falling to my death. Adrenaline rocketed through my body. The building moaned, shifting on its foundation. A loud crash somewhere toward the back of the shop, followed by what sounded much like footsteps, sent blackened bits of burnt wood raining down on me. A lump of smoke, snot, and bile clogged my throat. But I pushed on. "Lollie!" I screamed again.

Another faint cough echoed up ahead. I ran toward the sound. "Lollie, where are you?" I yelled. The coughs grew louder. The apartment door hung loosely on one hinge. I kicked it free and stormed into the room.

Thick smoke lingered in the air. The room, or what was left of it, was in shambles. Broken furniture and glass littered the scarred floor. My eyes scanned the ground, searching for signs of life.

In the corner, buried under a charred wooden beam, was a trim ankle. Heart in my throat, I shoved away the timber, revealing a soot-coated woman. For a second I thought it was Sleeping Beauty lying on the floor, and then I noticed the familiar tank top and tattoos.

"Kermit?" she croaked in a weak voice.

"It's okay, Lollipop. I've got you." I bent down next to her, gathering her up in my arms. Her body felt so fragile against me. Each breath she took racked her body as if it would be her very last. "Just take it easy. I'll get you out of here." I lifted her up and rolled her over my shoulder in a frog-prince-carry. She weighed less than the little piggy who ate roast beef for every meal. My eyes and throat burned from the acidic sting of smoke, or so I told myself.

Staggering blindly, I knocked Lollie's head against the doorway, causing her to cough. "Watch it, Kermit." I gave a grateful laugh. "Oops." Relief filled me. She'd be all right. With her tightly gripped in my arms, I maneuvered my way down the battered steps, surveying the damage around us. I shook my head, amazed Lollie had survived the explosion.

"Sir," Karl called from the front of what used to be the tattoo shop. "Help is on the way." Distant sirens emphasized his words.

"It's okay, Karl," I said with a cough. "I found her."

Karl's hand flew to his heart. "Oh, thank God. I was so worried about the princess."

Princess? Oh shit! I nearly dropped Lollie. I'd forgotten all about Sleeping Beauty. "Here." I pressed Lollie into

Karl's arms. Bits of charred ceiling crashed down around us. "Hurry. Take her outside. I'm going back upstairs to search for Beauty."

Lollie grabbed my arm. "No, Kermit. Don't..." She broke into a coughing fit. "It's...too..." Her soot-coated face grew even paler, and her eyes fluttered shut.

The building groaned and more debris fell, nearly whacking me in the head. I ducked, pushing Karl to the door. "Go," I ordered. "I'll be right out."

Karl looked to Lollie. "Please, sir—"

"Just keep her safe." I took a deep breath of soot-filled air and headed back upstairs to find my bride. I prayed I wasn't too late.

An hour later, exhausted and covered in ash, I staggered into my hotel room. My mind replayed the emotions of that morning—terror followed by relief, and ultimately total and utter confusion. What had happened to Sleeping Beauty? I'd searched for her for an hour, shifting through piles of burnt debris, finding no sign of my bride except for a slightly melted arm floatie.

"Sir." Karl handed me a towel. "I've started your bath water. It's a perfect 102 degrees. Just the way you like it."

"Thanks," I muttered.

He cleared his throat. "If I may speak freely?"

Like he'd shut up if I said no. "Very well." I wrapped the towel around my neck and motioned for him to continue. "What's on your mind?"

"Ms. Bliss, sir."

Unfortunately, she'd weaseled her way into way too many of my thoughts as well. At a time when my only concern should be for Sleeping Beauty, I found myself unable to concentrate on anything except for the injured woman asleep in the room down the hallway. "What about her?" I asked, glancing to the closed bedroom door as if it was an omen.

Taking a deep breath, he said, "Do you really think it's a wise idea for her to stay here? You being...well... you."

"Hey," I said. "What kind of prince do you think I am?"

"I prefer not to answer that, sir. I would like to keep my job, such as it is." He let out a drawn-out sigh. "Anyway, back to Ms. Bliss."

"Why the sudden concern for Lollie? Two days ago you couldn't stand her, and now you're playing Mother Goose. What's that about?" Too tired to wait for his answer, I waved him off. My mind filled with images of Lollie's soot-coated face and singed hair. I could've lost her, I thought, terror clogging my throat. "Never mind. It doesn't matter. Lollie will be staying with me, whether she likes it or not."

"But—"

"It's not up for debate."

"Very well, sir. You're the boss." His lips curled into a sneer, unsightly on many a manservant, but especially on a bald one with delusions of grandeur. "Shall I unpack the handcuffs? Perhaps tie Ms. Bliss to the bed so she doesn't escape?"

"It's a little early for the kinky stuff." I scratched my ten forty-five o'clock shadow. Flakes of signed hair and ash rained down. "Let's at least wait until she's awake."

Chapter 41

"Going somewhere?" I flicked on the lamp next to the couch, and the hotel suite burst to light. Lollie froze, hand on the doorknob. Anger flashed in her eyes, but her face remained impassive, cold. "Oh, I didn't see you there," she said with a hard smile. "Sitting in the dark. Like some creepy pervert."

I motioned to the drink in front of me. "Care to join me?"

Her eyes darted between the doorknob and me, as if gauging the distance. Finally, she nodded and released the knob. She crossed the room and poured herself a glass of something amber in color, much like the color of her eyes in the moonlight. She raised the drink in salute. "So what are we drinking to?"

I picked up my own drink and twirled it in my fingers. The warm liquid lapped at the sides of the glass. "How about we drink to ever after? The not-so-happy kind." The kind of happily-ever-after where you develop a craving for flies and licking your own butt.

Lollie gave a little laugh, but didn't drink. "What's going on in your very small mind, Kermit?" she asked, crossing her arms over her chest. A chest covered in one of my oxford button-down shirts that hit her mid-thigh. Various swirls of ink climbed along her tanned legs, disappearing into a pair of soot-coated combat boots. Tattoos of faraway places and exotic languages. Places and things I would never experience once I was locked away inside my amphibian prison. Anger seethed inside me. Damn her and damn this curse.

Lollie cleared her throat, gaining my attention. "Are you going to say anything, or were you planning to stare at my legs all night?"

As tempting as my continued leering was, I decided to get straight to the point. "You lied to me. Again," I said, watching her closely for the slightest sign of guilt.

"Did I?" she prompted.

I leapt from the couch, needing to distance myself from Lollie before I did something I'd regret. Something we'd both regret. I paced back and forth until the urge to choke her lessened to an acceptable, princely level. "Sleeping Beauty was at the Rose today."

"Says who?"

"That." I motioned to Karl's GPS device sitting on top of the table. "Machines don't lie, Lollie. Unlike tattooed girls with ulterior motives." My lips curved into a hard grin and I resumed my seat on the couch, leaning back as if we were discussing the weather. "So either one of two things happened."

"Do tell, Kermit." She raised a singed eyebrow, slammed the rest of her drink, and crossed the room to stand in front of me. "I'm all atwitter with anticipation."

Heat mixed with anger and pooled in my lower body as I gave her a slow once-over. For a chick who'd nearly died, she looked remarkably beautiful, and calm. Much too calm, to my way of thinking. I decided to give her a little push to see how she'd react.

"The way I see it," I paused, hating the words pouring from my mouth, "you lied to me yesterday. Spindle is very much a part of your life, so much so that you helped him kidnap Sleeping Beauty."

"Did I now?"

I nodded. "You used your," my eyes lowered to her ample breasts, barely contained within my shirt, "assets to distract me from finding and marrying Beauty. But why? Is this all about a ransom of some kind? Or is it something more?"

Her husky laugh sent shivers down my spine. "That's quite an imagination you've got there," she said, plopping down on the couch next to me. Her hand stroked my thigh and she purred. "So once I distracted you, as you so quaintly put it," she licked her plump lips, "I what? Blew myself up!" She thwacked me in the inner thigh, narrowly missing my smaller, if not smarter, little frog prince.

"Hey!" I hopped off the couch, avoiding another punch to the bollocks. "What's your problem?"

"My problem," she said through clenched teeth, "as you so kindly put it, is you."

"Me?" My hand flew to my throat. "What'd I do?" I stabbed my finger at her. "You're the one who used me. I'm the injured party here."

"You will be when I'm done with you." She straightened off the cushion, rising to her full height, about four inches shorter than mine. "In case you've forgotten, I was the one who almost died today when the Rose, a business I've worked my ass off for two years to make a success, exploded with me inside."

"Um..."

Her finger jabbed me in the chest, hard. "And why do you think that is, Kermit?"

This time I had the perfect answer. I slapped my forehead. "Of course." I nodded. "Your lover is trying to tie up any loose ends." I grinned. "And you, Ms. Bliss, are looser than most."

In hind-smack, my words sounded a little rude. But that wasn't what flashed through my brain when the pain in my smashed nose from her less-than-flat fist receded to a mind-numbing throb. Instead, I grabbed Lollie's arm, yanking her against me. Her chest heaved in anger, igniting something infinitely more dangerous than my temper.

"Lollie," I whispered, my gaze locked on her bottom lip and the sheen glistening on it. Said lips parted, and the tip of her pink tongue darted out in welcome. That was the only invitation I needed. My mouth crushed hers, my lips hard and insistent until she yielded to my will. I wasn't taking no for an answer, not that Lollie planned on stopping my assault. In fact, at one point, her greedy mouth ravished mine like some hero in a Regency romance novel. I feared for my lips, if not my life.

Once Lollie's teeth drew blood, I pulled away to catch my breath before I lost all control. Her eyes locked on mine, and what I saw inside her gaze scared me to my very toes.

She was the One for me.

Chapter 42

Without thinking of the consequences, of Sleeping Beauty, of my greener future, I grabbed Lollie's hand and pulled her toward my bedroom. Her skin against mine felt right, like we belonged together. But we didn't. Not truly, I reminded myself, fingering the B-shaped birthmark over my heart. Beauty was my One; if I belonged to anyone, it was her serial-killing self.

We reached the doorway to my bedroom, and Lollie pulled to a stop. "Make me a promise, Kermit," she said, her fingers sliding down my arm.

I nodded, mostly because, even under the threat of death, forming a coherent response was beyond my non-frog-sized brain. Thoughts of sex did that to a guy, especially when said sex involved a smoking-hot chick on the verge of fulfilling a multitude of fantasies.

"If we do this," she began.

"Oh, we are doing it." I grinned. "If you're lucky we might do it twice."

"Be still my heart." Her hands flew to her chest as she let out a peal of laughter. "Where have you been all my life?" Her words acted much like a cold shower as memories of my former lonely froglike existence flashed through my head. My heartbeat slowed and the rush of lust that had blinded me a few moments ago faded. I still wanted

Lollie like I'd never wanted another woman. But was I willing to give up the rest of my life for a taste of her?

She seemed to share my hesitancy, if not my dwindling libido. Biting her bottom lip, she took a step back. "I want you, Kermit. I want this."

"But?"

"No but," she said, her voice growing stronger. "More of an aside."

I tilted my head. "An aside? I'm not familiar with that position. Is that from the Fairy Sutra?" I asked, referring to the ancient sex text featuring all sorts of woodland animals in a variety of graphic positions.

"Cute." She grabbed the collar of my shirt. "But I'm serious. You have to promise me," she paused, her fingers curling in the fabric, "whatever happens tonight, nothing changes between us. We have tonight. That's it."

My eyes narrowed. "What'd you mean?"

"I won't fall in love with you," she vowed.

My heart gave a small squeeze, but I ignored the pain. This was just what I needed. A quick pre-wedding affair with no strings attached, I told myself. "Good to know," I said with a smile.

"I mean it, Kermit." She crossed her arms over her chest. "Tonight will be about sex. Nothing more. Just two people enjoying each other's bodies. Tomorrow we act as if nothing happened. I won't be your mistress. I won't love you." She swallowed hard. "You'll stupidly go back to your tired princess, get married, if she doesn't kill you first, and have a bunch of arrogant, narcoleptic brats."

"And you, Lollipop? What will you go back to? That bastard Spindle?" I pictured her burned-up tattoo shop, her ash-coated face as I lifted her into my arms, and the lump of terror in my throat when I'd thought I'd lost her. All because of Spindle.

I stepped toward her, taking her in my arms. My head rested on top of hers. We stood together for a few minutes, not speaking as thoughts of tomorrow swirled around us. As right as Lollie felt in my arms, we could never be more than this, a one-night stand. I wanted her body, her mind, her soul. Craved her in a way I'd never craved a woman before. She was beautiful, standing in the hallway, her arms swirls of ink and heat. My mouth went dry at the thought of her body mingling with mine.

Lollie gazed up at me, her eyes dark with questions. I swallowed and nodded. She grinned back, turned off all the lights before taking my hand and leading me the rest of the way to the bed.

From there things grew. . . .

Chapter 43

Harsh desert light spilled through the hotel room window, illuminating the colorful array of purple flowers sprouting over the small of Lollie's back. Flowers that resembled the ones imprinted on my lumbar region. Damn her, I thought with a satisfied smile. My finger trailed over a particularly sensitive bloom at the base of her spine that disappeared into her backside. Lollie groaned and snuggled deeper into the soft bedding.

I glanced at the bedside clock. Seven A.M. One day closer to my birthday. One day closer to a black fly birthday cake. Unless I found Sleeping Beauty, and quick. Yet, lying here, next to Lollie, my impending doom didn't seem to matter quite so much. It probably had something to do with my complete exhaustion and lack of fluids.

Or not.

Spending the night with Lollie proved to be an adventure of fairytale proportions. We explored each other's bodies for hours until every curve, nook, and cranny took us over the river and through the woods. And then we slept, arms around each other as we drifted off. Or rather I did. It seemed Ms. Bliss suffered from insomnia, or so she said when I caught her watching me sleep a few hours later. I wasn't sure if I believed her, but rather than argue, I wrapped my arms around her and did my best to tucker her out.

This morning, exhausted, I leaned against twelve-hundred-dollar pillows, tracing Lollie's inked flesh with the pad of my thumb. My mind filled with what-ifs. Questions like, what if Sleeping Beauty wasn't my *One?* What if all this was some sort of mistake and I was truly meant to be with Lollie?

"Don't be stupid, Johnny," Elly's voice squeaked from somewhere on my left. "I'm never wrong."

I jumped, quickly covering my nakedness from the prying eyes and vicious wand of my godmother. "Damn it, Elly. Can't you see I've got company?" I growled as she suddenly materialized next to the bed in a cloud of sparkling silver fairy dust and toxic gin breath.

Lollie groaned, but didn't fully wake. A good thing too since Elly was standing over her, her wand poised for damage. Glaring at my godmother, I hissed through clenched teeth. "What the hell are you doing here?"

"Is that any way to talk to me? A woman who's spent her best years protecting you from evil." She smashed her wand against the back of my head. "Now apologize and get away from that . . . person. We have work to do."

"Work?" Even on the best of days, the only work Elly ever did was nag me. At times it seemed like more of a full-time career for her.

"Yes, work." She crossed her arms over her sagging bosom. "Unless we locate your missing bride in the next . . ." She glanced at a freckle on her arm where a Rolex from Tiffany's I'd bought her for Christmas last year used to sit. A watch she must've pawned to pay her latest gambling debt. "Well, soon. You will spend the rest of your days mating with," her eyes scanned Lollie's taut body, "prettier, albeit greener females."

"Hey—" I began.

"Hush your mouth." Elly swatted me with the pointy

end of her wand. "What do you even know about this girl, Johnny? Other than she's mentally unstable."

My eyes narrowed. "Why do you say that?"

"She had sex with you, dear boy." Elly shook her head and snorted. "The girl obviously has issues."

I sat up, frowning at a black stain on the pad of my thumb, unsure where the smudge had come from. Shaking my head and pulling up my boxers, I said, "Mental health aside, Lollie's . . ."

"What?"

"I don't know . . . She's . . ."

Thwack. The wand smacked me across the side of my face, and for a few seconds my brain exploded into little silver stars. "Idiot!" Elly hit me on the other cheek for good measure. "You're in love with her. I can't leave you alone for two minutes without you . . ." On and on she ranted, but I'd stopped listening. The words "in love" blazed through my head. Was Elly right? Had I stupidly gone and fallen in love with Lollie?

Not possible, I assured myself. I was the Frog Prince, a man too smart to feel any emotion, let alone fall in love. I'd had sex with hundreds of women, women far hotter than Lollie, women skilled in the art of seduction, women who knew how to make a man beg, not that Lollie hadn't given it a good ole college try.

Lollie and I had great sex. Amazing, if I thought about it, but love? Hell, I barely even liked her. She was sarcastic and crazy. Not to mention she had an assassin for a boyfriend who'd kidnapped my future wife. Plus she lied to me at every opportunity. Love. Ha! I'd be stupid to fall in love with someone like her. Someone who laughed at my jokes. Someone whose eyes lit up when I entered the room. Someone who made me feel . . . not so alone.

I wasn't in love.

So why did the B-shaped birthmark on my chest ache when I pictured my life without ever seeing her again?

Chapter 44

An hour later, dressed in a pair of designer jeans and an absurdly expensive T-shirt, I gently nudged Lollie awake, careful to avoid the right cross she threw my way. "Hey," I said, shaking her again. "Get up."

One long-lashed eyelid rose. "Coffee?"

I grinned, passing her a cup of her favorite sweet, milky brew. "Fresh from room service. Now get moving. Karl will be—"

Before I'd finished my sentence, Lollie was out of bed, searching the floor, lampshade, and finally the balcony for the clothes she'd worn last night. As she located each wayward piece, she glared at me. I shrugged innocently. Picking her bra out of the mini-fridge, she raised an eyebrow.

"What?"

Rather than comment, she rolled her eyes and quickly finished dressing. "So what now?" she asked, pulling on her combat boot still stained with ash from the fire.

I took a deep breath, feeling guilty as hell. "Apparently Spindle contacted Elly. He wants two hundred thousand dollars or he'll kill Beauty." All last night, while I was making love to Lollie, my soon-to-be bride had been in the hands of a madman; whether by her choice or not, the point was moot.

"What! A ransom? That can't be." Lollie reached for

my arm, but I twisted away, my eyes burning into hers. Lollie knew too much to play innocent now.

"Why would Elly lie?" I scratched my head. "To me?" The "unlike you" part of the statement hung in the air between us. I was finding it hard to keep track of the sheer number of mistruths Ms. Bliss had supplied in the last few days.

Lollie's lips curled into a snarl. "I have no idea. Perhaps she's merely mistaken, but I swear to you, Jean-Michel, Beauty is safe. Spindle won't hurt her."

"Nice try, Lollipop," I straightened to my full six-foot height, "but it's time I met your boyfriend, man to man."

She snorted, not an attractive sound, but it turned me on nonetheless. Yeah, I was hopeless. I sighed. "The ransom drop is at a warehouse downtown. Spindle wants me there in an hour."

"Don't go." Her nails dug into my arm, leaving half-moon welts along the vein. "It's some sort of setup."

"I have to." I peeled away each of her fingers. "I can't risk Sleeping Beauty's life."

"Are you serious?" Her eyes flashed with violence. "You're still on this Sleeping Beauty thing? After everything that happened?"

I glowered, taken aback by her quick change of mind regarding our relationship. "Wait. What? Last night you said—"

"I know what I said." She stomped from the bed and into the living room. "I wasn't talking about last night. I was referring to yesterday. Remember the big explosion? Me almost dying? Ring any bells, Quasimodo?"

"Hold on." I trailed after her. "First of all, are you implying that Sleeping Beauty had something to do with the explosion yesterday? Second and most importantly," I patted my back, "does this shirt make me look like I have a hump?"

"No."

"Good." I nodded, relived. Turning back into a frog was bad enough, but a humpbacked frog? I'd never get laid again.

"I wasn't implying it, Kermit." She spun toward me, her hands fisted on her hips. "I'm outright saying it. Someone blew up the Rose, and it wasn't Spindle. You do the math."

"Are you crazy?" I giggled. "If anyone blew anything..."

"Don't you dare say it!" She poked me in the chest, hard. "I'm not in the mood for your lame attempts at humor. Not after I'm going to have to spend the day on the phone with my insurance company."

So much for the afterglow. "I was going to say," I paused to gain her attention, "if anyone blew anything up it *was* Spindle. He wants you out of the way, Lollie. Whatever the two of you had is over. Can't you see that?"

"Really?" Her finger scraped the collar of her shirt. "Why? What's Spindle's motive? According to you we're lovers, remember?" Her words sent a spark of pain through the center of my chest. "Isn't it far more likely that your demented fiancée blew up *my* shop to try and kill you?"

Goldie's warning echoed in my head, loud and insistent. Beauty was a cold-blooded killer. "But I wasn't even there," I said.

"But you were. Yesterday morning." She dragged her bottom lip through her teeth. "The bomb was meant for you. No one else."

"How can you be so sure?"

She took a deep breath. "I never saw Sleeping Beauty or her phone, Kermit. I swear it."

If Lollie was telling the truth and Sleeping Beauty was in on yesterday's explosion, my impending froghood looked more and more like a possibility. I didn't want to eat flies and poop in a swamp for the rest of my life. After all, frogs, even the princely ones, got mold in some very weird places.

"I'm sorry." Lollie reached for my hand. "I know how important marrying Sleeping Beauty is to you. But don't worry. You'll find the right princess soon. Maybe she won't be as rich as Sleeping Beauty . . ."

I pulled away from her surprisingly strong grip. "Whoa." I gave a small laugh. "You think I'm marrying Sleeping Beauty for her money?"

"Of course." She nodded as if my greed was a foregone conclusion. "Why else would you marry a woman who annoys you, much less wants you dead?"

Maybe it was time to come clean with Lollie. What did I have to lose? Beside my dignity—not like I had much of it left after the second Fairy Sutra position we'd tried last night. Who knew a frog price was so bendy?

Lollie snapped her fingers in front of my face. "Earth to Kermit. Are you going to answer me?"

"Oh. Right. Sorry." I groaned, erasing from my head the image of Lollie's long legs wrapped around my ears. "Do you know what the name La Grenouille stands for?"

"Arrogant idiot?" She grinned. When I didn't share her humor, she rolled her eyes. "I took French. La Grenouille stands for 'the Frog,' hence why they call you the Frog Prince. So?"

"So thirty-five years ago my parents fell in love. And I'm not talking the kind of love we shared last night." Not the sort of love that took a mop and bucket to clean up, not that I'd minded swabbing Lollie's decks. "I'm talking about the real deal. L.O.V.E. The happily-ever-after kind."

"Gross." Her lip curled. "What's this got to do with your fancy French name or why you're so desperate to marry Sleeping Beauty?"

"I'm getting to it." Crossing the room, I stopped at the bar to pour myself a cup of coffee. "A few years into their happily-ever-after, my grandfather ordered my father to give him an heir. My father didn't want anything to interfere with the time he spent with his bride, but he finally agreed when my grandfather threatened to cut him off." A sort of family tradition, I supposed, noting my own current financial quandary. The only difference was, I wouldn't let the Frog King's money rule my life. I was my own frog prince, damn it.

"It's not the worst reason to have a kid, I guess." Her eyes narrowed. "So what happened?"

"A curse happened." I shivered, my voice thick. "Try as they might, my parents couldn't conceive. My grandfather grew more desperate, pressuring my father until . . . well, one day, he—"

"I still don't understand what this has to do with you," she interrupted as she plopped down on the hotel room couch. "You weren't even born yet."

"Precisely."

"What?"

"My father did the only thing he could think of. He offered a witch riches beyond compare if she would give him a son."

"Huh." She nodded. "Your mother's a witch?"

"No. The witch cast a spell and soon after, my mother became pregnant with me. Mother rejoiced for nine months, until the night she went into labor. The labor was hard. So difficult that my mother . . ." I took a deep breath, the horror of that night infused in every word. "Died. A brain hemorrhage the doctor declared."

"My God." Lollie's hand flew to her heart. "I'm so sorry. I lost my mother when I was young too."

"If only it was that easy." I smiled sadly. "The thing is, my mother didn't stay dead, Lollie. You see, my father, in his great wisdom, did what any fool in love would do. He sacrificed everything."

"What do you mean?"

"The Frog King, then only a prince like me, called for his guards to bring the old witch to my mother's bedside and demanded the witch save my mother. She told him that nothing could be done to save her. But my father refused to listen." I gave a bitter laugh. "He was next in line to be the Frog King, after all."

I turned to watch the tourists on the Cin City strip below. My voice sounded odd to my ears, mechanical, as if the story I told was nothing more than a fable. But it wasn't. It was my life. "My father loved my mother so much that he offered the old witch his most prized possession if she would save his queen."

"Rookie mistake," Lollie said.

I nodded. "The witch accepted his offer, waved her hands in the air, and sure enough my mother began to breathe once again."

"And the witch?" Lollie leaned forward, enthralled with my tale. "Did she take your father's most prized possession?"

"I wish it was that easy," I said. "Rather than pay her price, he had the old witch arrested and charged with witchcraft."

Lollie sucked in a sharp breath. "He didn't."

I nodded. "Ten days later, on the morning the witch was to be hanged for her black deeds, my father awoke to find my mother standing over my crib, crying." My throat tightened. The queen still cried, to this day, locked away in her tower. Inconsolable with grief. I hated my father for that.

"How sad. Your poor mother." Lollie's hand covered her mouth. "Why was she crying? Were you missing?"

I turned to face her. "I was there."

"So what caused her distress?"

"A frog."

"I don't understand."

I stared into her dark eyes, so devoid of color like the

darkest recesses of my soul. "The witch had her revenge. She took what was most precious to my father. His most prized possession."

Lollie lowered her gaze. "Your mother."

"Yes." I vowed to never fall in love, to never allow someone to wield that much power over me. Being cursed and forced to marry a serial-killing nitwit was bad enough.

"But how?" she asked.

"By turning the queen's baby into a frog."

"No."

I swallowed, afraid, as if saying the curse aloud could somehow make it all the more true. "And she will have her revenge again in a couple of days."

"How?"

"On my thirtieth birthday, unless I marry the One, the curse strikes again."

"The One?"

"The woman, well, she was more of a girl really, when we first met at the pond, who broke my curse twenty-two years ago."

Lollie's face lost all color. "Sleeping Beauty."

I nodded.

"Son of a bitch!"

Chapter 45

Lollie's reaction wasn't quite what I'd expected. Rather than run away, disgusted by the fact she'd recently made love to a man who'd once digested flies, she paced the room, muttering, as if my curse was now her burden. I caught the words "pond," "girl," and "greenish moron" as she flew by.

I reached for her arm, stopping her mid-mutter. "Are you all right?"

"What?" She ducked her head. "Of course I'm all right. I just need to think."

"Okay," I said slowly in the voice I reserved for the village idiot. "I'm going to meeting Karl downstairs so he can drive me to the warehouse. Do you want to join us?" Not that I wanted her within a hundred feet of Spindle or my soon-to-be bride, but it didn't feel right to leave her locked up in my hotel room either, especially after I just dropped a frogshell like that in her lap.

Besides, what if she was right and Sleeping Beauty really did want to remove both Lollie and me from the picture? Leaving Lollie here would be like inviting an ex-girlfriend to my wedding and handing her a knife to cut my throat as well as the wedding cake.

"You're going to the warehouse. Now?" Lollie's face paled and her lips started to tremble. Then her face relaxed as something occurred to her. "What about the money? It will take you a couple of hours at least to gather that much cash."

I walked to the hotel safe and punched in a four-digit code. The safe opened, revealing stacks of cash, all neatly laundered and pressed, a job I often forced upon Karl when he annoyed me. I picked up a stack, weighed it in my hand, and then shoved it in a black bag. "That should do it."

Lollie's eyes grew wide as she stared at the money. "A little walking-around money?"

"Petty cash. Besides, my fairy godmother told me, always be prepared. That's the frog prince motto," I said, raising my hand in a Prince Scout salute, which equaled a raised middle finger.

"Hmm..." Her tongue flicked out to wet her lips. "In my experience, princes salute in a very different manner." Her face quickly sobered. "Didn't your dad disown you?"

"Yeah."

"So..." Her hand motioned to the petty cash and the safe.

I shrugged as my p-Phone jangled. "Hey, Karl. What's up?" I answered after a quick glance at the caller ID. I listened for a few seconds while he blathered on and on. For a bald, not-so-charming manservant, Karl could talk. I rolled my eyes at Lollie. She grinned back, but her smile slipped as soon as I stepped away. Distress was etched in every inky line on her body. Was she worried about Spindle? The thought caused a small—tiny really, nothing to even be concerned about—pain in my chest.

"Okay, we'll be down in a few minutes." I hung up and grinned at Lollie. "Karl ordered you some fresh clothes. Once the maid gets here, you can change and then we'll be on our way. But, Lollie," I began, my voice growing cold, "don't make me regret this. You'll do as I say. Stay in the car and keep quiet. I don't want you to get hurt." The very thought made that tiny ache explode into full-on indigestion.

She beamed up at me, the picture of innocence in a body designed by the devil himself. "You're the boss, Kermit. Your wish is my command."

I wished she'd stop saying that. It made focusing on the matter at hand all but impossible. Yet even as she promised complete wish fulfillment, I knew like a punch in the gut I'd regret ever bringing Ms. Bliss anywhere near my bride. Probably had something to do with the evil gleam in Lollie's dark, almost mauve in color, eyes.

Rolling up to Spindle's warehouse in an ugly yellow Ford Princess probably wasn't the smartest move. The car screamed for attention; add a slightly-olive-in-the-face prince, a bald manservant, and a tattooed lady, plus two hundred thousand dollars in unmarked bills, and we looked much more like a circus act than a rescue team.

"Are you sure this is the place?" Lollie asked, her eyes darting around. "It looks sort of . . . abandoned."

Karl checked the map on his BlackFerry. "This is the address Elly gave us."

I waved off any concern. "This is the place. I can smell the greedy bastard lurking inside."

Lollie raised a perfectly arched eyebrow, a trick only a woman could pull off. When I tried the same expression I resembled Humpty Dumpty after the fall. "Smell him? Really?" She fingered the big black bag sitting on the seat next to her. The same bag I'd found while searching remains of the Rose following the explosion. Or as Lollie put it, "all she had left in the world." What a drama queen.

Her royal pain in the ass flicked my ear to gain my attention. "Hey, Kermit. Be careful. You don't understand what you're dealing with." Her concern for my continued breathing warmed me.

"And you do, mademoiselle?" I grabbed her chin and kissed her, hard. Pulling quickly away before she could protest and/or smack me in the face. "Stay in the car. Karl and I will handle this. I don't need you messing it up with your . . . youness," I ordered, wincing as Lollie glared daggers at me.

Truth be told, I was more worried about how Spindle might react when he found his former lady love now loving my princely self. Not that Lollie loved me. We were just . . . I shook off that particular terrifying line of thought. Besides, if I brought Lollie inside, she could get hurt, and I wasn't about to risk her life again. One explosion per lifetime was enough. Of course, I didn't relish the thought of grilled frog legs either. I turned to Karl. "How do you feel about bullet wounds?"

"I'm opposed to them, sir." He heaved a long, world-weary sigh. "Please try and not get me shot."

I nodded. "Sounds like a plan. Let's hit it."

Before Lollie could comment or throw something, as she was prone to doing, Karl and I piled from the vehicle, the bag of cash in my hands. The street looked as abandoned as the rest of the neighborhood. Cars from the 1970s littered the landscape, a Chevy Aladdin with missing magic floor mats, a Buick Dwarf, one of its two seats ripped asunder. Most of the vehicles lurched to one side, engines, tires, and sometimes even the doors pilfered by villains.

I nodded to Karl, and together we headed for the warehouse and whatever lurked inside, namely my annoying and possibly murderous future wife. I shuddered at the thought.

"Wait!" Lollie leapt from the ugly Princess.

"What?" I ducked, preparing for a pummeling at her tiny hands. Rather than punch me, she wrapped her arms around my neck and kissed the breath from my lungs; her mouth ground into mine while our tongues played a game of ring around the tonsils. My hands tugged at the belt loops of her jeans, dragging her body even closer. She moaned, low and deep in her throat, kissing me as if the world was about to end.

And maybe it was. For us at least.

"Get a room," Karl said in a bored tone. "I mean, come on, his lordship will be right back. It's not like he's running away with the dish and a spoon."

Lollie pulled away, wiping a string of my saliva from her mouth. "Right. Sorry. But, Kermit, wouldn't it be safer if you left the money here? With me."

My eyes narrowed.

"She does have a point, sir." Karl nodded. "If Spindle is inside, what's stopping him from killing us and taking the money? If we leave it with Ms. Bliss, he won't outright murder us."

"But—"

Lollie's own dark eyes narrowed. "But what? Don't you trust me? After," she lowered her voice, "last night." Before I could answer, she reached out to take the bag from my hands. "I'll just wait right here like a good little girl until you give me the all clear."

I frowned.

"What do you have to lose, sir?" Karl asked with a shrug. Two hundred thousand dollars came to mind, but I could afford it, for the moment. On the other hand, walking into a trap with that much money in hand sounded stupid, even to me, a prince who'd failed Heroes 101 at charming school. When I still didn't release my grip on the bag, Karl patted my arm. "The sooner we do this, the sooner you can start your happily-ever-after."

And resume my real life, I added silently, *one without tattooed beauties much too intelligent to trust.* I took a second to run my fingers across the faint freckles sprinkled across Lollie's cheek before finally letting the bag drop. "Don't make me regret this," I said, voice thick with equal parts lust and suspicion.

Lollie gave me a wink and headed back to the ugly Princess to wait for me. I liked the sound of that, maybe a bit too much. Something shifted in my chest. My feet felt touched by Midas, heavy, leaden, as if I was slowly being swallowed by the concrete below me.

This was it. Once I had Beauty back, safe, we'd get married and I'd lose Lollie forever.

"Sir?" Karl motioned to the warehouse.

"Right." I shook my head to clear the taste of Lollie from my mind and focused on the task ahead—saving Beauty without dying in the process.

How hard could it be?

Chapter 46

Opening the front door of the warehouse took a few minutes, mostly because neither Karl nor I realized it was unlocked. A shiver of dread ran up my spine as we pushed the door wide, sort of like when the mouse ran up the cat-faced clock. He too was never seen again.

The warehouse was a perfect place for an ambush. A part of me wanted to turn around and rush back to Lollie, to protect her from whatever secrets, lies, or sleepy brides waited inside. Karl shined a flashlight inside the darkened building, illuminating thick black oil stains on the concrete. Otherwise there was no sign of life. I strolled farther into the dark interior, my ears straining. If Beauty was here, she was either asleep (a likely possibility) or dead. I swallowed past the lump in my throat.

"What's that?" I pointed to the back of the warehouse. Karl swung the flashlight in an arc, illuminating a metal staircase. It appeared rickety and old, every other rung rusted beyond repair. The staircase screamed certain death, perfect for a bald, slightly pudgy manservant to climb.

"What d'you think?" I nodded to the stairs.

Karl tilted the flashlight up higher, toward the second floor. The weak beam skirted the stairwell. "Seems like the kind of place a devious villain might stash a tired princess." Karl motioned me forward. "Why don't you check it out? I'll wait here to ensure Spindle doesn't escape."

I scratched my chin. "How about you go up there, and I'll wait here. You are my manservant, after all. A man paid to take a bullet for me."

"No, sir." Karl straightened to his full five-foot-seven height, bald head gleaming in the dim light. "I'm paid to scrub the stains from your boxer shorts, not risk my life, even though the two seem mutually inclusive at times." Karl pointed to his knee. "But alas, I can't go upstairs for you. Old college football injury."

"Oh. In that case . . . ," I said, taking a step toward the staircase. "Hey, wait a minute. You didn't go to college."

"You got me." He grinned. "I see your Ivy League education was money well spent, sir. Your father must be so proud."

I snatched the flashlight from his grip. "Mock me if you will. But I'm not the one wearing tights."

"Touché." His smile widened. "That's French, in case they didn't teach you that at Olly, Olly, Oxford, Not-So-Free."

Ignoring Karl, I slowly climbed the stairs to the second floor, scanning the dark interior. My foot slipped a few times, but I stayed upright.

"Sir," Karl called from below. "As much as I'm enjoying this adventure, would you climb a wee bit faster? Surely it's been over an hour and you're only three feet up."

"It's only been a few minutes!" I shouted back, continuing my ascent.

By the time I reached the top step, I was out of breath and regretting my late-night amorous activities. Princes weren't made for endurance, even frog princes as fine as myself.

Switching off the flashlight to make myself less conspicuous, I stepped into the darkness of the second floor of the warehouse. A small squeak echoed somewhere to my right. I jumped at the sound. Images of blind man-eating mice flashed through my brain.

A loud thump followed another tiny squeal. I flipped on the flashlight and shone it around the room. Cobwebs covered every inch of the space, except for the corner, where an old rocking chair sat, eerily rocking back and forth. If I was any other prince, the whole empty but still moving chair might've freaked me out. But I was the Frog Prince, damn it. It took a lot more to scare me.

A hand grabbed my shoulder and I screamed like a little girl. I spun to face the threat, nearly wrenching my spine in the process. The flashlight fell to the floor, casting an eerie glow throughout the room. Yet it emitted just enough light to see into my future, and trust me, what I saw wasn't Pretty, but her older sister and my forthcoming wife, Beauty.

"Hi." Beauty opened her arms in welcome, yawned, and then punched me in the nose.

Pain exploded behind my eyes as snot leaked from my injured nostrils. I stumped back, holding my face until my eyes stopped tearing. "What the hell was that for?"

"Took you long enough."

"What?"

"To find me." Her arms crossed over her chest and she tapped her foot. "Well?"

"Well what?" What did this crazy woman want from me? Blood? Apparently so, I thought as I wiped away a stream of red pouring from my nostril.

Her sigh reverberated around the empty room. "Apologize."

"For what?" Shit. Did she know I hired Spindle to kill her? If so, I had a hell of a lot of explaining to do. Not that I even knew where to begin. "Sorry" didn't quite seem to cover it, especially since I'd spent last night in the arms of another woman while Sleeping Beauty spent the night locked away with a madman. Or had she? Was she a victim or villain? Not that it mattered; I would marry her either way.

Her drawn-out yawn brought me back to the matter at hand. "Apologize for taking so long to rescue me. I've been waiting," she glanced at her bare wrist, "for a really long time for . . . you to come."

"Are you all right, mademoiselle?" My eyes roamed over her from head to toe. She wore a white robe that covered her from neck to ankle. She didn't look hurt. In fact, with the exception of a small emblazed "A" on the lapel of the robe, Beauty appeared as fresh as snow. I frowned at the lapel, trying to remember where I'd seen it before. Nothing came to me.

My gaze moved to Beauty's face, hidden partially in shadows. One lone purple-lollipop eye stared out at me from behind a veil of kinky blond hair. "Did Spindle harm you in some way, mademoiselle?" I asked, motioning to her obviously demented head.

"No," she said with a bright smile. "I'm fine. Just a little sleepy. I'm glad you're here." She finished with a loud yawn.

"I see." I raised an eyebrow. "And in your excited gratitude, you punched me in the face?"

Her sigh was so forceful a cloud of dust swirled to life. "I was waiting a really long time."

I bowed low. "For that, I do apologize. Now, if you don't mind," I reached for her arm, propelling her forward, "we should really get out of here before Spindle decides to kill us."

Her eyes narrowed as if I was now the crazy one. "Kill us? Why would anyone kill us? We're very nice," she said, nodding for emphasis. "At least I am."

"Be that as it may—"

She pulled to a stop. "Say it!"

"Say what?"

"Say I'm very nice."

What was wrong with this chick? Serial killer my ass— the only way Beauty was capable of murder was if she annoyed someone to death. Her missing fiancés suddenly made sense. The poor bastards had faked their own disappearances to keep Beauty away.

Oh, how I longed for a tower.

Or a gag.

"Well?" she prompted when I failed to respond to her previous demand.

"Well what?" I held my hands up. "Fine. You are a very nice princess. Happy now?"

"Ecstatic," she mumbled.

I rolled my eyes, again taking her arm and heading for the stairs before Spindle arrived on scene to slaughter us. Which was odd. Where was Spindle? He'd orchestrated this whole thing, dragged me to this abandoned warehouse with two hundred thousand dollars . . .

Lollie.

"Son of a bitch." I stopped fast, Beauty knocking into my back. She gasped and her hand flew to her mouth. "Forgive my language, mademoiselle," I said with a frown, wiping at a red spot on my T-shirt, a spot over the B-shaped birthmark covering my heart. "I did not mean to offend—"

"Look out," she screamed, launching her body at mine. We tumbled to the floor. The blackened window in front of us exploded as a swarm of high-powered bullets fractured the glass like the mirror, mirror on the wall after a full frontal view of the ugliest stepsister in a bikini.

I wrapped my arms around Beauty, taking the brunt of her weight on my body as we smashed to the cold concrete. The noise of gunfire deafened me, as did the wild beat of my heart. I knew Sleeping Beauty's rescue was too damn easy. Spindle had set me up. And now I would die with a woman I didn't even like in my arms.

A woman who'd just saved my life.

Staggering to my hands and knees, glass digging into my palms, I crawled toward the stairs. Beauty grabbed at my leg. "Are you insane? Stay down. Before you get us both killed," she said, her eyes round with terror.

"Shh," I said. "I made you a promise, remember?"

She nodded, looking anything but mollified by my statement. In fact, my words seemed to enrage her all the more.

"What did I say?" I prompted when she failed to respond.

A volley of shots garbled her response.

". . . hurt me," she finished.

"That's right." I reached for her arm. My blood stained the sleeve of her nightgown. "I won't let anyone hurt you."

For the first time in our association, her eyes cleared and she looked real, alive, and even more pissed. "Even you?"

I swallowed, hard. "Even me," I vowed, which seemed to satisfy her if her nod followed by a yawn was any indication. The gunfire abruptly ended. Gun smoke and dust floated in the air around us.

"Sir?" Karl called out. "Are you dead?"

"I don't think so."

"Oh. Good then," came his disheartened response. "In that case, maybe we should make a hasty escape before the villain can reload."

"Great idea." I glanced at my future wife. "But there's one small problem."

Karl bounded up the stairs as nimble as Jack, old college injury forgotten. "Are you hurt, sir?" Real fear entered his voice as he poked his head up from the stairwell. He looked around, a wrinkle forming between his bald brows. "Sir?"

I motioned to Sleeping Beauty, who lay on the floor, her hand curled under her head like a pillow. With the exception of our dire circumstances and the string of drool slipping from her mouth, she looked quite beautiful. A light sprinkle of freckles danced across her nose. "It seems that all this excitement has made my bride a wee bit sleepy."

Beauty let out a loud snore.

"Oh, I see." Karl climbed the rest of the way up the steps and helped me lift Beauty into my arms. Her eyelids fluttered, but she didn't wake. I carried her down the staircase, careful not to bang her head. The last thing Sleeping Beauty needed was further brain damage. She was weird enough as it was.

When we reach the bottom step, Karl offered to take Beauty from my arms. I shook my head. I'd promised to keep her safe, and I would honor that vow. I owed her that much. "Any sign of the shooter?" I asked Karl.

"No, sir." He peeked through the dingy window.

"You ready?" I nodded through the door to where our yellow ugly Princess was parked on the curb less than fifty feet away. It could've been a mile for all it mattered. Once we stepped outside the warehouse we'd be sitting rubber ducks.

Karl swallowed. "Not quite, sir."

"Buck up, Karl." I shot him an eye roll as I took a step toward the door, Beauty still asleep in my arms. "If I don't make it..." I paused, my face expressionless.

"Oh, please don't speak like that, sir." His voice broke. "You will live to carry on the La Grenouille name."

"But if I don't," I took a deep breath, "bury me in the Armani."

Karl gasped. "Not the Armani."

I nodded.

"But, sir." Fat tears welled in his eyes until they rolled down his equally plump cheeks. "It's Armani."

I lifted an eyebrow, and when he still didn't agree, the other followed.

He sighed. "Very well."

"Thanks." I grinned. "I knew I could count on you.

Now open the door, and let's get this over with." Karl did as I ordered. He opened the door, and we prepared for certain death.

I stepped outside.

Much to our surprise, nothing happened. Even Beauty appeared shocked by the events, if the way in which she lay sprawled across me was an indication. The tired princess blanketed me from head to toe, making walking to the ugly, yellow Princess nearly impossible. I shifted the burden in my arms as I ran the rest of the way to the vehicle.

I froze mid-run, realizing three things.

The ugly Princess was gone.

So was my two hundred thousand dollars in unmarked bills.

And let's not forget, Ms. Lying Lollie Bliss.

"Bitch!"

Sleeping Beauty awoke momentarily, just long enough to smack me in the nose again before the sandman carried her away.

Chapter 47

"What do you think of this?" Sleeping Beauty, dressed in a new flannel gown, held up a bouquet of plastic flowers. They looked like tiny petrified roses with fluorescent green stems. I hated them on sight, almost as much as I hated the thought of marrying the woman standing next to me. Four days had passed since the incident at the warehouse. Four days of spending every waking hour with my future bride. Four days of pure hell.

"They're nice," I said with a shrug.

Her smile froze. "Nice? Is that all you have to say? Nice?"

"Yeah. Nice." Was Beauty tired, bitchy, and a little deaf too? I straightened off the gold-plated recliner where I'd spent the last hour relaxing in the king's library, drinking his private stock, listening to my annoying bride go on and on about wedding this and reception that while a minister in black ordered us around like servants. Less than twenty-four hours separated me from wedded bliss or frog legs. After the last couple of days, I wasn't too sure which I preferred.

The only time Sleeping Beauty stopped squawking was when she suddenly and inexplicably fell asleep, often mid-sentence, and while standing.

Oh, how I longed for those times.

I pictured the next forty years with my chattering bride. Frog legs looked better and better with every passing second. The king sat on the chair next to me, his gaze as glazed with boredom as mine.

Pretty seemed to be the only one in the room enjoying the pre-wedding festivities, which sent a shiver of suspicion up my spine. Pretty beamed at Beauty. "You will make such a beautiful bride."

"I know," Beauty said, fluffing her blond hair. "Too bad I can't say the same for my groom. I mean, is a haircut and a shave too much to ask? Does he have to look so . . . so . . . ," she paused, "French?"

I rolled my eyes. For the last four days, I'd tried to see past the flannel and whiny voice to the woman underneath. The woman who'd kissed a frog and broken my curse. The woman who was fated to be my One.

While Beauty was rather beautiful, she couldn't hold a candlestick to Lollie. At the very thought of her name, something, rage most likely, filled me, churning hot and deep in my gut. I tasted her on my lips, pictured her tattooed skin, pictured her running away with my two hundred thousand dollars in cash.

"Now, after you recite your vows," the minister paused in his pre-wedding rehearsal speech, "we'll move on to the ring ceremony. You do have the rings, right?"

I nodded, rubbing the huge five-carat black diamond ring in my pocket. The same ring the jeweler had couriered to my hotel yesterday afternoon. A ring I didn't remember buying, though the jeweler insisted I'd called him in the middle of the night, blackout drunk, and forced him to come to the Rose to pick up a golden ball I wanted made into the diamond ring.

Whatever had happened that night, the ring was still beautiful, one of a kind actually, or so the jeweler promised. Not that I trusted the guy. After all, he also tried to sell me a bag of magic beans and a Rolex.

Beauty's sigh brought me back to the annoying conversation at hand. "I want everything to be perfect. I've waited so very long to find..." Sleeping Beauty's eyes met mine as she sneered, "you."

God help me.

The minister rolled his beady eyes. "Good for you. Now, son," he addressed me. "Will your mother be joining the precession?"

"No," Sleeping Beauty and I declared at the same moment. My eyes narrowed on my bride's face. "Excuse me, mademoiselle. How did you know that my mother would not be attending our nuptials?"

"Oh." She blinked. "I thought we were talking about my mother. She can't make it. She's dead." Without pausing for breath, Beauty asked, "Have you seen the wedding cake? It's the loveliest shade of jade." Her eyes bored into mine. "I know how you enjoy the color green." With that statement hanging in the air, Beauty spun on her heel and abruptly exited the room, leaving the four of us, including the stern minister, staring after her.

My p-Phone rang a few seconds after she'd left. I checked the caller ID. Karl. "I have to take this," I said, slipping from the library and out the back door to the oddly overgrown garden. My eyes scanned the plant life for any prying ears. Finding none, I answered on the fourth ring. "Did you find her?"

"I'm sorry, sir," he said. "I've called everyone I can think of. There is no sign of Ms. Bliss."

"And her cell phone?" I swallowed, hating the emotion that leaked into my voice. "Did you try tracking it?" I remembered the flash of rage in Lollie's eyes when she'd learned about my tracking Sleeping Beauty's cell signal and grinned. What would she do if she learned I was doing the same to find her? I doubt I'd like the answer.

"Yes, sir."

"And?"

"And it's off." His tone suggested more than Lollie's phone was off. "No signal. No sign of the yellow Princess either. The rental company is going to charge us a fortune in fees. I knew I should've taken the theft insurance."

"Forget the insurance. I'll buy a fleet of those damn cars." I glanced to the greenish water of the pond. "Just find Lollie. I don't care what it takes. I need to . . . get the ransom money back."

"Is that all, sir?"

"Yes." Something caught my eye, and I peered harder into the overgrown foliage just past the pond. There, hidden in the thick greenery, were rows of tiny wooden crosses, twenty-nine in all. On the very end, in front of the final cross, was a fresh mound of dirt and an empty hole. I glanced from the hole up to Beauty's bedroom window two stories above. In the reflection of the glass I saw my future, as well as my future bride. She shot me a wicked, knowing smile and then disappeared from view. A shiver ran up my spine.

Shaking off the feeling of impending dread, Karl's next words caught my attention. "Very well," he said, pausing as if weighing his words. "I do have a lead on Spindle, sir." His voice grew soft. "But you have to promise me something."

"What?"

"You won't do anything stupid."

I grinned into the receiver. "Stupid? Give me some credit. I'm not nineteen anymore. I've matured. Hell, I will be a married man by this time tomorrow." Or not, I thought as I read the name on the twenty-ninth tiny cross. The one that said: "La Grenouille."

"Uh-huh." He heaved a long-suffering sigh. "Call me when you need bail."

Chapter 48

An hour later, I found myself on the front porch of a fairly nice cookie-cutter house in a pleasant neighborhood on a much-too-quiet street on the outskirts of Cin City. I checked the address Karl had supplied for the third time. Yep, 1067 Three Bears Lane.

This was it.

Spindle's not-so-evil lair.

A group of kids played red rover in the yard next door. I bit my lip, considering the suburban nightmare surrounding me. Karl had to be wrong. There was no way Spindle lived here. Not with its perfectly manicured lawn and yellow welcome mat on the front step.

Yet a tiny part of me longed for its peaceful landscape. This was the sort of place where nothing bad ever happened. A place a frog prince could be happy. A place a frog prince would never be alone again.

What the frog was wrong with me?

My impending nuptials had messed with my head. I wasn't the wife and two-point-five kids kind of prince. I didn't buy my clothes at King*Mart, nor get my hair cut at a strip mall. My shoes were Prada not pleather. I didn't want to spend the next forty years, let alone forty days, waking next to the same woman.

Variety was the spice of a frog prince life.

Lollie Bliss was awfully spicy, the little voice in the demented part of my brain whispered. Not true, I fired back. Lollie was a thief and a liar. She'd used me. I was here for the ransom money. That was all.

Liar, liar, pants on fire.

I checked my nose to make sure it hadn't reached telephone-wire proportions. It hadn't. My knuckles hovered above the door, poised for knocking.

"What are you doing, Johnny?" Elly grabbed my hand and twirled me around to face her. "You're supposed to be getting ready for your bachelor party tonight and then your wedding tomorrow."

I closed my eyes, dreading the thought of yet another dimly lit strip club, filled with dim, naked, barely legal women. I wasn't sure which I feared more, the bachelor party or the wedding itself. "Elly, I don't know if I can—"

Whack! Her wand slammed into my right ear with enough force to rattle my teeth. She raised her wand again. I held up my hands to protect my handsome face. "Don't even think about it," she screeched. "You will marry Princess Beauty tomorrow. I won't let you ruin everything for a thieving tattooed slut."

"Lollie has nothing to do with this," I lied. "Don't you want me to have a happily-ever-after?"

"Will you be happy with frog legs, Johnny? Because that's what will happen if you don't marry Princess Beauty."

My stomach bubbled at the thought of eating grilled flies for the rest of my days. "You're my fairy godmother, for frog sakes. Can't you fix this?"

Elly's face fell and tears welled in her eyes. "Oh, Johnny, I'm so sorry. I'm a terrible fairy godmother. You deserve so much better." She sniffed, her wand falling to the porch as her head dropped into her hands. "God knows I did my best . . ."

Filled with guilt, I awkwardly patted Elly's large shoulders. After all, when I was growing up, Elly had tried to make up for my father's indifference and my mother's insanity, in her own drunken, dysfunctional way. "Hush. You are a wonderful fairy godmother. I don't know what I would've done without you for all these years."

Her wet, mascara-streaked face looked up, lips trembling. "Really? Do you mean it, Johnny?"

"Of course," I lied. "You're right. I was being selfish. I'll marry Beauty."

She sniffed once and gave me a watery smile. "That's a good boy." She tapped my arm, and then poof, in a cloud of gin fumes, she vanished, leaving me standing alone on Spindle's porch.

I looked down at my hand, ready to knock on the door, and groaned. Elly was right. Wedding Beauty was my only chance for a real happily-ever-after, even if it was with a demented bride. I turned to leave.

The front door of Spindle's abode creaked open. I spun around, prepared for an attack. But the doorway stood empty. "Hello?" I called, taking a small step forward. "Is anyone home?" A dog barked in the distance. I glanced around, debating. I could stand on the front porch all day, staring at the open doorway, or I could step inside.

A no-brainer. I pushed the door open all the way and entered. I took a few seconds to get a feel for the place. Homey. Warm wooden handcrafted furniture filled the otherwise empty living room. A coatrack stood next to the door, a worn, leather gun holster hung on a wooden peg. I guess I'd found the right place.

I strolled casually toward the back of the house, pausing to listen for signs of life. Nothing. No dripping faucet. No half-eaten pizza boxes. Nothing to indicate anyone really lived there, other than the faint stench of Old Spice and gunpowder.

Once inside the kitchen, I scanned the room. A wooden

table with three chairs sat below a large bay window. Each seat looked brand new, as did the other appliances all neatly lined up like toy soldiers.

I moved from the kitchen to the sunken family area. A dining room table sat in the corner of the room across from a black leather couch and a wide-screen TV. Here, the scent of fresh-baked cookies tickled my nostrils.

A sense of wrongness filled me. Could this really be Spindle's house? The man was an assassin for frog sakes. A man capable of killing without thought. A man meant to be feared. At the moment I couldn't even muster up a whiff of anxiety, let alone actual terror. The most I felt was hungry.

I gazed around the room, taking in an array of paintings in bold colors and style. They practically screamed Lollie, and yet, upon closer inspection, the signature on the bottom wasn't hers; rather, the painting was signed with a large "S." Lollie had learned more than how to tattoo drunken princes at Spindle's hand. Jealousy burned in my gut.

No matter what I said or did, Spindle's connection to Lollie could never be broken. Unless . . . my eyes fell upon a fireplace poker, sans fireplace—we were in the desert, after all—and for the first time in my life I contemplated outright murder. One quick smack to the noggin and Lollie would be mine, as long as she never found out I'd bashed her lover's head in and she was willing to engage in an abomination or two.

I winced. Women tended to detest murder almost as much as they disliked living in a swamp.

Go figure.

Not that I cared one way or another about Lollie's reaction. She meant nothing to me. Yeah, we'd had our fun, but all that changed the minute she'd stolen my ugly yellow car along with a stack of cash, all for her stupid boyfriend.

Sadly, the missing money didn't bother me. Not nearly as much as the fact that she'd up and left without even a good-bye. For a frog prince with abandonment issues, her callous betrayal angered me all the more. I wasn't the kind of prince women walked away from. I was the kind that walked away, after an acceptable number of orgasms. I hated Lollie for leaving almost as much as I hated myself for caring.

With a sigh, I ventured through the rest of the house, finding nothing of interest. No smoking guns. No hit lists. No suitcase full of ransom money. At best Spindle was a fanatic housekeeper, a trait that did little to endear him to my heart. On top of that, bits of Lollie were everywhere. Her brand of shampoo sat on the side of the tub next to a razor. A bottle of henna ink stood next to the sink. I picked it up, inhaling the scent. Lollie's scent.

Dropping the bottle, I moved to the bedroom. A suitcase sat open on the bed. Brand-new tank tops and lace panties lay folded inside, bearing price tags, all in Lollie's size. New clothes bought with my cash, I assumed. Silk sheets marred with smudges of black lay across the queen-sized bed. A sketchbook filled with tattoo designs and other drawings lay on the nightstand.

I sat down on the bed Lollie likely shared with Spindle and picked up the sketchbook. Flipping through the pages, I grinned at a caricature of Karl, his overly bald head filling the entire page. Two pages later, a young tattooed woman with kinky black curls lay on a mound of pillows, a wicked smile on her lips. A smile that appeared so familiar it hurt to look at. I quickly turned the page, to an image that shocked me to my soon-to-be-webbed toes.

It was a drawing of a frog sitting on a lone lily pad, his eyes filled with longing and arrogance. A frog who'd seen it all, and yet, wanted something more. Something deep. Something real. Was this what Lollie saw when she looked at me? The thought brought wetness to my eyes. Manly wetness. I quickly blinked it away and closed the sketch-book.

Brushing off my trousers, I stood, surveying the rest of the bedroom. I smiled at the red curtains, so much like the ones I'd promised to buy Lollie only a couple of days ago. It looked like Spindle and I shared more than the same taste in tattooed ladies.

The sun had just started to set, spraying shadows along the bedroom walls. I glanced at my watch. Eight o'clock. I'd been inside Spindle's house for over an hour, and yet, it felt as if time had stopped. But it hadn't.

Much too soon, I'd vow to honor and cherish a woman I hardly knew, a woman who hardly knew me, and for what? To appease a curse born before either of us? For the first time since Sleeping Beauty had kissed (nearly eaten) me, I seriously considered saying "Frog it!" and walking away from everything. What's the worst that could happen? I turned back into a frog? Big deal. At least my life would be my own.

The creak of the front door acted much like a cold shower, snapping me from my fantasy and back into reality. I carefully crept to the stairs. Boot heels clicked on the hardwood floor below me, a familiar click. Lollie's click. Rage and lust filled my chest, a feeling I'd often experienced around Ms. Bliss.

No sign of Spindle, though. Was he lying in wait somewhere downstairs? Or perhaps he was preparing to woo Lollie with roses?

Only one way to find out.

With a deep breath, I climbed down the stairs and into the assassin's den, literally, since the staircase led straight into Spindle's den, not to mention a pissed-off chick with a gun.

Chapter 49

"Jesus, Kermit!" Lollie dropped the tattoo gun she was cleaning as her hand flew to her chest. "You scared me to death. What are you doing creeping around here?"

My eyes slowly scanned her body from head to toe, noting the slight bloom of color on her cheeks. Was it a flash of guilt? Or something a little more interesting? Desire, perhaps?

"Where's Spindle?" I asked, taking a step closer to her. Her scent filled the air between us, ink and Lollie. I swallowed back a wave of longing. Longing for what I couldn't say, but it was there, in the pit of my stomach. So when I repeated the question, my tone dripped with ice. "Where's your boyfriend, Lollipop? He and I need to have a little talk." I cracked my knuckles in anticipation. Spindle would feel my wrath. That was a promise.

She wet her lips, the tip of her pink tongue jutting out enough to twist my rage into lust and then back again. I wouldn't be played again. "Why are you here, Kermit?" she asked with a sneer. "Shouldn't you be with your fiancée, to stay at her side day and night until you say 'I do'? That's what a good frog prince would do."

"Where I should be and where I am are very different things." I crossed my arms over my chest. "I came to get what's mine."

Her eyes flashed. "And what's that?" I stepped even closer, like a fairy to a flame. Our bodies stood mere inches apart. Her minty breath tickled the stubble on my chin. "What do you want from me, Kermit?" Her hand brushed my chest, lightly, slowly. Pink lips parted, welcoming.

The blood in my head drained in a rush, filling other, more vital organs. My fingers gripped her chin, pulling her mouth toward mine. "I want..."

"Yes?" She exhaled.

"I want," I said, our lips a centimeter apart. "I want my money back." I shoved her away. She stumbled, her knees hit the table, and she fell back. I grabbed her before she landed on the hardwood. Her fingers locked on mine for a second, and then she let go and dropped to the floor. She lay there, glaring up at me. Had she not used and then robbed me, I might've felt a wee bit guilty.

She slowly rose to her feet, shaking off my outstretched hand. Brushing at her leather pants, she shot me a bitter smile. "I'm sorry to disappoint you. But I don't have your ransom money. So I guess that means that you'll be on your way, unless you came here for something else?" She looked up at me, her dark eyes glowing almost blue-black with violence.

When I didn't comment, she nodded once. "That's it, then." She pulled the door open and motioned for me to leave. "Good-bye, Kermit."

"Not so fast." I help up a hand. "What do you mean you don't have the ransom money? Last I remember you snatched it from me and vowed to protect it with your life. So tell me, Lollipop, just what happened after you and your boyfriend tried to kill me?"

Her screech of outrage nearly knocked me back a step. At the very least my ears would ring for the next week. "I had nothing to do with that."

"Uh-huh." I scratched my chin like I'd seen many a TV

prosecutor do. "So who did? Because I wasn't shooting at myself."

"Not that you'll believe me." She paused, her eyes shifting around the room. Was she waiting for Spindle? Was this yet another setup designed by the one woman I couldn't stop thinking about? "When I heard the first shots, I stuffed the money under the seat and ran to help."

"How sweet of you."

Her hands flexed into fists. "Why do I bother? You obviously can't see the truth. So, fine, I did it, Kermit. I'm a terrible person. I deserve your scorn, your hate. It's easier that way, isn't it? Leave before you get hurt." Her voice cracked. "Simply walk away and never look back. It's what you're good at."

What did she know? I wasn't some wimp who cried over his spilled milk. No, I got a mop and cleaned up my own mess, which was exactly what I was doing now. Lollie Bliss was a tattooed mess in need of wiping away. That was all.

Frustration, unfairness, and anger of the last year clogged the back of my throat. I took a couple of steps through the door, pausing on the welcome mat outside. "Have a nice life," I sneered. "I'm sure you and your lover will be miserable together for years to come."

Lollie chuckled and started to close the door. "Probably. But I promise you that it won't be nearly as bad as you and your precious bride." Yet before the door closed completely, her words floated from the crack. "I'll see to it."

I made it as far as the sidewalk before her words churning in my ears sent me back to the front door. Was she threatening Beauty? My vision grew red. I pounded on the wood until it nearly rattled off its hinges. "Open the door, Lollie. Now!"

I pounded harder. No one bullied me, especially not some slip of a woman covered in ink. Her boyfriend wasn't around to protect her now. The chain lock rattled as she pulled the door open a crack. "Forget something?" she asked with a smirk.

At the sight of her heart-shaped face, my rage vanished, replaced once again with longing and desire. I could deny it till Bo Peep's wayward sheep came home, but the truth was, I wanted Lollie. Needed her. If only for one more night. Then I could walk away, marry Sleeping Beauty, and live out the rest of my days unconcerned over unwanted green and moldy bits.

At least that's what I told myself, over and over again until that cold place in my heart started to believe it. I leaned against the door frame, my face an inch from hers. "Are you going to let me in?"

She tilted her head to one side, showing off the slope of her neck and a small rose tattooed at the base of it. Either she'd got a new tattoo or I'd missed it during last night's intimate inspection. In my defense, her neck wasn't my primary focus during that excursion. Hell, anything above chest height, with the exception of her hot mouth, was neglected in my tender assault.

"If I let you . . . in . . . for a nice chat," she said with a smile, "just this once, you'll have to be on your best behavior."

"Oh, I promise." I held up a hand. "Frog prince honor."

Like I had any when it came to Ms. Bliss.

The door floated open, leaving Lollie and me standing inches from each other. The heat from our desire fogged the front windows. She opened her arms, and I fell into her, my mouth hot and hard against hers.

Tomorrow vanished under the feel of her fingers kneading the muscles of my arms. I had regrets, those that often kept me awake at night, but being with Lollie would never be one of them. In her arms, the rest of the world fell away, leaving just the two of us. Together. Until tomorrow night, that was, when I'd either marry Beauty or return to a strict fly diet.

Chapter 50

Later that night, I grinned as Lollie let out a soft snore and then snuggled closer to me, her perfectly formed backside molding to me. Twisting a long black lock of hair around my finger, I stroked the side of her cheek. My finger dipped lower, brushing the soft inky outlines of exotic characters that ran down her spine.

"Hi," Lollie whispered when my fingers reached a particularly interesting part of her anatomy. Her hand reached for mine, stilling my roving appendage. "We need to talk, Kermit. I need to tell—"

"Later," I said against the softness of her stomach. *Much later,* I thought, unable to articulate anything, let alone the lies Lollie needed to hear.

I awoke an hour later, alone. A sketchpad lay open on the pillow next to me. The harsh planes of my face stared back at me from the open page of the paper canvas. I stared into my own eyes, not liking what stared back. Lollie seemed to see right through me. Self-reflection was not the way I planned on spending my last day as a single man. Yet my plans did include plenty of self-satisfaction, and maybe even a little satisfaction for Ms. Bliss.

I pushed the sketchpad away and slowly rose, listening for any sign of Lollie. The shower down the hallway turned off with a squeak. I pictured a sudsy Lollie, tattoos glistening with water. My mouth went dry at the image. Footsteps sounded in the hallway. Lust swelled inside me. I wanted her, even after hours spent in her arms, exploring every curve and inky line of her body. The longer I touched her tattoos, the blurrier the inky lines became until I lost all control. The bedroom door started to open as I pulled back the silk sheet to show Lollie just how glad I was to see her.

"Ah!" Handsome screeched. His formerly handsome face crinkled with disgust as his hand hovered dangerously over the gun strapped to his hip. "What are you doing in my house? In my bed?"

Yanking the sheet back in place, I struggled to find my voice. His house? What the frog? A sudden and horrifying thought occurred to me. "You're Spindle!" I jabbed my finger at him. "You bastard." Launching myself from the bed, bare-assed naked, I charged Handsome, grabbing the gun on his belt and tossing it to the floor. "Hey," he began, but I cut him off with a shove, sickened by the thought of Lollie and Handsome together. I wanted to kill him. And then kill him again. Perhaps kill him a third time for good measure. What had Lollie seen in Handsome? He was an arrogant, self-absorbed prince. Sure, one could argue I shared the same traits, but I wasn't also obsessed with my stepsister. So there.

Spindle aka Soon-to-be-not-so-Handsome jumped back, raising his arms to protect his pretty face from my fist. "What are you doing? I don't even know this Spindle person."

My hand grabbed his lapel and twisted, effectively choking him with his Armani silk uniform shirt. I shook him, hard. Like a puppet on a string, his legs dangled back and forth. The terror in his eyes cooled my rage, but only a little. I pictured Lollie trapped inside the burning cinders of her tattoo shop and twisted harder. "Don't lie to me. Karl tracked Spindle here. To this house." My voice grew colder. "Your house."

"I don't know what you're talking about." Handsome's arms flapped like a hummingbird. "No one has a key but me." He paused, his eyes widening as I squeezed a wee bit harder. "And Beauty. Beauty has a key," he squeaked.

Beauty? What the frog? What connection did Lollie have to Handsome or Beauty? And just where was Spindle in all this? Frustration and confusion boiled inside me, so much so that I tossed Handsome across the room. He bounced once on the bed and then over the bed, landing in a heap of less-than-handsome prince parts. Lollie's sketchbook, which was sitting on the bed, crashed to the floor as well. Handsome moaned. I came around the bed, still naked as the day Beauty had tried to eat me.

"Ow, my head," Handsome whined, but I wasn't paying any attention to him. My focus was on the open sketchbook and the sketch half-finished on the page, a picture of a frog in the hands of a kinky-haired girl with violet eyes.

The little girl smiled with womanly knowledge.

My stomach clenched. Could it truly be? I snatched the sketchpad from the floor, staring at the drawing in front of me. A picture I should've seen days ago. "Damn you," I whispered, seeing the truth for the very first time.

Similar features.

The same crooked grin.

Lollie's smile on Beauty's face.

Chapter 51

Throwing on a pair of trousers, I grabbed the damning sketchbook and silently made my way down the staircase, broken pile of Handsome all but forgotten upstairs.

The scent of strawberry shampoo and ink floated up the stairwell. I hated the smell. Hated the way Lollie's laughter sent a rush of pleasure through me. Hated the fact that even though she'd betrayed me again and again, I still wanted her.

Taking a deep breath, I pushed open the kitchen door. "Hello, Lollipop." I licked my dry lips, lips that only an hour ago had kissed her treacherous mouth. "Or should I call you Spindle?"

Lollie spun around, dropping the wineglass in her hand. It crashed to the floor, shattering on impact. Dark liquid pooled around us, filling the physical void between us. Wincing, Lollie raised her eyes from the mess on the floor to the mess she'd created of me. "What are you talking about?"

"No more leapfrog, Lollie. I'm done playing games with you." Everything we'd had was a lie. From the moment we'd met, she'd played me, and I'd chased after her like the dish after the spoon. Well, I was done being her frog prince on a string.

"Kermit, wait." Lollie grabbed my arm. I shook her off,

too angry to listen to another lie fall from her succulent lips. Been there, done that, quite a bit actually. My stomach gurgled with rage and hunger. I hadn't eaten since the rehearsal dinner, and even then I found it hard to choke down something called Frog Eye Salad. An aphrodisiac, the king assured me with a wink.

"Wait for what?" I grunted. "You to think up yet another lie? No thanks." I shoved the sketchpad at her. The pages fluttered as if they too wanted to hide from the truth. "Tell me I'm wrong. Tell me Sleeping Beauty's not your sister."

"Sister?" Her brow wrinkled. "Give me a minute and I can explain."

My eyes narrowed on the sketchpad and the sketch of Sleeping Beauty. I should've seen the resemblance days ago. Sisters. Hell, maybe even twins. Perhaps I hadn't wanted to see the truth. "Explain?" I snickered, a bitter, harsh sound. "What's there to explain? Explain why you've been lying to me since the day we met? I'm pretty sure I already know the answer."

"Kermit—"

"Beauty didn't want to marry me." I swallowed, hating the hurt and need in my tone. I didn't want to care. Not about her or her demented sister. Not now. "But the king insisted, so Beauty went running to you, her sister. And you promised to take care of everything."

"It's true," her eyes gave me a slow once-over, "Beauty didn't want to marry you. Not at first."

"So you did everything in your power to get rid of me, even going so far as to make up an assassin. How sisterly of you," I said, rage licking at my every word. I pictured the sisters huddled together while they plotted to ruin my life.

"Hold on a second. Spindle was your idea." Her lip curled into a snarl. "Not mine."

"What are you talking about?"

"The day after we met, you came into my shop and accused me of protecting my assassin lover." She laughed, not a pretty sound. "You even gave him a name. No matter how many times I told you differently, you persisted in your delusion. So, after a while, I agreed. Why not?" She pulled from my grip and slowly sat down on the kitchen chair. "Besides, none of this was supposed to happen."

"Isn't that nice."

Her eyes flashed, and she abruptly stood, jamming her index finger into my sternum. "Why couldn't you be a shallow, self-absorbed jerk and walk away? Things would be much easier."

"Whoa," I said, grabbing her hand before she could do any lasting damage. "For your information, I am very shallow and self-absorbed."

She shoved me away. "But you didn't leave." The fight suddenly left her, and Lollie again sank into her kitchen chair. "At first I thought, maybe you weren't the one. . . ."

My eyes narrowed. "The one? What one?" Was I missing something? Was Lollie cursed too? Was that what drew me to her? Like calling to like and all that?

"It doesn't matter." She reached for my hand, but I stepped away. "I was wrong. I'm sorry. I never wanted you to get hurt."

I snorted. "No, that was all Beauty's idea, wasn't it?"

Lollie's brow wrinkled. "What are you talking about?"

"Oh, let's start with," I stuck my index finger in the air, "trying to run me down. Twice. Not to mention blowing the Rose sky high."

"That wasn't Beauty."

"Then who was it, Lollipop?" My eyes narrowed. "You? The imaginary assassin Spindle?" I took a step closer to her. "Come on, face it. Your sister is a killer."

"You're wrong, Kermit." She took a deep breath. "Not that it matters one way or another. What's to be is meant to be. We can't stop fate." Lollie slowly rose from her chair like an old man who'd just rolled home after a long night of giving a bone. She walked to the bay window. In the shiny surface of the glass, her dark gaze met mine.

"Bullshit."

"No, it's true." Her voice quivered with emotion. "Tomorrow you will marry the girl from the pond, the only one who can save you. Beauty."

"And you, Lollipop?" I reached out to comfort her, but my hand dropped before it touched her shoulder. "What happens to you? Do you live happily ever after?"

"Perhaps," she said, a small tremor entering her voice.

"So what?" Anger and fear swelled inside me, boiling over into my words. "We see each other at family dinners, and I'm supposed to smile politely and forget the things you allowed me to do to your body?"

She swallowed, hard.

"And what about Beauty?" I closed my eyes, picturing the woman I was to marry in a few hours. "Does she know that her beloved sister's been frogging her fiancé mindless for the last couple of days?"

"Kermit, you can't tell anyone about me. About us." She grabbed my arm, her nails digging into my skin. "Please, promise me you won't say a word. The danger is too great."

I hesitated; a rush of loneliness so deep it stole my breath filled me. Lollie smiled softly, as if she shared my pain. "Promise me."

I gave her a curt nod.

Licking her lips, Lollie nodded to the cat-faced clock on the wall. "It's almost time."

I nodded again.

"Good-bye, Kermit." Lollie brushed her lips against my mouth and quickly backed away. "I hope you find happily-ever-after. I really do." With one last shaky smile, she spun on her heel and ran up the stairs as the grandfather clock in the living room gonged midnight.

Chapter 52

Almost twenty-two hours later, back at the Vaniteuse palace, yet another grandfather clock gave a mournful bong, but I might've been projecting. Yeah, I was definitely projecting. My mind, heart, and body felt raw after leaving Lollie's; exhaustion plagued my every step. "You've tripled the guards, right?" I asked Marvin for the third time in the last hour.

"Yes, sir." He nodded toward Beauty's bedroom at the end of the hallway. "There are three guards at her door, two below the window and another two in the passageway. Princess Beauty is safe as snow." And even more importantly, she wouldn't be pulling another runaway bride anytime soon. I'd wasted enough time and energy on the Vaniteuse sisters. It was time to marry Beauty and settle into my "happily-ever-after." Lollie be damned.

"Add two more guards at the front door," I ordered, my eyes drifting to the room next to Beauty's. The one with the fancy sewing machine. Was that Lollie's old room, long forgotten like the black sheep sister? My dislike of the king increased tenfold.

"As you wish, sir," Marvin said as he opened the door to another bedroom a few doors down from Beauty's. "If you'll come with me." He motioned inside the ornate room. "Your tuxedo is in the closet, and per your request, the king's finest scotch is on the nightstand. Can I get you anything else?"

A plane ticket to Never Never Island? One last taste of Lollie's lips? "No, I'm good," I told Marvin. "Thanks anyway."

But a part of me, a larger part than I cared to admit, couldn't stop thinking about Lollie Bliss. Everywhere I looked, every memory, reminded me of her. Hell, I couldn't even look at the most recent painting of the Vaniteuse family sans their black sheep tattooed relative hanging on the wall in front of me without seeing the ghost of Lollie reflected in Sleeping Beauty's lollipop-colored eyes like some damn omen. I sat on the bed, staring at the painting until my vision blurred.

The bedroom door swung open suddenly. In the archway stood a man dressed in black, his bearing regal and a bit pudgy. His face beamed with self-satisfaction. Like a king who ate the canary, or in his case, would marry off his demented canary in just over an hour.

I should've locked the damn door.

"King Vaniteuse," I said, turning to the mirror on the wall to adjust the sleeve of my wedding tux. The green cummerbund, courtesy of my bride, brought a grim grin to my lips. "To what do I owe the pleasure?"

Without a word, the king closed the door behind him and moved across the room. Our eyes locked in the reflection of the mirror. "Second thoughts, son?" he asked.

I dropped my gaze and reached for the scotch bottle on the bedside table. Pouring a healthy amount, I downed the drink. My fourth in the last twenty minutes. "Of course not," I said over the rim of the glass. "Why do you ask?" Did I look like a groom with frozen feet? Good thing I'd packed—or rather Karl had packed—wool socks made in Scotland from terrified sheep.

"No reason." The king shifted uncomfortably on what were likely three-thousand-dollar shoes. "No reason at all. It's just . . ."

"What?"

"No exchanges. No refunds, son. You break it, you buy it."

"What?"

The king cleared his throat. "That came out wrong. I . . . like my stepdaughter. Hell, I . . . care about all my children." *Even Lollie?* I wanted to ask, but stayed silent. She'd begged me to keep our relationship a secret, and I'd agreed like a smitten fool, when what I really wanted to do was smash the king in the face for all the pain he'd caused. What kind of man forced a sixteen-year-old girl to live on the streets? Or forced his demented stepdaughter to marry the first idiot prince who lived long enough to say "I do"? I swallowed my rage and tried to focus on what the king was saying.

"Beauty, like her mother, God rest her soul . . . well . . . she has flaws, son . . . But I only want what's best for her." His eyes flickered over my silk shirt and tie with disgust, as if I was wearing knockoff Armani. "And maybe that's not you."

"Why do you say that?" Days ago, the king begged me to marry Beauty, and now he looked at me like Rapunzel after a lice outbreak. I wondered at his sudden change of heart. Unless he'd learned about my father's recent visit. . . . "I'm not broke," I said. "Far from it, in fact."

"Oh." A few seconds later, his face split into a wide grin. "In that case, welcome to the family!" He spread his arms and pulled me into an awkward, one-sided hug.

"Thanks for your compassion in my hour of need." I pulled away, nearly stumbling over my loafer. "If you'll excuse me, I have a wedding to prepare for."

He nodded. "Of course, son. Good luck to you."

Right now I needed only one thing, and it wasn't luck.

Lollie's ink-covered body and bent smile flashed through my mind, but I shook the image away and poured another drink.

Once the king left and I was alone again, I stared into the mirror as I twisted the silk fabric in my hands into a perfect Windsor knot. "The rabbit goes around the loop, and in his hole . . . and viola," I sang. T-minus thirty minutes until the wedding march chimed. I swallowed, hard, trying to calm the rapid beat of my heart. Had I lost my mind? I was about to marry a woman who didn't want to marry me and in fact had tried, repeatedly, to kill me. Not to mention, a woman whose sister I'd recently played with naked, all around her mulberry bush.

The bedroom door flew open again. This time Pretty, looking fetching in a pink satin gown, stood in the entryway. What was wrong with these people? Didn't anyone knock anymore? "I see that you and your father are very alike in manners," I said, a thin smile plastered on my lips.

Rather than comment on her rudeness, her eyes slid over me in an appraisal illegal in thirty-three kingdoms. "Don't you look handsome," she purred.

God, I hoped not. I motioned inside the room. "Make yourself comfortable. I'll just be a minute." I ducked into the bathroom to throw up, which I followed up with half a bottle of mouthwash, fairymint flavor. Stomach empty, teeth brushed to a pearly white, I stared into the bathroom mirror. My face looked a ghastly color green, at odds with the frog green of my tie. It was happening. I was slowly turning back into a frog. By midnight the transformation would be complete unless I married a chick who didn't want to marry me.

Frog!

With a sigh, followed by a minty hiccup, I stumbled back to the bedroom. I stopped, rubbed my eyes, and then quickly turned and ran back to the bathroom, slamming the door behind me. I considered the sight I'd just witnessed. Pretty was beyond beautiful, as well as stacked, not to mention buck-naked and sprawled on the bed like a *Fairyboy* model. The thought *Pretty and her other half sister Lollie share some very similar attributes* flashed through my pickled brain.

"Bad idea. Bad idea. Bad idea," I said, mostly as a reminder to my penis of our upcoming nuptials, not to mention the very real possibility Lollie would neuter me. Once the retina-burning vision of Pretty naked against satin sheets faded from my brain, I once again opened the door, keeping my eyes tightly closed. "So . . . ," I said, quite the frog prince with the ladies.

"Why don't you come sit down?" The whack of hand against bed resonated through the room. "I promise I won't bite. Unless you like that sort of thing."

Eyes still tightly closed, I swallowed back waves of intoxicated lust. "As nice an offer as that is, I can't."

"It's Beauty, isn't it?" Pretty's voice rose, no longer sultry, but much more dangerous. "It's always Beauty, Beauty, Beauty. What does she have that I don't?"

"Sanity" popped to mind, but I quickly discarded the notion. Nobody in the Vaniteuse family appeared quite stable.

"Well, it was . . . great to see you. . . ." I trailed a hand along the wall, guiding me to the doorway. With a flick of the wrist, I popped the door wide and gestured for her to leave. "Thanks for dropping by. See you, fully dressed, at the wedding," I added for good measure.

A gasp from the hallway grabbed my attention. My eyes shot open. In the doorway, Sleeping Beauty stood, her violet eyes filled with violence.

"It's not—" I began.

Her fist caught me upside the head, sending me flying back against the plaster wall. The drywall crumbled under the assault, leaving a prince-shaped hole. I waved away a cloud of plaster dust obscuring my vision in time to see Beauty running down the hallway to her bedroom, her white gown swirling around her ankles. She paused at her bedroom door, shot me a cold glare, and then slammed the bedroom door with enough force that my teeth rattled.

Pretty's laughter followed.

I closed my eyes again and sank to the floor.

Chapter 53

My naked brush with Pretty sobered me up considerably. Good thing too, since I now had less than twenty minutes until the wedding procession began, *if* the wedding procession began. The look of hurt in Sleeping Beauty's eyes would haunt me for a lifetime. The pain in her gaze went beyond the typical betrayal.

She looked . . . devastated.

Frog! I staggered to my feet, thankful Pretty had dressed and vacated the room minutes ago. Her nakedness was a distraction I didn't need. Not right now. Hell, not ever. In fact, out of all three Vaniteuse sisters, Pretty terrified me the most. Probably had something to do with the blatant greed in her cold, green eyes.

Callous eyes unlike the passionate inferno burning in Beauty's gaze only minutes ago. I grabbed the Windsor knot around my neck and yanked the forest green tie off. How could I not have seen it earlier? Sleeping Beauty was in love with me. It was so obvious. She'd tried to fight it, and even enlisted Lollie's help to end our engagement, but in the end, like all the others before her, she'd succumbed.

And really, who could blame her?

Guilt pooled in my intestines.

Beauty probably thought that I loved her back too. She

wasn't the first woman to fall under the frog prince spell. Why did I have to be so damn charming?

Not to mention handsome beyond compare.

And rich, even without my father's money.

A sudden thought occurred to me. How jealous was Beauty? Jealous enough to kill her own sister? I pictured the Rose as it exploded into a fireball with Lollie locked inside.

The farther I stayed from Lollie, the safer she would be. The thought sent a sharp pain through my heart. Either that or the leftover Frog Eye Salad I'd eaten for breakfast was taking its revenge on my organs.

I needed to set things straight with Beauty. If only to protect Lollie. I headed for the door, acid swirling in my gut. I had to convince Beauty that loving your significant other was no way to start a marriage.

I reached for the doorknob, rehearsing exactly what I would say to my demented bride. "I'm sorry for sleeping with your one sister, but I swear I didn't do your other sister" didn't seem quite right. My fingers started to twist the knob when the door flew open and smashed me in the face. I staggered back, purple pansies filling my eyes as tiny princesses circled my damaged noggin. A few seconds later, my world went from emerald to black.

Chapter 54

I blinked against the lamplight filling the bedroom, my head pounding like all five monkeys jumping on a bed. Once my vision turned from black to merely semi-blurry, I glanced around the bedroom, unable to move more than my head. My hands and feet were bound tightly with some sort of pink ribbon.

Frog! Was this Beauty's final revenge? Would I soon find myself slaughtered and stuffed in a grave out back? I wasn't ready to die. Not yet. Not until I told Lollie...

A crackle of maniacal laughter filled the room. "I see you're awake," a small voice whispered.

"Beauty?" I called out. "I swear it wasn't what it looked like. Pretty was just showing me—"

"Shut up, you dolt," my attacker cut me off.

My stomach rolled as I recognized the tiny voice, if not the words. Words I'd heard before, outside this very room. Panic filled me. I pulled against the ropes binding my arms, feeling a lot like Gulliver when he took that wrong turn and wound up at an S&M club.

The faint sound of the wedding march floated from the hallway. I swallowed hard and glanced down in time to see my small assailant pointing a very large pistol at my head. I was going to miss my own wedding thanks to the manic insect with a Napoleon complex, a top hat, a tiny shovel, and a gun.

"Jimmy, good to see you. Now how about you be a good cockroach and untie me?" I glared down at the miniature assassin, barely visible against the shag carpet.

He cackled with insane, malicious glee. "I think not."

"That's a shame." I sighed. "So what's the deal? Did you come here to wish me luck on my wedding or something?" Oh, I hoped it wasn't the "or something" because I really didn't want to die. Not on my birthday, for frog sakes.

"Or something. Something slow and painful, I think." He cocked the gun, which sounded like a cannon in the silence of the bedroom.

"Whoa. Wait a minute," I said quickly. "You can't kill me yet. Where's your grand, probably incredibly boring, reveal? The one where you tell me why exactly I must die. Come on, man. Don't short yourself now."

His beady eyes blazed at the short comment, but he lowered the gun a quarter of an inch. "If you insist," he said, "it all started—"

"I take it back," I said. "Just shoot me."

The roach scowled, his tiny face growing red.

"Please?" I added.

"In due time, I assure you." Jimmy cleared his throat. "As I was saying . . ."

"Oh, what's the point?" I blew out a harsh breath, and then in a rush outlined his dastardly plot. "You're in love with Beauty. She's in love with me. So you decided to take me out of the equation. Blah. Blah. Blah." I paused to take a mouthful of air-conditioned air. "You die and I get away in time to marry the love of your life. The end."

"It's rude to interrupt when your better is speaking." He jabbed the gun at me.

"Not as rude as attempting to murder me." My eyes narrowed to slits. "Three times so far."

"Five," he said.

"What?"

His beady eyes rolled in his tiny-top-hat-wearing head. "Five times. I've tried to kill you five times, and until today, I've unfortunately failed. I cannot abide inaccuracy of any kind."

"Five? Are you sure?" I mentally counted the number of attempted murders.

He nodded. The smug bastard.

"The black Unicorn attacks? Sleeping Beauty's bedroom? The warehouse? The bomb? Those attempts were all you?" I felt sick. Lollie was telling the truth. Beauty had nothing to do with any of this. She was nothing more than an innocent, albeit sleepy bystander. I owed Beauty a major apology.

"Sadly, you arrived a bit late for the bomb to work." He caressed the gun with his tiny fingers. "I blame myself. I did not take into account traffic on the strip." He gazed down at his tiny, manicured fingernails, black with grave-digging dirt, and then glanced back up. "As for the other misfortunes, I will make up for my failures soon."

"But why kill Beauty's fiancées? Why not just tell her that you love her and see what happens?" I scratched my chin. "Hell, you gave us your blessing, for frog sakes. What was that about?"

"If you would pay attention, I'll explain." He jabbed the gun at me, the barrel looming even larger in his small hands. A bead of some nasty insect secretion dripped down the trigger. "Many years ago, young Beauty was cursed with a terrible fate." He started reciting the curse, the one written on the back of the picture frame in Beauty's bedroom: *"A pin-pricked finger, will sleep eternal, until his true heart Be."*

"Not exactly Shakespeare." I pulled against the silk ropes. "Besides, as of a few minutes ago Beauty looked just fine to me. No eternal sleep or pinpricks to speak of."

I motioned to the doorway with my head. "So suck it up and tell her how you feel." I pictured Lollie's face last night when she ran up the stairs and out of my life. Swallowing past the words I should've said, I croaked, "Curse be damned, before it's too late and you lose her forever." Like I had.

"If only it was that simple." The gun wavered in his hand. "Princess Beauty has not yet been stricken by her curse. She has taken great care over the years to avoid any prick." His eyes narrowed on me.

"Ha, ha." I gave an affected laugh. "So she's not actively cursed. Good. What's the problem?"

"The only way Sleeping Beauty can avoid her sleepy fate is by true love's kiss. *Until his heart Be.*" He grimaced. "For some ridiculous reason, she believes that heart is yours." My mind flashed to my B-shaped birthmark, the birthmark that sat squarely above my heart, but Jimmy wasn't finished. "I tried to tell her how stupid that was, but she refuses to listen."

"What makes you think I'm not the guy?" I asked. She was, after all, my *One*. It only made sense that I would be hers. Of course, curses rarely made sense. In fact, they just loved to frog with you. Take my curse, for example. As if it wasn't hard enough to sit around and eat flies all day, they had to top it off with finding a princess willing to kiss a frog, and not one of those hippy chicks who lick toads either, but a bona fide princess.

He snorted, aiming the gun at my chest. "Look at you," he said, waving the gun at me. "You don't love her. You don't love anyone but yourself."

Again, an image of Lollie's crooked smile filled my head.

Cocking the weapon with one hand, Jimmy backed up to the door and gave me a tiny finger wave. "Good-bye, Jean-Michel. I'll give Beauty your regards."

Chapter 55

"Sir? Have you seen my rose petal potpourri? I had it specially delivered to the hotel for the flower girl..." Karl called as he flung the bedroom door wide, knocking Jimmy to the floor. The gun flew from his hand and bounced under the bed. "Karl," I shouted. "Look out!"

But it was too late.

Karl stepped into the room and right onto Jimmy Cockroach, assassin and marriage broker to the stars. The awful squish of shoe meeting killer insect filled the room.

Karl glanced down and glowered at the goo on the bottom of his shoe. "Sir, did you leave gum on the floor again? How many times have I told you..." His eyes narrowed on my tied-up form on the bed. "Oh, shame on you, sir. Playing sex games while your guests wait downstairs. I have half a mind to—"

"Hurry up and untie me, Karl." I pulled against the ropes. "I have to find Lollie—"

"I'm sorry, sir." He lowered his gaze. "But Ms. Bliss isn't downstairs."

"What are you talking about?" No woman would dare miss her sister's wedding, not even Lollie, the black sheep of the family. "Fine," I said. "If she's not downstairs, I'll go to Handsome's place."

"She's not there either, sir." Karl's eyes filled with tears. "Ms. Bliss is gone, sir. Forever. She asked me to tell you . . ."

"What?"

"To forget her. Marry Beauty and live happily ever after."

I closed my eyes, letting Lollie's final good-bye sweep over me. She was right. I wouldn't make the same mistake my father had. I was my own prized possession. Not some tattooed girl who I couldn't stop thinking about. I would marry Beauty, end my curse, and have my happily-ever-after.

Or not.

Only one way to find out.

Karl glanced at his watch as the faint chorus of the wedding march began again. "Princess Beauty awaits you downstairs."

Chapter 56

Standing at the altar, Handsome at my side per Beauty's "suggestion," my palms started to sweat. I wiped them on my tuxedo pants and swallowed back a wave of regurgitated scotch. I caught sight of RJ and Asia seated in the fourth pew.

RJ, the bastard, winked.

My mouth grew as dry as the desert air.

My gaze shifted to the front row. Karl beamed at me from his seat next to Candi, who wore a surprisingly un-stripper-like dress and ballet flats. Karl wrapped an arm around her thin shoulders and smiled. The two of them looked mismatched, Karl pudgy and eager in contrast to Candi's jaded gaze and blatant, albeit diluted sex appeal, but as a couple, they couldn't have looked happier. Which both pissed me off and warmed my heart. Why couldn't I fall in love like that? Why didn't anything come easy for me?

On the other side of Karl sat my father, the Frog King, who was the only man in the room wearing a rented tuxedo. Shortly before I'd made my way downstairs, the Frog King had knocked on my bedroom door. He apologized for disowning me and had welcomed me back into the froggy fold. I wasn't sure what caused his change of heart, but right now, it hardly mattered.

Nothing mattered.

I tried to smile at the crowd, but my lips, now fused to my teeth, refused to comply. I looked to my father's right where a subdued Elly sat, avoiding my gaze. What was up with her? If anyone should be happy about my upcoming "I do," it was Elly.

The wedding march began again, loud enough to rattle my back teeth. The temple doors opened. A flash of white caught my eye. Frog! This was it.

I closed my eyes.

Handsome gasped.

The crowd sucked in a collective breath.

My eyes flew open, nearly bursting from their sockets at the sight in front of me. Sleeping Beauty stood, alone, at the back of the room. White lace and satin swirled around her. Gone were her sleepy eyes and disdain, replaced by a thin white lace veil that covered her face. Her long hair shone like spun gold, falling around her shoulders in waves. Her eyes shimmered like the purest of violets at dawn through the lacy curtain obscuring her face. She looked absolutely beautiful and terrified.

I shot her a small, hesitant smile.

She glared back.

Oops. Someone had missed her afternoon nap.

Anger quickly replaced the terror in her gaze, and she stomped up the aisle toward me, apparently still a little upset about our earlier run-in. The king ran up the aisle behind her, followed by a fully dressed Pretty.

We all took our places, Beauty at my side.

Forever.

The room grew even hotter.

Sweat beaded my upper lip.

"Dearly beloved," the minister began.

I sucked in a deep breath as the room spun around me.

The scent of strawberries tickled my sense.

And something else.

Something familiar.

I spun around, searching the crowd for Lollie's face.

"Do you...Princess...this...man...till death do you part..." the minster droned on, but I wasn't paying any attention. My heart pounded in my chest. My fingers itched to take Lollie into my arms, to feel her skin against mine, if only for one last time. But we weren't meant to be. My future lay with the sleepy princess next to me, the one who looked ready to, and probably would, murder me in my sleep.

For a second my attention returned to Beauty. A woman I would never love. "I do," Beauty mumbled, a slight hitch in her voice.

"Do you, Jean-Michel La Grenouille," the minister began.

Did I what? Know I was making the biggest mistake of my life, one that would haunt me, like the taste of Lollie on my lips, until my dying day? Yeah, I had an idea.

I pictured Lollie's tattooed skin and her slightly slanted smirk. I pictured her holding a baby, our baby, in her colorful arms. The words "prized possession" flickered through my mind.

"...your lawfully wedded wife? In sickness..."

The scent of strawberries grew stronger. My eyes searched the pews. No sign of Lollie, but she was here. I had no doubt about it. I could feel her. Almost taste her inky flesh.

"...till death do you part..."

A lump formed in my throat from the urge to shout her name, to end this charade once and for all, to spit in the face of fate. Green wasn't that bad a color.

A low murmur swept through the guests.

"Jean-Michel?" the minister prompted. "Do you take her?"

What? Take who? I tried to focus on the question, but the smell of strawberries had addled my thoughts.

"Jean-Michel!" the minister yelled again.

I snapped to attention. "Sorry. What was the question?"

Beauty screeched, "Just say 'I do'!"

"I do," I repeated dully.

Sleeping Beauty let out a choked laugh. Or maybe a snore. Could've even been a sob for all I knew. One could never tell with her.

"All right then." The minster paused to glare at us, and then at the rest of the wedding guests. "Now, if anyone has reason to believe these two," the minister's eyes darted between Beauty and me, "should not be wed, let them speak now of forever hold their—"

"I do."

"Me too."

"Not the best idea . . ."

"I could use a drink."

The minister rolled his eyes as he stared out at six raised hands of those unable to hold their peace for a second longer. One of the hands was mine, and another, well, that hand belonged to my not-so-sleepy and currently enraged bride.

Chapter 57

"If you'll excuse us for a moment," I said to the crowd as I grabbed Sleeping Beauty's hand and pulled her down the aisle. I pushed through the doors and into the garden. The overpowering smell of roses tickled my nostrils, replacing the succulent scent of strawberries and ink from my mind.

"Achoo!" Beauty sneezed.

"Bless you," I mumbled, staring into the miniature reflecting pool in the center of the garden. My greenish face stared back. For once the color didn't bother me so much. The weight that had settled on my heart about the time I met Lollie had lifted. I was finally a free man, albeit greener.

Silence lengthened between Beauty and me, each lost in our own thoughts. Finally, I turned to my supposed *One*. "I didn't touch Pretty. I swear it."

"I know."

Another stretch of silence.

A fly buzzed around my head, and I had a strong urge to snatch it out of the air and stuff it into my mouth.

"I have something to tell you. Something I should've told you days ago," Beauty said, staring into the distance. Roses and dirt surrounded us, not to mention the twenty-eight graves of her former lovers. Crickets chirped, perhaps in warning.

I stared into Beauty's violet eyes, regretting a future that would never be. I was in love with her sister. She was my One. My most prized possession. "I already know, and I'm sorry."

"Sorry?" Beauty asked, her head tilted to the side.

I nodded.

"Huh." Her bottom lip started to tremble as hurt flickered in her eyes. "Why didn't you say something?"

What was there to say? She was cursed. So was I, and you didn't hear me whining about it. Not right now, at least. We had far more important things to discuss.

Beauty twisted the plastic rose bouquet in her hand. Red, green, and white swirled together in a dizzying array. "I'm sorry I lied," she said. "It's just . . ."

Lied? What was she talking about?

". . . at first I didn't want to marry you." Blond curls danced around her face as she whipped her head back and forth. "Or anyone, for that matter. And then I—"

"I can't marry you," I interrupted.

"What?" she shouted, adding a foot stomp for good measure. "But you have to!"

"I'm sorry. I really am." I bit my lip, unable to meet her stare, my eyes lowered to the reflection of the two of us in the greenish water of the pond. "But I'm in love, true, real love." I paused to gather my courage. "With your sister."

Rather than terrifying me, speaking the words out loud only made my feelings stronger. I loved Lollie Bliss. The kind of forever love my parents had shared, the kind of love that no matter what vindictive, deceitful thing Lollie did, I would always love her. She could lie to me a million times, steal everything I owed, kidnap a hundred tired princesses and my heart would still yearn for her.

I glanced up from my reflection in the pond to see how Beauty was taking the news. I winced. She did not look pleased; in fact, she looked as if she'd swallowed a fly.

Her fists clenched at her side.

"I hope we can still be friends—"

Violet eyes blazing with violence, she grabbed my tuxedo jacket and shoved me backward. My feet hit the edge of the pond; arms pinwheeling wildly, I tried to regain my balance, but half a bottle of scotch had taken its toll, and I tumbled headfirst into the murky pond water.

Spitting a mouthful of sludge out of my mouth, I yelled, "What the—"

"Damn you, Kermit! You can't love Pretty. I'll—"

I shook the water from my ears in case I'd misheard her. "Kermit? Did you just call me Kermit?"

Her hand flew to her mouth, a very familiar mouth.

Son of a frog! "Lollie? Is that you?"

She nodded once.

Stunned, I sat in waist-deep pond water. Slowly, a smile crossed my lips as my heart swelled. My One truly was standing in front of me. Lollie wasn't Beauty's sister. She was Beauty. Or rather Beauty was her. The same princess in different clothes, a wig, colored contacts, a magnetic nose stud, and press-on tattoos. I staggered from the pond, water pouring off my tuxedo, and reached for her.

We would have our happily-ever-after, after all.

"Lollipop—"

Lollie's eyes grew wide and then fluttered closed as she dropped into my arms. Pretty stood behind her, Lollie's tattoo gun with its very large bloody needle in her manicured hand.

Chapter 58

"No!" I screamed as Lollie fell into my arms with a soft snore. Karl appeared behind Pretty, knocked the gun from her hand, and then grabbed her around the waist.

"Oh, what happened?" Pretty tittered with sick glee as she struggled to free herself from my servant's grip. "Did your princess fall asleep?"

Rage, so dark and violent I feared for Pretty's safety, let alone my own sanity, filled me. If I wasn't so worried about the princess in my arms, I would've choked the life out of the one standing in front of me. "What did you do?" I growled.

Pretty's face twisted into a mask of jealousy. "I did you a favor, Jean-Michel. She would make a terrible queen. I mean, look at her." She motioned at the pale face of my beloved.

I took a step forward. "She's your sister, for frog sakes."

"Half sister," she corrected. "And not a good one either. You should've married me. Not Beauty." She stomped her slipper clad foot. "Me!"

Through gritted teeth, I exhaled a harsh breath. "Her name is Lollie." I don't know why, but insisting on Pretty using Lollie's name seemed vital to me. As if the curse, Beauty's curse, couldn't touch the woman I loved, the woman asleep in my arms.

"Whatever name you use," she said, "it doesn't matter. She's not your true love, and you're not hers. You can't save her. The curse says so. Only her true love can awaken Sleeping Beauty."

Pretty's words sliced through me as if she slashed my flesh. What if she was right? What if I wasn't the One for Lollie, the one who could wake her from her eternal slumber? My hands began to shake, and for the first time in my life, I knew how Karl felt on a daily basis. Much like a hooker, inferiority sucked.

Lollie moaned in my arms. Locked in some kind of inescapable nightmare, her eyes fluttered, but stayed closed. I glared at Pretty and then turned to Karl. "Get her out of my sight before I—"

"Yes, sir." Karl bowed before he dragged Pretty away. Her damning words echoed in my brain: "You can't save her."

In Beauty's darkened bedroom, I sat, staring at the rise and fall of Lollie's chest. Deep even breaths. A soft snore. And then silence. I'd watched Lollie sleep, the horror of her curse growing with each passing minute, as did the fear that I wasn't her One.

"Just kiss her, sir," Karl said from behind me. "Then you will know the truth. You are her true love. Everyone can see that. Just take a chance."

"And if I'm not?" I asked, my voice raw. "What then, Karl?"

"You are, sir. I know it." He cleared his throat. "Please, you're running out of time."

Turning into a frog seemed like the least of my worries at the moment. My full concern centered on the woman asleep on the bed in front of me. Yes, she had lied to me, multiple times, in fact. Lied about her true identity. Lied about Spindle. About the kidnapping. But she'd also saved my life. And not just that day she'd broken my curse either.

What if I wasn't able to return the favor?

Someone cleared their throat behind me. I glanced up to locate the source and then glanced lower. Red, the redheaded midget, stood in the doorway, her eyes filled with tears. The first emotion other than affected hipster annoyance I'd seen cross her face.

"Pretty?" Red nodded to the sleeping Lollie.

Karl spoke up. "Princess Beauty is more than pretty, she's quite beautiful, and I'll tussle with anyone who says otherwise."

Red rolled her eyes.

A tiny smile flickered on my lips, but I quickly sobered. My eyes locked on Red's face, and I slowly nodded. "In the garden. Why, Red? Why did Lollie keep her identity a secret from me?" I thought of the hours of lost time we could've had together, had I but known.

Red licked her lips, taking a step closer to Lollie's sleeping form. "All Lollie's life she had to live by someone else's rules."

I pictured the precocious four-year-old from the pond and smiled. She sure as hell hadn't followed any rules that day. I had the teeth marks in my skull to prove it.

"Lollie tried to live up to the king's standards for most of her life." Red's face grew hard. "But she could never please him, so eventually she quit trying."

"And Lollie Bliss was born?" My mind flashed to Lollie's tattoo-covered body. Press-on tattoos. Fake, I reflected. Just like her name. Was everything about her, about us, a lie? I shook off the thought, focusing on Red's next words.

"Lollie Bliss was born long before Beauty was." Her lips curved into a grin. "You see, the king decided to change his stepdaughter's name to Beauty on her fourth birthday. The day she met you." The smile on her face slipped a notch. "The king thought it would increase her value."

A wrinkle formed on my forehead. "Value?"

"On the marriage market." Red gave a bitter laugh. "Subliminal advertising. What better way to snag a rich prince for a son-in-law?"

I grinned, motioning to the small recorder I'd found tucked inside her nightstand. A recorder filled with the sweet sound of loud, annoying snores. "But Lollie found a way to thwart him and it."

"Exactly." Red brushed her hand over Lollie's arm. "Everyone knew of the curse, of course. Lollie took advantage of that fact. She developed a," Red curled her fingers into air quotes, "disorder of the sleepy and annoying kind. And it worked. The king would find a suitable prince via Jimmy Cockroach, the oblivious prince would meet Beauty, and by the next day, he'd be halfway to New Never City, glad to be far away from Beauty." She hesitated, looking thoughtful. "Or so we assumed, until someone tried to shoot you in the head. It was then that Lollie realized her former fiancés weren't happy at all, but dead."

I pictured the tiny grave markers in the garden and frowned. Jimmy Cockroach was one sick insect. I shook off my near-death experience and focused on Red's tale.

"Lollie's plan to live two separate lives worked great until the day she met you." Red grunted. "You made her crazy with your threats to marry Beauty, no matter what. She pulled out all the stops, was whiny and annoying as possible, but nothing seemed to work." Humor flashed in her gaze. "Then something changed."

"I told her about my curse." A lump formed in my throat. "That's why she agreed to marry me. She felt sorry for me."

"You really are stupid, aren't you?" she continued be-fore I could comment. "Must be all that royal blood."

"What do you mean?"

"Lollie fell in love with you. That's why she dumped you. Saving you was all that mattered to her." Red blew out a harsh breath. "And look what that got her."

With those parting words, Red left the bedroom. I sat, staring at Lollie's beautiful face. For the first time, a spark of hope blossomed in my chest. Maybe I was her *One?* Maybe we could live happily ever after.

Lollie's eyelids fluttered as a world of dreams filled her mind. I glanced up at Karl. He mumbled something I couldn't catch over the thundering of blood in my ears. This was it. The moment of truth.

Squeezing my eyelids shut, I mouthed, "I am the One."

Then I crushed my lips to her cold ones.

Chapter 59

Not a damn thing happened. Lollie's lips, frosty to the touch, remained unmoved by the warmth of my embrace. I kissed her harder, adding a little tongue for good measure. One had to try, right?

Still nothing.

I wasn't her *One*.

A tear rolled from the corner of my eye, down my face, and hung on the edge of my chin for a second before it splashed against her cheek. Shrinking into myself, I held the only woman I would ever love in my arms, squeezing her against me as if willing her to awaken and end the aching sorrow filling me.

For a minute, no one moved. Shock registered on Karl's face. There would be no storybook ending. No happily ever after.

Lollie would stay asleep, forever.

Unless . . .

An idea formed in my head. I straightened, laid Lollie back down against the pillow, and motioned for my manservant. "Karl, come here. Quick."

"Yes, sir," he said, hovering inches from my head.

I grabbed his hand and yanked him down on the bed next to me. "Kiss her!"

His eyes went wide. "What?"

"Kiss Lollie." I shoved his wet, pudgy lips toward her face. "Do it. Now."

"But, sir. I don't think . . ."

Grabbing the back of his neck, I forced his face to Lollie's. "It's the only way," I whispered. "I can't let this be the end. She deserves a life. Even if it's not with me." I swallowed, a tide of fear lacing my every word. "Please, Karl. I have to find her *One*. The only thing that matters is her happiness."

He nodded once and then pressed his pudgy lips to hers. Again, nothing happened. Lollie remained fast asleep. Karl's face fell and tears streamed down his cheeks. "I'm so sorry, sir. I—" He let out a choked cry.

I patted his shoulder, my gaze on Lollie's beautiful face. "You did your best." Wincing, I wiped away a string of Karl's drool from Lollie's lips.

"Thank you, sir."

Taking a steadying breath, I turned to the growing crowd outside her bedroom doorway. Wedding guests and servants dressed in their finest attire eavesdropped outside the door. My father stood toward the back, his rented tuxedo standing out against the other trappings of wealth. He caught my eye and nodded. I nodded back. I wouldn't make the same mistakes he'd made. Not with Lollie. She deserved better. Better than this stupid curse. And better than me. I would gladly give up everything to see her smile once more.

"Ladies and gentlemen." I cleared my throat. "If I might have your attention for a moment."

The crowd quieted.

"I need all the men to form a single-file line." I wagged my finger at Handsome. "No cutting."

Marvin the butler frowned. "But why, sir? This hardly seems like the time for games. Not when our poor princess is lying there in eternal slumber."

"No games, but there is a prize." My gaze locked on

each and every person in the room. A few of the ladies fainted under my gaze while the men shifted from foot to foot. "For the man who awakens my lady love . . . he will get everything. All my money, cars, palaces. My title. Everything."

The grandfather clock in the downstairs hallway bonged once. My eyes lifted to the bedside clock.

Midnight.

My time was running out.

I fingered the black diamond and gold ring in my pocket, a ring made from a small golden ball I'd carried around for years, the same ball that had sent my wet-dog-smelling lady love to me so many years before.

Lifting the ring from my trousers, I set it in Lollie's cold hands. The warm glow reflected off her blue-tinted skin as if warming it. In that moment, I knew that I'd made the right decision.

For both of us.

The clock bonged again.

"Everything," I repeated with absolute confidence.

Once more, the clock gonged.

I swallowed, hard. "RJ?" I called out to my oldest friend, tattooing aside. After all, if it wasn't for him, I would've never met the real Lollie Bliss.

My oldest friend stepped forward, his face dark with concern. "I'm here, Jean-Michel."

"You're up." Motioning to Lollie, I added, "Kiss her. No tongue."

RJ laughed without humor. "No thanks."

"What?"

"One bride is one too many for me, my friend. You'll have to find someone else to kiss your girlfriend." His face twisted into a sad smile. "But if you ask me, you're going about this all wrong. Trust me. I made the same mistake once."

How dare he question my plan? What did a villain know about curses anyway! "Forget it," I said to him. "Karl, after I . . . you know . . . you start the . . . kissing."

"Yes, sir."

"And, Karl," I said. "When she wakes up . . . I wouldn't mention any," I waved around the room to the line of eager males already out the doorway and down the corridor, "of this. Not if you want to live." I rose from the bed and crossed the room, my head high. Inside me the transformation had already begun. I would never again be the man Lollie had loved.

The clock bonged for the twelfth and final time.

I sat bowlegged next to the pond, listening to the water gently lap against the rocks. My eyes stayed locked on the window above me, waiting for some sign that Lollie's One had arrived. At the castle gates, hundreds of princes, commoners, and even a king or two stood in line waiting for their chance to kiss the woman I loved.

Jealousy choked me enough that I let out a sound much like a ribbit. But then envy passed, and a feeling of despair settled around me once again. I rubbed at the B-shaped birthmark over my heart, trying to ease the ache.

Bliss would never be mine.

Chapter 60

Dawn streaked the sky, spraying orange and pink ribbons along the horizon. Sunlight glinted off the sleeping princess's window. Suddenly, the room exploded in a golden glow, so intense it blinded anyone within a hundred feet.

A forlorn frog at the edge of the pond croaked and then dove beneath the plane of the water, barely making a ripple in the greenish pond. A single bubble floated to the surface and then popped.

A minute later, a high feminine scream rang out, "Ow, my lady. Why'd you hit me?" Footsteps soon followed. The door leading from the palace to the garden burst open, and out tumbled a very angry woman, her blond hair sticking up at impossibly geometric angles, her purple irises glowing.

"No. no. no," she muttered like a madwoman as she rushed through the garden, pausing only long enough to let out a sneeze before returning to her mission.

A few seconds after she opened the garden door, she arrived at her destination, the lily-pad-infested pond. A pudgy manservant, his bald head gleaming much like the black diamond and golden ring in the lady's hand, ran up behind her. "Princess, please. I assure you, the Frog Prince, he only wanted your happiness."

"Really?" The princess sneered. "My happiness? In the form of mononucleosis? Or how about a nice festering cold sore?" She shuddered prettily. "Did you see some of those degenerates?"

Karl winced. "We were scraping the bottom of the barrel with the last hundred or so." He lowered his voice. "I'm not even sure the last one was of age."

"I can't believe Kermit's stupid enough to think a slobbery kiss from some idiot would solve everything. When has that ever worked?"

Karl winced, his eyes darting to the slimy green pond.

"Oh, right." The princess blushed before plunging her hand into the pond water. She dug around, finally emerging with a large green frog.

"Ah, my lady . . ."

"Quiet," she ordered as she puckered her lips. "Here goes nothing," she muttered. The frog squirmed in her fingers, his froggy eyes wide. The smacking kiss echoed around the quiet garden. Lollie dropped the frog and waited.

And waited.

"Damn it!" she yelled before once again stabbing her hand into the murky water.

"My lady, please." Karl's face turned as green as the second amphibian Lollie yanked to the surface.

Lollie glared the servant into silence. "None of this would've happened if Kermit trusted me in the first place. We'd be married and living happily ever after. But no, he had to go all princely on me at the last minute. Who does that?" She closed her eyes and puckered her lips. The amphibian in her palm grinned as if he'd hit the fly lottery.

"Madam, are you cheating on me already?" I called from the other side of the pond. "With a toad? I thought you had better taste."

Her eyelids flew open, and she stared at me, the human

me, for a long minute, her gaze dissecting every inch of my body. "Apparently not." Dropping the poor disappointed toad back into the water, she slowly rose. "I thought . . ."

"I didn't."

"But how?"

A smile curved across my lips. "No curse."

"What?" Her hands fisted at her sides. "You jerk! You lied to me about your curse? To what? Trick me into marrying you?"

I straightened away from the stone pillar. "Since no actual wedding took place, your complaint is moot." I took a step toward her, unsure if I wanted to shake or kiss her. "And speaking of lying, I wasn't the one who created an entire fake persona to keep would-be suitors at bay. Mind you, I'm happy you did."

She winced.

"But, Lollipop, I didn't lie to you about the curse, or anything else. Not once." Which in itself was a lie, but it felt good to turn the tables. After all, she'd played me since the moment we'd met, twenty-two years ago.

A small smile curled on her lips. "If you weren't lying, why aren't you much smaller and green?"

"The blame belongs to you, my sweet." I stopped, staring into Lollie's beautiful face. "You broke my curse. Again."

A wrinkle formed on Lollie's forehead. "I don't understand. To end your curse, you had to marry Beauty, the same girl who kissed you at the pond. Not me, Lollie. The king had changed my name by then. So . . ."

"You tried to force me to marry the fake you. Beauty."

"It was the only way to save you," she said, her lips drawn tight.

"True."

"Then, and follow my logic here, since we didn't actually marry, you should be much greener and let's not forget, shorter. So," she motioned between us, at the pond, "what happened? Was it all some kind of mistake?"

"You tell me."

"What'd you mean?"

"Who's the lucky guy?" At her blank look, I added, "The guy who broke your curse. The one who now owns my palace, my cars, and a couple bazillion dollars, not to mention a pair of handmade leather boots from Italy."

She gave a bitter laugh. "Your most prized possession. I should've guessed."

Karl cleared his throat. "In his lordship's defense, they're a really nice pair of boots."

I beamed at Karl. "Thanks."

"You're welcome, sir."

Lollie huffed. "Can we please get back to the subject at hand?"

"Of course, my lady. I'm a pauper, and some other dude is your happily-ever-after. Why wouldn't I want to discuss this in greater detail?" I said, bowing low.

"You're not."

"Not what?"

"A pauper."

"I don't understand." The full weight of my actions settled in my brain. For the first time in my life I was totally broke. Not a frog prince cent to my name. "I gave away my fortune to whoever broke your curse. You're awake, so, follow *my* logic here, I'm now flat broke."

"No, you're an idiot." She held out the ring I'd left in her hands the night before. "This broke my curse. The ring made from the golden ball I dropped in the pond twenty-two years ago. The ball found and returned to me by the man with the letter 'B' over his heart." She pointed at her chest. "You, Kermit." She then lifted her hand to the sky. "With a little help from the sun. Apparently you missed the fine print where I would awake at first morning light."

She frowned. "Perhaps you should invest in a pair of reading glasses?"

Ignoring her last comment, I considered her curse: *Until his true heart Be.* I rubbed at the B-shaped birthmark and smiled. "My doctor worried it might be skin cancer," I said. "He wanted to remove it, but I refused."

"Only because you're afraid of needles, not to mention you're a really big chicken," Lollie said with a grin.

She knew me so well. "Lollie, pay attention," I said, crossing the short distance between us, and pulled her against me. "I like my boots."

Her lips curved into a frown. "A lot, apparently."

"But I love you," I said as I covered her mouth with mine. The kiss lasted for a few seconds before I pulled back. "You, Lollipop, are my One. The only One for me, and that's what broke my curse. You are my most prized possession."

She raised an eyebrow.

"Not possession," I quickly amended. "Object?"

Her eyebrow climbed higher.

"Asset? Accessory? Acquisition?"

She pressed her finger to my lips, halting my diatribe. "And don't you forget it. Now shut up and kiss me."

And they lived happily ever after.
For the most part.
Or so the rest of the tale goes.

Miss the first F∗∗∗ed-Up Fairytale, *Curses!*,
and didn't see how RJ wound up with Asia?
Buy it now in paperback or e-book before
it turns back into a pumpkin!

I'm no hero. In fact, up until a couple of days ago, I was the villain. Kidnapped maidens, scared kids, stole magic tchotchkes—until I got into a little scrape with the union. Now I'm cursed with the worst fate in New Never City— no matter what I do, I gotta be nice.

So when a head-case princess named Asia barges into my apartment and asks me to find out who whacked her stepsister, Cinderella, I have no choice but to help her. And I'm more than willing to head back to her parents' castle and do some investigating if it means I can get into her black leather catsuit. Except this twisted sister has a family nutty enough to send the Biggest Baddest Wolf running for the hills—and a freaky little curse of her own. . . .

"More than f∗∗∗ed-up. Demented. Hilarious."
—Mario Acevedo, author of *Werewolf Smackdown*

"Forget everything you know about Cinderella.
J. A. Kazimer sets the record straight with
humor and a hell of an imagination!"
—Jeanne C. Stein, national bestselling author

"A thoroughly fun read."
—Nicole Peeler, author of the Jane True series

Prologue

Once upon a time (about nine minutes and forty-seven seconds ago) in a land far, far away (the corner of West Fairy-Second Street and Sugar Plum Lane, to be precise) stood a beautiful princess, a woman without compare in beauty or sweetness. Every man, woman, and child in the land loved her, from the most villainous villain to the wickedest of witches.

"Hello there." The princess smiled at the bluebird pecking at a bit of cocoa on the sidewalk. "Aren't you a pretty bird?"

The bluebird chirped, dancing around the beautiful princess. Its tiny claws scratched against the pavement as it bopped figure-eights around her trim ankles.

The princess laughed a high feminine laugh of pure delight. The bird paused, and then continued its acrobatic tricks. The princess bent down to run her manicured hand over the brightly plumed bird. The bird fluttered its wings, edging closer to the busy avenue. A taxicab blaring a bibbity-bop version of "Some Day My Prince Will Come" whizzed by, a little pig at the wheel.

What a lovely day, the princess thought, watching the bird rise into the cloudless sky as it chirped a familiar tune.

Yes, it was a lovely day.

Too bad it was also her last.

Sadly, the princess never saw the crosstown Fairy-Second Street bus.

Chapter 1

A delivery kid stood in front of me in the pastel hallway of my four-story walk-up on the edge of the Easter Village. His hands juggled a grease-stained bag. My own arms juggled a week's worth of junk mail. I shoved an official-looking paper toward the kid. "This is bollocks."

The kid shrugged.

I waved the paper under his nose. "The union thinks I need a vacation. That I'm suffering from some kind of post-villainous-related stress." My eyes bulged and spit flew from my lips. "What kind of crap is that?"

"Whatever," the delivery kid said. His spiked green hair and facial piercings gave him a clownish appeal. The aroma of red curry noodles from Villainous Van's Corner Bistro wafted in the air between us.

"What are they thinking?" I shook my head, counted to ten, and ran a hand through my already rumpled black hair. "Mandatory mental health leave? Are they afraid I'll go postal or something?" This made little sense since I didn't even work at the post office. "Come on. I've suffered greater defeats and managed to pull through."

"Listen, Mac," the teen said to me. My name wasn't Mac, or anything that resembled Mac. Some people called me RJ, at least to my face.

"The total's ten bucks," the kid said. "Either pay me or

I'll feed your dinner to the rats." The kid motioned from my dinner to the furry creatures dressed in tiny felt hats that roamed my darkened hallway like a demented version of *Dancing with the Villains* rejects. I rolled my eyes, muttered something about kids today, and dug into my jeans for some cash.

"Don't forget my tip," the kid added.

I'll give the little shit a tip. I smashed two fives into his palm and snatched the bag from his hand. My boot kicked the door closed with a loud bang. The kid yelped, sending me into a fit of villainous laughter.

A few seconds later, the kid said, "Thanks, mister."

He sounded happy, which made me unhappy.

Shit.

Yanking a wad of bills from my pocket, a wad considerably smaller than it had been a minute ago, I pulled open the door and watched the teen practically tap-dance down the hallway, a hundred-dollar bill clutched in his hands.

My crisp hundred-dollar bill.

"Darn it," I yelled, booting the door closed again. "I can't take much more." I'd been out of work, suspended without pay, for six days. Six long days. Six days of fluffy bunnies and happy thoughts. All due to one little slipup and the union's subsequent curse. The worst part was, now, no matter what I did, it turned out . . . good . . . nice.

Take yesterday, for example. I'm walking down the avenue, minding my own business, when a little old lady calls out, "Son, would you mind helping me carry this package? It's a basket of cookies for my granddaughter. She's five. . . ."

On and on she went.

Rather than telling her to shut up and snatching her cookie basket, I found myself lugging twenty pounds of pastries four blocks up Avenue XYZ while exchanging recipes with the demented old dame.

What kind of villain does that?

I hated being nice, even more than I hated helping people. And I hated that more than curds and whey. But the union had voted, and I would remain cursed, forced to be nice to any idiot around, until they deemed me mentally stable enough for bad-guy duty.

Feeling sorry for myself and hungry to boot, I stalked across my living room and dropped down in my favorite chair.

My favorite chair screamed in response.

"Wha—?" I jumped up and flicked on my lamp.

A redhead in tight black leather glared at me from my seat. Her vivid emerald eyes sparkled with anger, and just a hint of something else. Something not very nice, but infinitely more interesting than a basket of cookies.

"Don't you look before you sit?" The redhead's lips curved into a frown, which only added to her beauty. She looked like sin, the dirty kind with plenty of sweat and saliva. Long copper hair curled down her shoulders, clinging to the outline of her C-cup breasts. The rest of her body was smoking with long, toned limbs and lots of pale skin.

"Who the heck are you?" I pointed the greasy bag in her direction. Before I could stop her, she snatched it from my fingers. I watched in amazement as the interloper dove into my curry noodles with the gusto of Goldilocks during a bout of bulimia.

"Hey." I stabbed my hand in her direction. "That's my dinner." I would've snatched the carton back, but I was afraid of losing a finger.

After a few minutes of gluttony, she paused to glance my way. "Sorry, but I'm starving. I haven't eaten since five."

I glanced at my watch and frowned. "That was like forty-five minutes ago."

"Really?" She cocked her head to the side, showing off the pale skin of her throat. "It feels like an hour at least."

"While I'd love to chat more about the relativity of

time, I'd prefer you tell me exactly who you are and how you got into my apartment." With each word, my voice grew louder and my tone grew more dangerous. While I might have lost my villainous powers, I could still make one little redhead cry.

Or not.

"Do you have any soda?" She smiled up at me. "Maybe a Diet Pepsi? All that MSG makes me thirsty."

With an eye roll I started for the kitchen, pausing to berate my treacherous legs for obeying her command. But I couldn't help it.

Literally.

I did whatever anyone asked, my own will completely ignored, as long as the requestor's intent was pure. Twenty-eight years of bad luck guaranteed any request made by a knockout redhead in black leather was as pure as Sleeping Beauty. Damn it.

Reluctantly, I opened my refrigerator and popped open the last can of mead. A rush of bubbles rose to the surface, foaming over the can and dribbling down my fingers. I sucked the foamy goodness from my thumb and grinned. The mead would have to appease my uninvited dinner thief. I returned from the kitchen, sat down on the edge of my coffee table, and handed her the can.

She glanced at my saliva-soaked fingers and then at the can. "Thanks," she said after taking a long drink. Tilting her head, she studied me for a moment. Her eyes examined every inch, from my scuffed boots to the top of my hair. "You're not what I expected."

"Oh, and what exactly did you expect?"

"Someone a bit shorter." She frowned. "What are you? Six foot?"

I nodded.

"What do you weigh? Sixteen stone?"

Again, I nodded.

She shook her head. "Puny."

"Hey—" Six foot, two hundred pounds was not puny, not by a long shot. Moreover, I was as fit as Hey Diddle Diddle's fiddle. In my line of work, it paid to be, with all that running from angry mobs with pitchforks and such.

"No offense." Her lips lifted into a smirk. "Maybe you could bulk up for the job? Eat more."

Rage flashed through my bloodstream like a boiling cauldron. "Eat more?" I strangled out, my eyes burning into my nearly empty carton of curry noodles and back at the redhead with a dollop of curry on her upper lip. What I should've said was, "Job? What job?" But I didn't. I blamed my dropping blood sugar for the mistake.

The redhead grinned, lifting the nearly empty carton my way. "Oh, was this your dinner? There's an egg roll left." As she said those words, her eyes locked onto the greasy cabbage roll, as if debating eating it.

I grabbed the egg roll, crammed it in my mouth, and spewed leafy green strands at her as I repeated my earlier question. "Who the heck are you? And why are you here?"

"My name's Asia." She paused, her eyes boring into mine. Don't say it, my brain begged, but just like a woman, she said it anyway. "I need your help."

Chapter 2

"Asia..." I tapped my finger to my chin. The vaguest of memories flickered at the edge of my mind. "Your name's familiar somehow. Have we met before?" I doubted it. She wasn't a Villain Vamp, as we called the girls who lowered their standards enough to date my kind. So how did I know her?

She blew out a long sigh. "My full name is Asia Elizabeth Maledetto." At my blank look, she added, "My stepdad's King Maledetto." She paused long enough to roll her eyes. "King of the land of Maledetto. You know, the kingdom that borders the northeastern part of New Never City?"

"Doesn't ring a bell." I shrugged. What the fuck was with the geography lesson? If I wanted to learn, I would've stayed in Charming School.

"Fine." Her hands lifted to her round hips and she glared at me. "My stepsister's Cinderella. Striking midnight now?"

Holy crap. I leapt from my seat on the table and paced around the room. Not that there was much room to pace. In fact, my whole apartment could fit into one of the three kittens' missing mittens. "You're the ugly stepsister!" I said with a frown. Yet this chick wasn't ugly, not by a long shot.

"I'm one of them." She shrugged as if the nickname didn't bother her, but the look of hurt in her eyes spoke more than words could. The villainous, still hungry part of me took satisfaction in her pain. It served her and her princess-stuck-in-an-ivory-tower kind right.

"I'm sorry about," I winced, "your sister's accident." Smashed under a bus was a bad way to go. I should know. I'd run over quite a few jesters and even a prince or two in my time.

"Thanks," she said. "But it wasn't an accident."

I scratched my chin, not liking where this was going. "I have an alibi. I was at my mother's in Queens of Hearts."

Asia arched a flame-colored eyebrow. "Why would you need an alibi?"

"No reason." I tried to smile, but it came off more like a grimace. "You were saying?"

"My sister's death wasn't an accident." Her eyes met mine. "She was murdered. And I need your help to prove it."

Damn. There was that word again. I started to say fuck no, but instead, the following string of words flew from my stupid lips: "Of course. Whatever you need."

God, I hated myself. In an act of revenge, I chomped down on my treacherous tongue until it bled. Served it right.

"Are you eating your tongue?" For a brief second Asia appeared terrified at the prospect. "I'm so sorry. I didn't realize you were that hungry." She shoved her hand into the pocket of her leather pants and removed a lint-covered breath mint. "Here. Take this."

Before I could stop her, she shoved the mint into my mouth. I wanted to yell "Are you fucking nuts," but it came out more like, "Thanks."

Damn it.

She smiled. "So you'll help me track down her killer?"

"Why the heck not?" I stared into her green eyes, losing

myself in their beauty. If a woman's eyes were a window to her soul, I was in big trouble. Because the only image inside Asia Elizabeth Maledetto's eyes was my own evil reflection.

"I'll come back in the morning," she said, "and we can begin our investigation."

I nodded, watching her heart-shaped butt walk out my door and disappear down the hallway. Ugly stepsister, my ass. Hell, even the gayest of the rats surveyed her strut down the corridor.

"I'd do her," said Tate, a pink felt hat-wearing rat with a lisp and a pronounced swish. The other, straighter rats rolled their beady eyes. To which Tate replied: "What?"

I closed the door before things got ugly and dropped into my favorite, now-empty chair. A cloud of dust exploded from the fabric and the sweet scent of pumpkin pie floated around me. I picked up the remnants of my dinner, surprised to see Asia had left a fortune cookie. I smiled at the plastic-wrapped goodie, picturing Asia's emerald eyes.

Peeling the cookie open, I licked my lips in anticipation of its sugary goodness and informative, if not valuable, summation of my future. The cookie read:

THE DELIVERY KID LICKED YOUR EGG ROLL.
HAVE A NICE DAY!

Damn! Foiled again by a teen with more metal in his head than Snow White had sugar midgets.

Hi Ho, Hi Ho . . .

Off to scrub delivery-kid spit out of my mouth I go.